IF CATFISH HAD
NINE LIVES

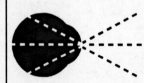

**This Large Print Book carries the
Seal of Approval of N.A.V.H.**

A COUNTRY COOKING SCHOOL
MYSTERY

IF CATFISH HAD NINE LIVES

PAIGE SHELTON

WHEELER PUBLISHING
A part of Gale, Cengage Learning

GALE
CENGAGE Learning·

Farmington Hills, Mich • San Francisco • New York • Waterville, Maine
Meriden, Conn • Mason, Ohio • Chicago

GALE
CENGAGE Learning·

LIBRARY OF CONGRESS CATALOGING-IN-PUBLICATION DATA

Shelton, Paige.
 If catfish had nine lives / by Paige Shelton.
  pages ; cm. — (A Country Cooking school mystery) (Wheeler Publishing
 large print cozy mystery)
  ISBN 978-1-4104-7704-0 (softcover) — ISBN 1-4104-7704-5 (softcover)
  1. Cooking schools—Fiction. 2. Murder—Investigation—Fiction. 3. Large
 type books. I. Title.
 PS3619.H45345I334 2015
 813'.6—dc23   2014043930

Published in 2015 by arrangement with The Berkley Publishing Group,
a member of Penguin Group (USA) LLC, a Penguin Random House
Company

Printed in the United States of America
1 2 3 4 5   19 18 17 16 15

For my husband and research partner, Charlie, who happily drove the car and brought along good music when I told him we needed to go out to the middle of Utah (which turned out to also be the middle of nowhere) to see a "real" Pony Express station, and that we needed to add a few hours to a road trip just so we could go to the Pony Express museum in St. Joseph. Your support and enthusiasm for my stories is beyond measure.
Thank you.

CHAPTER 1

"Believe it or not, I do know how to fish," I said. "I've done this a time or two."

"I do believe you, Isabelle, but why would you use a worm that isn't real?" Jerome asked as he leaned back against the tree and folded his hands on his lap.

"Because I don't like the feel of real worms. They're slimy and alive and gross. These fake worms are wonderful inventions. And I believe we call them lures now. To lure the fish, you know."

"Lures," Jerome said with a disgusted sigh.

"Missing the good old days?" I said.

Jerome smiled his half smile. "Always. Not in the ways you might think, though."

I was sure that Samuel Clemens himself would have been inspired to pen another great American novel if he saw Jerome and me in the woodsy setting.

I wore my oldest, most faded overalls and one of my mom's straw hats. If the hat had seen better days, they were days before my time. My white T-shirt was new and clean, but surely Mr. Clemens would have forgiven that minor fault in my country look. I'd even had the urge to pick a long piece of grass and hold it between my teeth, but so far I'd resisted. Jerome was Jerome, dressed in his cowboy hat and cowboy-ish clothes — the clothes he was wearing when he was killed in 1918.

For the fishing excursion, I'd picked a spot in the woods that I was familiar with. It was close to town, very close, and still a secret to most of our visitors — the tourists who ventured to Broken Rope every summer, as well as the current group, who'd been more a surprise than a plan. The river was one of Missouri's more narrow rivers and about a hundred feet back from the jail side of Broken Rope's Main Street, the place where the buildings and businesses were set up to duplicate their original Old West incarnations. I'd fished this river a number of times, and I knew about the abundance of catfish it held. Well, it might not be so abundant at the moment, but it would replenish quickly, even after Broken Rope's recent run on catfish fishing. It was only two days earlier that many of the town's full-time residents, Gram and me included, had been standing side by side up and down the river with our lines in the water. We'd all had a successful outing.

As a town, we had — well, Jake had, and the rest of us had gone along — agreed that Broken Rope could feasibly host a cowboy poetry convention this year, since the cowboy poets' normal campsite had been destroyed by fire the previous summer. For our contribution, Gram and I would be teaching a couple outdoor cooking classes — frying catfish over a campfire and Dutch oven techniques. Along with the frying, there'd also be large amounts of catfish eaten over the next four days. We'd had to stock coolers and freezers with enough fish to support a bunch of healthy, fueled-by-fresh-air appetites.

The convention was almost a day and a half old, and if Jerome and I listened hard, we could hear sounds from the skit currently being performed on Main Street — something about a pioneer wife's disloyal ways that would, of course, result in a gun battle. We'd already heard a gunshot. I hadn't been needed for this particular skit, so I'd decided to take a few hours of downtime just for me. Before Jerome arrived I was just going to go for a head-clearing drive. There were a couple reasons I felt I

9

needed to get away from the activity. A little quiet time might help me refocus; the convention had conveniently been scheduled over the cooking school's April spring break, and all the students had left town, so they didn't need any immediate attention, but the timing also meant I'd gone from busy cooking school teacher to busy convention-planning assistant. My normal spring break day or two of recharging wasn't going to happen this year. Fortunately, even though the cooking school year had started off rough, things had been sailing along smoothly, and busily, since January.

But with Jerome along, my biggest reason for ditching the long drive idea and escaping a hundred or so feet into the woods was that I wanted and needed a place other than my car or my house to talk to him without the possibility of being overheard or interrupted by something more than a fish tugging on the line.

He'd arrived the previous night. I awakened briefly and thought I smelled wood smoke, but he hadn't appeared in my bedroom like he had the last time he'd visited. When I smelled the smoke and didn't see the ghost attached to it, I attributed the scent to my slightly open window and someone's fireplace. April in southern Missouri was somewhat unpredictable, weather-wise, but lately the nights had been comfort-able enough to either open the windows a crack or light a fire, depending upon your temperature preference.

Instead of the awkward bedroom appear-ance of his previous visit, he'd waited until I left the house and then joined me in my old blue Nova — he'd simply appeared and said hello. He'd startled me, but at least I'd been fully dressed this time.

We'd sat in front of my house for a few minutes and caught up in the awkward way of catching up that we'd become accus-tomed to. If any of my neighbors had been watching, they would have wondered why I was sitting in my car talking to myself, but that sort of scene isn't too strange anymore, considering cell phones' hands-free features. After a few minutes of initial greetings, I called Jake and Gram to confirm that nei-ther of them truly needed me until later in the day, changed into my favorite overalls, grabbed my tackle box, and drove us out to the woods.

"So, you think you're here to save me?" I said, repeating a question I'd asked when we were in the Nova. The question had been one of many, and I didn't think it had been answered yet to my satisfaction.

"I think so, Isabelle. I'm still fairly certain that's why I come back now, to keep you safe from harm."

"But you don't know why I'm in danger?"

"No."

It looked like that question, among others, might never be answered to my satisfaction.

"So maybe you're just here for a visit? Maybe you were only meant to save me the last time or two you showed up. The rules do keep changing."

Jerome thought a long minute and then said, "S'pose that's possible."

I smiled, but it wasn't a totally happy smile. I appreciated his seeming raison d'être, of course. Even though there was a healthy-sized part of me that thought I was pretty good at saving myself, who wouldn't want to be rescued by a handsome, long-dead cowboy? However, the ability to communicate with ghosts had made me somewhat less effective when it came to protecting myself from dangerous situations that included one or more of the spectral beings. I thought it commensurate that one should be able to save me every now and then.

The ghosts of Broken Rope's past were now a solid part of my life. I'd never been much into history, but my fairly new, and apparently inherited from my gram, awareness of their existence had changed everything, including my interest in our Old West legends, as well as my personal definition of *safe*. The ghosts had certain uncanny and unpredictable abilities that had put me and people that I loved in harm's way more than once. And, more than once, Jerome had saved me from a grim outcome.

Unfortunately, I also felt things for him that might be defined as unsavory and were most definitely strange. I liked him a lot; I'd talked myself out of being in "love" with him, but, truthfully, I wasn't sure yet. I was one hundred percent sure that I loved my alive and still-breathing-oxygen boyfriend, Cliff (who didn't know about and couldn't communicate with the ghosts), so I'd decided that *that* love should trump my uncertainty about Jerome. It was a stupid thing to feel anyway — love for a ghost I'd only recently met. But, even though we hadn't known each other long and even if he was technically not alive, no matter how hard I tried, I still couldn't quite ignore those stupid and confusing emotions. I was working on it, though.

"But I don't seem to be in much danger. Even the river's not running too quickly. If

I fell in, I could probably get out just fine. And I haven't seen a ghost since the last time you were here, when Gent visited."

Jerome squinted and thought a moment. "I surely don't know, then."

I pulled my attention away from the water and peered at him from under the brim of my hat. Though we were in shaded woods, a few stripes of sun were able to shoot through the high limbs and new spring leaves. Jerome was patterned; the parts of him in shade were more solid than the parts that were being hit by sunlight. In the dark — and when I was in the general vicinity — the ghosts became dimensional and touchable, though they didn't feel like people as much as they just felt like something solid.

"You're just going to hang around, then?" I said.

"I don't have much choice," Jerome said, but then he cleared his throat. "I mean, if I had a choice, Isabelle, of course I'd want to . . . what were the words you used? Hang around? I'd want to hang around with you, but my coming and going isn't something I control, you know that."

I smiled fully and tipped my straw hat back. It was a gesture I'd seen him do many times with his own hat. Suddenly, I felt a tug on the line.

"Oh, here we go." I stood from the fallen tree trunk I'd been sitting on. I pulled the pole and wound the line.

"That was quick," Jerome said as he stood and moved next to me.

"Much better than real worms," I said, but I was startled by the strong pull from the sunken end of the line. "Hey!"

"Don't lose him," Jerome said as he crouched down and peered into the murky water.

The water was too dark and just slightly too deep to see the fish until I got it a little closer to the surface. But as I wound and pulled some more, it fought hard.

"It's a big one," I said.

Jerome looked up and tipped his hat back, just like I had done a moment before. "Once I caught a catfish that was so big it might have wrestled me back into the water."

My forearms already felt twinges of pain up to my elbows.

"This one might be related to that one," I said.

"I don't know. I bet mine was bigger. I used a real worm."

I laughed, but only for an instant. I had to pull and wind some more.

"I might have to let this one go," I said.

Those were words I'd never uttered before and never thought I would, but this creature was besting me quickly.

Jerome stood and put his hands on his hips.

"No, you can pull him in. Don't give up yet."

As much as I didn't want to give in to any fish, this one was rapidly becoming not worth the effort.

"I don't know," I said.

"Here, let me help," Jerome said.

Neither of us took a moment to consider that it would be impossible for him to help. Though he'd been striped in shadow and slightly more opaque in parts, we weren't surrounded by darkness, so he couldn't be completely solid.

Nevertheless, he put his hands over mine and together we pulled, yanked, and wound the line.

An eternity of about half a minute later, the fish was at the surface.

"That is the biggest fish I've ever seen," Jerome said. "Keep bringing him in."

The Loch Ness Catfish Monster, as I'd suddenly decided to name him, fought, writhed, twisted, yanked back, and might have growled, if such a thing were possible.

"On three, one last big pull," Jerome said.

"One, two, three!"

The fish, which truly was one of the monsters of the river, I was sure, sprang up and into the air in front of us. Even as he was flying up, he was writhing and spitting. He was probably the biggest catfish I'd ever caught, but he wasn't gigantic; I thought I should be able to handle him. He looked me in the eye right before he spit out the line, hook, and lure, and then splashed back into the river, drenching me from straw hat to cute tennis shoes. The force of the release sent me, Jerome, and the pole with the masticated fake worm to the ground.

An instant later, Jerome and I looked at each other and laughed.

It wasn't long, though, before I sobered and the laughter transformed into something not funny at all.

"Wait, I felt your hands on mine," I said.

"Oh?" Jerome held his hands up and looked at them.

"I'm not supposed to be able to feel you unless it's really dark. It's not really dark; it's not dark at all."

Jerome looked up toward the high treetops. "It's not bright sunlight in here either."

"But still." I wanted to reach out and see if I could feel him. But I didn't. I did not want the ever-changing rules with the ghosts to be changing again. I couldn't keep up with all the edits, and accepting each new change took me time and contemplation.

Jerome looked at me, his eyebrows tight together. "Maybe I showed up to save you from the fish."

It was an absurd statement, of course, but I didn't laugh.

"No, you're still here," I said.

"That's true."

"Let me see," I said as I tentatively reached for his hand again.

I'd placed my cell phone on another fallen tree trunk a little farther back from the river. It suddenly buzzed and vibrated and slid onto the ground. I pulled my hand back and got up and hurried to gather the phone.

"Gram?" I said. "What's up?"

I listened to her words and tried to focus on their content, but she was saying some pretty unbelievable stuff.

When she was done, I said, "I'm on my way back. Stay inside and Cliff will get to you in a second, I'm sure."

"What is it, Isabelle?" Jerome said after I ended the call.

"I've got to get back into town. There's been a shooting. Someone was killed," I said.

The details Gram had given me were so

gruesome that I couldn't bring myself to repeat all of them for Jerome.

"I'm going with you," he said.

"That's probably a good idea."

All thoughts of testing Jerome's solidity were left beside the river with my tackle box, pole, and probably an amused Terminator catfish. But, eventually, all things forgotten would have to be remembered.

CHAPTER 2

At first I couldn't find Gram. She'd said she'd gone inside the saloon, but she wasn't there. The place was crowded, but mostly with people I didn't readily recognize. There were so many convention attendees — we had dubbed them *the poets* — and I didn't know most of them well enough to approach anyone and ask if they'd seen Gram. We had a number of visiting actors as well. I knew a few more of them because I'd helped with skit rehearsals, but my quick search didn't yield any actor, poet, or Broken Rope native that I recognized. I looked for Orly, the man who was in charge of the poet group. He was tall enough that I'd spot him quickly if he was there. I saw plenty cowboy hats, but none that reached up high enough to have been perched on the tall man's head. I moved out of the saloon and to the boardwalk to continue my search.

With what Gram had said on the phone, I was surprised that the crowd wasn't more panicked. Concern wavered throughout, but maybe shock was taking over, replacing the initial fear. I hoped Dr. Callahan, our local doctor, had some help.

"Jerome, see if you can find Gram. Tell her to call me," I said.

"Will do," he said after he pondered the request a moment and then disappeared. He was probably weighing the chances of me being in danger before he left my side.

We'd run back into town and directly to the saloon. It would have taken more time to drive. So far, I hadn't paid any attention to the spot where the victim had most likely been shot. I knew the skit had been performed at the other end of Main Street, opposite to where I now stood outside the saloon. Even though the street wasn't all that long, there were plenty of people on it and on the boardwalks — everyone unsure of where to go and what to do. It looked like some crowd control was needed, but I wasn't sure how I could help.

I stepped off the boardwalk and tried to see what was going on down the street. There was definitely a large crowd of people gathered, looking at one spot. I assumed it was at the body. I had no desire to join them, but I ached to know who'd been killed.

"Let's go, folks. Come on. Please move inside somewhere," an authoritative voice said from behind me. "Each shop or business has someone who will ask to check your purses and pockets and identification. We assure you that you'll be fine."

No one in the saloon had checked my pockets or asked for identification.

Jim Morrison, the police chief, was attempting to direct traffic, but it was an uncooperative crowd. Some of the officers had been dressing as cowboys in deference to the fun convention atmosphere, but Jim had kept with his official uniform, which at the moment seemed like a wise idea. His bald head was shiny, and though he was gifted with the ability to keep calm in horrible situations, I could see the concern in his eyes behind his thick black plastic-framed glasses. I hurried to join him.

"What happened, Jim? Can I help?" I said.

"Betts, just get inside somewhere. And try to calm down anyone who needs calming."

I looked back toward the saloon just as someone I recognized went inside through the swinging doors. Officer Jenkins, Broken Rope's newest police officer, would attend to everyone there.

I looked around. "I'll head to Stuart's." Stuart owned the shoe repair shop, and from where I stood, it looked like only a few people had sought refuge there.

"Good." Jim turned to the others on the street. "Now, folks, please, we've secured the area, but please get inside."

I didn't think the area had been secured, but I'd play along. Jim had done what he could to prepare for the unusually large April population, but there were just some things that a small-town police force could never be prepared for. Someone being gunned down in the middle of the street and in the middle of a skit was probably one of those things.

I turned to hurry to Stuart's but was interrupted by a pounding rumble that seemed too loud, and even though I heard the rumble, oddly, I couldn't feel it. As I looked toward the other end of the street again, I saw a man on a horse coming this direction.

"Jim?" I said, but my voice was quiet enough that he didn't hear me.

When the man and his horse rode directly through the concerned group without harming anyone or knocking anyone over or even stirring up enough wind to cause hair to flutter, I realized that no one else saw either the horse or the man. The sun was behind a cloud, but it was still bright enough that the new arrivals were mostly transparent. I could see them both fairly clearly, though.

With intense purpose, the man steered the horse directly toward me but didn't seem to notice that I could see him. It was the distinct scent of leather that came with animal and man that finally assured me that another ghost had come to visit, or rather two ghosts: the rider and the horse. The man seemed young, and he wore a cowboy hat that was even more beaten up than Jerome's. His dirty face, grimy long tan pants, and grungy white shirt made me think that his scent wouldn't be as pleasant as leather if he was alive. As he stopped the horse only a few feet away from me, I saw that he also wore a badge, but I didn't think it signified law enforcement. He sat on a satchel of sorts that was over his saddle. Something in the back of my mind sparked. I should know what that satchel was, but I couldn't quite place it.

"Missouri Anna Winston!" the young man proclaimed as the horse turned in place, impatient to get back to running.

The man's voice made me think he was more a boy than a man. I looked even more closely at his face, but it too was smudged with dirt and he was moving around too much for a thorough inspection.

"Hey," I said, trying to get his attention only and no one else's. "Hey."

He looked down at me. "You can see me, hear me?"

"I can. I'm Missouri's granddaughter." I looked around. Fortunately, the new ghost was the only one paying me any attention.

"That's amazing. Good to meet you. I'm Joe," he said.

"Joe who?"

"I don't have any idea," he said with a laugh. "Just Joe."

"Betts!" a voice called from somewhere behind me.

"Miz!" Joe said.

Gram had emerged from a crowd that was gathered in front of the Jasper Theater. She wore jeans and a red and blue Ole Miss T-shirt.

"You okay?" I said. I performed a quick visual inspection. There was no blood marring the red and blue. She looked unharmed, but not unharried.

"Fit as a fiddle that needs to be restrung," she said. "It hasn't been a fun morning." She looked up. "Hello, Joe. It's always good to see you, but you've picked an interesting day to visit. Come along, let's see if we can

25

find a place to talk without all this commotion."

But our efforts were thwarted.

"Miz, Betts, come help," another voice said.

It took a second to realize that the voice was attached to Stuart, the owner of the shoe repair shop I'd intended to go to before the ghost appeared. He was older than Gram, and I'd noticed that his short stature had gotten somewhat shorter lately. He was leaning out through his front doorway and signaling for us to come over.

"Sorry, Joe, we're going to have to confer later," Gram said.

"But, Miz, the letters? We've only got a few more," Joe said.

"Sorry. We're busy. Meet us back at the cooking school later."

Evidently, Joe thought his letter emergency was more important than the ruckus that was still going on in real life, but the ghosts were typically fairly self-involved. He harrumphed and then disappeared.

Gram sighed and shook her head at me. She didn't need to remind me how annoying she sometimes found our otherworldly visitors.

"Here we go again?" I said.

"Something like that," she said. "Well, I

like Joe, but now's just not the best of times. Come on, let's see what Stuart needs."

We hurried off the street.

Chapter 3

"I have a couple ladies in here, and I'm particularly concerned about one of them," Stuart said as he held the door open.

"Do they need medical attention?" Gram asked as we hurried past him.

"I don't know, but no one is answering any phones anywhere. I saw you two and hoped you'd have a better idea of what to do. I'm not prepared for damsels in distress."

If someone other than Stuart had used those words, it might seem like they were attempting a joke, but *damsel in distress* was still a contemporary phrase for the gentle, quiet man who spent most of his waking hours sitting at his back worktable either fixing shoes or crafting leather belts, which were selling at a brisk pace to both visiting tourists and Internet customers.

The repair shop was long and narrow. Akin to the scent that had wafted my direction with Joe's arrival, the shop also smelled of leather, but there were other scents inside Stuart's shop that made it one of my favorite places in Broken Rope. Polish, an assortment of oils, and Stuart's never-empty coffeepot added smells that blended perfectly with the leather. The smallish lobby was comfortable, with four old vinyl-covered, cushioned chairs. Two of the chairs were currently occupied.

"Hi. I don't know what to do for her. Can you help?" one of the women said when she saw us. Her words were tight with wiry nervousness. She was leaning toward the woman in the other chair, who had her head back with a cloth on her forehead. The woman leaning back was breathing quickly, and her cheeks were flushed.

They were relatively young; probably still in their mid-twenties. They both wore jeans and embroidered cowboy shirts, like so many of the poets and actors. The damsel in the most distress had a long black ponytail that hung down the back of the chair. The other woman had short, blazing red hair. I always considered my auburn hair to be almost-red. There was no "almost" about hers.

Gram crouched next to the woman in trouble and put the back of her hand against her flushed cheek.

"What happened?" Gram asked.

"I'm not exactly sure," the redhead said. "It was after the shooting — was someone shot dead, for real?"

"I don't know for sure," Gram lied.

The redhead nodded and blinked and shook her head all at once. "After whatever happened out there, it seemed like everyone was in a panic, running every which direction. Vivienne" — she looked at the brunette — "ran into me and was very upset. I thought she might pass out, so I brought her in here. It was the closest spot."

"Her name's Vivienne?" Gram asked.

"Yes, Vivienne. I'm Esther. She and I met yesterday, at the campsite."

"Vivienne," Gram said gently, "can you hear me?"

Vivienne swallowed and then nodded, the back of her neck still resting on the back of the chair.

"Good. Stuart, can you grab her a cup of water or something?"

"Sure," he said before he hurried behind the front counter and back toward his worktable and office.

Gram took a deep breath and said, "Vivienne, is there any chance you can sit up? I'm just going to be honest here — I need to see if you're okay. We're worried. My granddaughter has her car right outside. We can get you to a hospital if we need to, but we need to know how bad a shape you're in."

There were a number of problems with what Gram had just said: My car wasn't close by, but I could run and get it if I needed to, I supposed. The closest hospital was about an hour and a half away. And finding out how "bad" a shape someone was in might not be the most delicate way to handle the moment.

But Vivienne seemed to respond favorably. She pulled the cloth off her forehead and sat up straighter. "I think I'm okay. I just got freaked."

She was very pretty, even with splotchy skin. Her bright blue eyes were perfectly spaced over high cheekbones. She had a small mole above the right side of her mouth. Gram would call it a beauty mark; it worked well on her. Her full lips and bright white teeth made me think of plastic surgery and long hours in a dentist's chair, though the end result on Vivienne wasn't fake at all; just striking.

"That's understandable," Gram said.

"Here you go," Stuart said as he re-appeared with a bottle of water. He twisted the lid a little and then handed the bottle to Vivienne.

"Thank you," she said as she smiled briefly at him. She took a drink and then wiped her mouth with the back of her hand. She was still breathing a little faster than normal, but I wasn't as alarmed as I'd been a moment earlier. She turned to Esther. "Thank you, too. I'm sorry."

"Not a problem. I'm just glad that you're going to be okay."

Vivienne looked at each of us, one at a time. Gram answered the unspoken questions.

"I'm Missouri Anna Winston. This is my granddaughter, Betts Winston. And we're all in Stuart's shoe repair shop." She smiled at Stuart, who looked relieved that all damsels were most likely going to recover.

"Nice to meet you all. Thank you again. I'm okay, really, but can any of you tell me what happened out there?"

I had no idea, and Gram didn't go into detail.

"The skit was being performed in the street," Esther began. "It was about a woman who'd cheated on her husband."

I'd watched the short skit a number of times in rehearsal. I would have recognized the actors — one in particular. One of

32

Cliff's cousins had been given the role of the disloyal wife, and it had been fun to see her again, since her last visit to Broken Rope had been when Cliff and I were still in high school. Jake had scrambled for April actors. Most of Broken Rope's thespians somehow managed to take summers off from their real jobs so they could volunteer to entertain the tourists. But most of them couldn't make themselves available in April to help with the convention. I knew Jake had brought in some actors from Kansas City and St. Louis, but he'd still put a call out for more. Cliff's cousin Jezzie had already planned on visiting, and she thought it would be easy and fun to participate in a skit or two, so she volunteered.

I still hadn't heard who exactly had been killed. A cold string of dread suddenly ran through my gut, and I couldn't help but interrupt. "Who was killed? Man or woman? Tell me the details."

Gram blinked but seemed to understand my sudden need to know.

"Oh, she's fine, Betts," she said. "I'm afraid it was one of our visiting actors. I didn't know him, and I haven't heard his name, but he was playing the part of the good guy."

"Norman?" I said. "I think his name was

Norman." I hadn't known him, either, but I'd met him, and we'd shared a little small talk.

Gram's mouth pinched tight as she shrugged.

"It was horrible, but it also seemed to be a part of the skit — you know, a gunfight and everything — until it got awful and real," Esther said.

"The person who was killed was definitely named Norman," Vivienne said. "I met him last night at the campsite."

"I did, too," Esther said, "but I didn't talk to him all that much. Did you talk to him?"

"Not really."

"Was he shot during the skit?" I asked as I removed the straw hat that I'd forgotten about and that suddenly made me feel claustrophobic. I placed it on Stuart's front counter and wiped a few stray hairs off my forehead.

"Yes," Vivienne said. "It was confusing, because he was shot by the bad guy at the same time. We were all laughing because it was kind of a funny skit and then the bad guy pulled out his gun and fired it. It . . . I don't know, did it sound funny?" Vivienne asked Esther.

"Yes." Esther nodded. "It boomed, but from somewhere that didn't seem like the same spot where the bad guy was standing. Like behind us or something," Esther said.

"It startled us all," Gram added. "And then we all were uncertain and confused as to what was going on, or what we thought might be going on." Gram shook her head. "Then we saw the fella on the ground. It was bad."

"I'm so sorry," I said.

The door to Stuart's shop flew open, causing the bell above it to ring at the same time as it slammed into the wall. We all jumped and turned.

"Everyone here all right?" Officer Jenkins said. He was wearing jeans and a T-shirt. He normally worked the night shift at the jail. He'd probably been roused when the murder had occurred and hadn't had time to put on either his uniform or the more casual cowboy gear.

"We're all right," Gram said after she looked at each of us for a confirming nod or blink.

"Good. I'd like for you to all come with me. We're gathering as many people as possible at the jail so we can take statements and get contact information in a timely manner."

"I was just here in my shop, Officer," Stuart said. "I didn't see or hear anything. May

I just stay here? I won't leave until you okay it."

Officer Jenkins wasn't from Broken Rope. He also wasn't as conditioned as Jim, or even Cliff, who was fairly new to the force, at keeping a neutral facade. Concern and suspicion pinched at his eyes as he glanced outside.

"No, sir, we'd like to talk to everyone there," he said.

I interpreted that this was code for "We don't know if everyone is safe from danger yet and we'd like everyone where we can see them." A glance at Gram told me I wasn't the only one reading in between the lines.

"Come on, we'll be nice and cozy in there, but I imagine they won't keep us long — will you, Jenkins?" Gram said.

"No, ma'am, we'll have you out of there as quickly as possible."

"Let's go," Gram said.

As we exited the shoe repair shop, I saw Jerome standing beside the entrance to the Jasper Theater, which was the spot where I'd originally noticed him on his first visit to Broken Rope. The theater was only two doors down from Stuart's, but I thought that Gram might have been in too much of a hurry to get everyone to the jail to notice that he'd returned. If she saw or smelled him, she didn't give any indication. I lagged behind the group and then hurried to him.

I didn't hesitate to reach for his arm, and then his hand, and then his shoulder. My own hand went through him every time. There was nothing solid under my touch.

Jerome watched my movements, but didn't comment. When I finished he said, "I think you're fine for now, Isabelle. I can't go into the jail, but I'll be close by."

"Why could you help me with the fish in the woods, Jerome? Why could I feel you? It wasn't dark."

"I don't know, darlin'," Jerome said as he moved his hand gently toward my face, but he pulled it back before it got even halfway. "I don't have any idea."

I put my hands on my hips and looked around. I didn't know how the jail was going to hold everyone who'd been in town, but the boardwalk was emptying quickly.

"What about everyone else? I'd like to know that everyone is okay," I said.

Jerome sighed. "Can't help you there, Isabelle. I wish I could."

I wished he could, too.

"We'll talk more later?" I said.

"I think so." Jerome smiled. "I haven't left yet."

Actually, he'd left me a few times now, but he had come back, so I didn't point out that nitpicky and self-involved detail. For now, at least.

I tried to "feel" him one more time, but my hand went right through his shoulder again. I didn't want to leave him. I wanted to talk to him more, find out more, but I wasn't even sure what my exact questions were.

"I'll see you later," I said before I hurried to the jail.

CHAPTER 4

"I wasn't in town," I said. "I was back there, fishing." I pointed toward the back wall of the jail. I wished I was still there, beyond the wall and the crowd, with the fake worm in the water or hunting down the evil catfish. "I heard a gunshot, but I couldn't tell you if it was from a popgun or from something real."

"Catch anything?" Cliff asked.

"Yep. It was huge, but it freed itself, gave me the evil eye, and took off," I said with a sad smile.

"The one that got away, huh?"

There was no good reason for the two of us to have stepped back from the crowd for a moment just so we could both make sure the other one was okay. Cliff had a job to do, and taking time away from that job wasn't fair, but we'd done it anyway. He'd told me he was glad to see me, because he hadn't been able to find me in the crowd after the shooting.

"Do you think we were all in danger or just Norman?"

Cliff shrugged. "We don't know, Betts. This is bigger than anything we've ever dealt with. I won't say that Jim and the rest of us are in over our heads, but we simply don't have the manpower to effectively deal with something like this — someone shot out in the open who was in the middle of a larger crowd. We're doing the best we can, and we've called in some help."

"Do you know where the shot came from?" I asked.

Cliff nodded. "Yes, we think so, but we can't find any solid evidence; we're basing our knowledge on measurement and distance guesses, and Jim's the only one who has had any training with that stuff. Someone more experienced from St. Louis will be here soon to evaluate what we've come up with so far."

I bit my lip. Were we dealing with someone on the loose who was going around killing randomly, perhaps just building a list of victims, or had someone wanted Norman dead? How in the world could the police begin to figure *that* out with only measurements and distances?

As if reading my mind, Cliff said, "Betts,

there are ways to investigate this. I don't want you to think we're standing around wondering what to do next. We do have some ideas."

"I know," I said, even though I hadn't until he'd said so.

For a long moment, Cliff held my eyes with his. Though we were in a corner of the room, there was no real privacy. There were people everywhere. I'd been nudged by the elbows of passersby as we'd attempted the somewhat discreet conversation. And he was a police officer. Even though he was one who'd taken the casual-wear idea seriously, everyone still knew he was an officer. We had to keep it professional. A comforting hug would have been weird.

Cliff squinted. "I'll call you later, but it will probably be much later."

"I expected as much."

He put his hand on my arm, smiled, and then turned to get back to work. I watched him melt into the crowd.

"Betts! Hi! Is this crazier than a three-horned toad?"

Cliff's cousin Jezzie squeezed her shoulders through a small crowd on my other side.

"Jezzie, you okay?" I said.

She was still dressed in the period costume

she wore for the skit — a yellow dress with a starched white apron. Her long blond hair was pulled back into a low bun and her pleasant face was free of any makeup. I didn't think she ever wore any, which was only one of the things she and I had in common. We'd also both tried law school and both found that it wasn't for us, and we both adored Cliff, though her adoration was strictly cousinly. Just the day before, she told me that Cliff was her favorite relative and that she was grateful he'd found his way back to me and to Broken Rope. I told her I was, too.

"I'm fine, sweetie, just shaken up. The whole thing was so shocking. The skit happened, and then when Norman was supposed to be shot, he *really* was. Golly, I've never seen anything quite like it."

"I'm sorry," I said.

"No need for you to be sorry at all. Unless you were the one to pull the trigger, I suppose." Jezzie laughed and then put her hand to her mouth. "Good gravy, Betts, why in the world would I laugh about anything at all right now?"

"Stress, Jezzie. It happens. Don't be hard on yourself for that."

"I'll try not to be." She sighed. "He was a nice fella."

"Did you get to know him?"

"Only a little. We did the skit together, but I also saw him over at the campsite last night. I was going to talk to him, but he was busy with the ladies, if you know what I mean. Oh! And he was hanging out with Teddy, too."

"My Teddy?" I said, meaning my brother, Teddy.

"Yes, that one," she said.

"I haven't seen him today. Have you?"

"No."

There was no reason to be concerned about Teddy just because neither Jezzie nor I had seen him today, but the circumstances did make me wonder about his time at the campsite with the murder victim.

"What was he doing last night?"

"I'm not sure. I saw him with Norman, but I also saw both of them flirting with the girls."

"Teddy and the girls," I mumbled. Teddy's ways with girls had frequently caused issues, both when he was paying attention to them and when he was ignoring them.

"Yeah, he's adorable," Jezzie said. There was no added weight to her words, as if she wanted me to fix the two of them up — which was something I frequently dealt with. She was only stating a fact.

I nodded.

"Oh my, and the girls were so darn pretty," Jezzie said. "One had the reddest hair I'd ever seen, and the other looked like a young Elizabeth Taylor."

Her description fit the two women I'd met at Stuart's. I craned my neck to look for them so I could point them out to Jezzie, but I couldn't find them anywhere.

"Were they all together? I mean, were the girls together?" I thought back to the two women. Esther had said that she and Vivienne met only the night before. I hadn't sensed any sort of bond between them, but I wondered about the logistics of them both potentially vying for the attention of the same guys.

Jezzie seemed to be thinking about her answer, but I didn't learn anything further from her, because Jim called her over to a spot next to one of the holding cells. Apparently, it was her turn to answer some questions. Once again, I was left to my own thoughts amid the bumps and *excuse me*s of the crowd. I pulled my phone out and called and texted Teddy, but didn't make immediate contact either way. He'd call or text back when he got the messages. It wasn't unusual not to reach him on the first ten or so tries.

The area that contained the jail — the holding cells and office space for the police officers — wasn't big, and it was currently so crowded that it wasn't easy to spot anyone specific. I looked for Gram, for the two women — Esther and Vivienne — for Teddy, for Jake, and then for Cliff again. In due time, Jim called me over, but we didn't talk for long when he found out I'd been fishing at the time of the murder. As Jim questioned me, my attention went to someone sitting inside one of the holding cells. The doors to the two cells were open, and a few people had gathered in each space; some were sitting on the cots, and some were just standing.

I'd gotten to know Cody, aka the bad guy from the skit, as well as I'd gotten to know Norman. I'd made friendly acquaintance with them both, just easy small talk as I observed a few rehearsals and offered my little bit of input.

Cody sat on one end of the cot in the closest cell. He was slumped, as he was also leaning back against the wall. His face was pale and drawn and he seemed to not be in the moment.

"Jim, have you talked to Cody yet?" I pointed.

"Oh, yeah, poor guy. He's pretty shook up."

"But there's no evidence that he killed Norman, right?"

"Not at all. All indications are that he had absolutely nothing to do with it."

"He doesn't look well. Has he seen Dr. Callahan?"

"No, but you're right, he doesn't look well. I'll have an officer take him over to the doc."

"You're short-staffed as it is. I'll take him," I offered.

Jim looked around at the crowd and grimaced a moment. "All right. That would help, Betts. I appreciate it. We are certain we've secured the area around downtown, but stay alert."

I threaded my way through the crowd and into the holding cell. I lightly touched Cody's shoulder. He blinked and jumped before his eyes focused on me.

"Hi," he said uncertainly.

"I'm Betts," I said.

"I know."

"Come with me, Cody."

He didn't question my request, but lifted himself off the cot as I held on to his elbow and led him out of the jail.

"Phew," he exclaimed when we were

46

outside. "That place was hot and crowded."

Though he sounded relieved, he didn't look much better.

"You look a little pale," I said.

"Yeah, I needed to get out of there. When can I just go home?"

"Soon," I said. "But for now, let's get some air."

I'd changed my mind. Cody didn't need a doctor; he just needed some elbow room.

"Sounds good to me." He looked up and down the boardwalk as if he wasn't sure which way to go.

"This way," I said as I turned toward the Jasper Theater.

Cody was still in costume. He wore jeans and a black Western shirt. Our normal summer costumes didn't usually include jeans, but Jake had kept to a budget by asking the male cast members to bring their own denim. Cody was young, maybe barely twenty, which had originally given me doubts about his ability to play a husband whose wife had cheated on him, but he proved to be one of the best actors at the convention — one of the best I'd ever seen in Broken Rope, actually. His dark eyes belonged on someone much older and, frankly, much wiser. When he wasn't reciting lines, the word I thought best described him was *goofy.*

"Oh, man, Betts, I just want to get out of here. This was fun and all until Norman got killed. Now, well, now, it's just bad."

"I understand," I said as we sauntered, the wooden boardwalk creaking every now and then with our footfalls. "But I think the police want to make sure they know who all is here first. Check up on everybody."

I heard him gulp before he stopped walking. "Check up on us? What do you mean?"

"Questions and stuff." I kept it simple.

"Damn."

"Why are you concerned?"

Cody looked around. Up and down the boardwalk again. He was a good-looking kid, and even for someone who was goofy, he had an intensity about him that I suspected had made his high school years very social.

"I have a record," he said quietly.

Or maybe those high school years weren't social as much as they were just spent in juvie.

"Uh-oh, what'd you do?"

Cody put his hands in his pocket and sighed. "You won't tell, will you?"

"Of course not," I lied.

"I borrowed a car. The owner said I stole it, but he lent it to me, I swear. I'd just turned eighteen, so it'll show on my record."

"Oh. Who was the owner?"

"Just a guy I went to school with. A big group of us were out having a good time, and a girl needed to go home, so I asked if I could borrow the guy's car and get her home. He said I could, but then he called the police. The girl wouldn't even back me up."

I knew that wasn't the whole story, but I said, "I think you can explain that to the police, Cody. They'll understand." I didn't know if they would or wouldn't, but I doubted they'd care too much.

"Oh, good. That's a relief."

And, just like that, Cody seemed to feel better about everything. The color had even returned to his face.

"Hey," he said, "got any money?"

"Uh. Why?"

"You think that cookie shop is open? I'd love a cookie. I'd pay you back," he said with his actor's voice, and his actor's stance and stare, too.

I laughed at the almost perfect James Dean love-me eyes. I hadn't been around someone like Cody in a long time.

"I doubt they're open, but we'll see if Mabel, the owner, is in. I bet I could round up a couple cookies."

"And milk?"

"What good's a cookie without a little milk?" I said.

"Exactly."

So, instead of a doctor's appointment, I took Cody to Broken Crumbs and got some cookies for us both. I tried to learn more about what he'd observed with the goings-on at the convention, but instead I ended up learning more about Cody — his favorite music, television shows, movies, etc.

I convinced him that he shouldn't try to leave town, but it took three cookies to do it. I doubted he had it in him to kill someone, but he needed to stick around for another possible round of questioning. When we were done and as I watched him walk away down the boardwalk, I thought there was a small chance that he wouldn't listen to me, but only a small one. He was such a good actor that the thought also crossed my mind that one cookie might have done the trick, but he just wanted to see how many he could bilk. I had to give him credit.

CHAPTER 5

Even for April, downtown Broken Rope was way too quiet. There were no tumbleweeds in the area, but I could picture one rolling down the empty unpaved road and stirring up the dry earth.

"Excuse me," someone said from behind me.

"Yes?" I said as I turned. It was the redhead, Esther. "Hi again."

"Hi." Esther smiled. "Thanks for what you did back at the shoe repair place. You and your grandmother were great."

"Our pleasure. Is your friend okay?"

"Vivienne is fine. We're not really friends . . . oh, no matter. Yes, she's fine."

I had a few more questions for Esther, but it didn't seem like the right moment to add on to the police's interrogation, and without a little more information I wasn't sure how to approach the subject of whatever had happened between her, Vivienne, Teddy, and

Norman. I'd have to ease into that conversation, considering that her personal life was truly none of my business.

"I'm happy to hear that," I said.

She smiled and winced at the same time. "Look, I know it's been beyond a terrible day so far, and I'm upset, of course, but I have an ulterior motive for coming to the cowboy poetry convention, and I'm afraid we'll all be asked to leave soon or something now because of the . . . Well, I would understand and all, but I'd really like to try to do what I came here to do before heading back home."

"How can I help?"

"I was hoping to find some record of one of my ancestors, my great-great-grandfather. He lived here at one time."

"We're pretty good at that sort of thing. Can you tell me anything else about him? Do you know where he's buried?"

She shook her head. "No one knows where he's buried. He became a Pony Express rider and disappeared on the trail. I know he grew up here. His name was Astin Reagal."

I'd never heard of Astin or his disappearance, but that wasn't too surprising; I wasn't nearly as on top of our history as Jake was. However, a *ding* of sudden awareness chimed in my head when she described her ancestor. The Pony Express was pretty big around these parts. The route had originated in St. Joseph, Missouri, and then snaked through the western United States all the way to California. Even I had been to see the stable tourist attraction in St. Joseph. And there was a replica of one of the Express stations right in Broken Rope. The ding of awareness had rung because of Joe, the newest visiting ghost, with whom I had only become briefly acquainted. He was a young man, like most of the riders had been, and he had a satchel of sorts over his saddle. At one time I knew the name of the satchel that fit over the Express riders' saddles, but at the moment I was at a loss. That satchel; did people other than the Express riders use something like it? I didn't know, but I suddenly wondered if by some crazy chance Joe actually was Astin Reagal, Esther's long-lost relative. It seemed like the perfect coincidence. It also seemed like a wonderfully easy way to perhaps resolve whatever issues the ghost might have, and I was sure he had an issue or two. They all did.

Even more coincidentally, the Broken Rope Pony Express stop was right across from the field behind the high school, which was also the spot for the poets' campsite. It was set back in an area that had once been considered out in the middle of nowhere. I wondered if all the elements of whatever was going on would come together that easily, even though past experience told me nothing was quite that simple with the ghosts.

"The best place to start is with Jake," I said. "He knows the history of Broken Rope and its citizens more than anyone. His office is right there." I signaled with a nod. "Come on. I'll be happy to introduce you if he's in."

"Do you think it's a bad time?"

"I guess I'm not sure. He might not even be there, but if he was excused from the jail, I'm sure he went back to his building. He'll tell us if we need to come back later."

"Thank you."

Jake's fake sheriff's costume was cleaned, pressed, and put away until the summer tourist season, but in deference to the poets and their garb, he'd been trying to follow the same request he'd made to the actors and police officers. He'd been wearing mostly Western shirts, cowboy boots, and jeans. But today he was completely civilian in jeans and a nice blue pinstriped button-up shirt, the sleeves of which were rolled up to his elbows. He wasn't a big man, but he was surely one of the most handsome guys in town — maybe in the whole county. He'd been my best friend since high school, and I hoped we'd be friends forever. He sat on a stool behind the raised podium that was in the front room of his building. During the summer, he'd stand behind the podium as he recited his original Western-themed poem with his deep baritone voice. At the moment, he was somber and seemed to be concentrating on something on the podium.

"Betts," he said as he raised his head. When he noticed it wasn't just me, he stood and tried to erase the sadness from his demeanor. He stepped toward us.

"Hey, Jake, this is Esther . . ."

"Oh," she said. "Reagal. It's Reagal."

"Esther Reagal. She's in town with the poets, but is looking for some information regarding her great-great-grandfather."

"Okay."

"I'm so sorry," Esther said to Jake. "The timing is awful and probably rude and wrong, but I don't know what might happen now and I don't want to leave town without trying."

"I understand," Jake said. "It's fine. What was his name?"

"Astin Reagal."

"Hmmm, there's something familiar about that, but maybe it's just because it's such a great name." Jake smiled a friendly smile.

Ester smiled, too, and her cheeks blushed lightly. I was caught off guard for a moment. Jake wasn't much of a flirt, but that had definitely been flirting. Should I stay or should I go?

"He was a Pony Express rider," I interjected. I looked at Esther. "He disappeared on the trail. His body wasn't found, is that right?"

"That's right."

"Well, I've heard that story, of course." Jake looked at Esther and then at me. "I'm sure I have some information, though I'm not sure how much." He hesitated. I realized he was silently debating whether or not to share the location of his secret room with an outsider. Ultimately, he probably concluded that Esther was harmless enough, or maybe just cute enough to want to spend more time with. "I have an archive room in the back. Would the two of you like to join me?"

I didn't really want to. I would have rather left to go about my own business, but I was suddenly under the impression that I was being asked for the purpose of either witnessing or chaperoning. Jake had done as much for me a time or two.

"Sure," I said.

"That'd be great," Esther said.

Jake led us through the door on the back wall. I'd become used to the transformation from the front office to the back room. The front room was decorated with remnants from an Old West sheriff's office, but the spacious back archive room had tall, packed shelves, a large worktable, and the old saloon chandelier that had been wired for our century. I was one of the lucky few who got to frequent the room. Jake didn't like to share his archive space with lots of people.

"Wow," Esther said as she glanced around and then behind us to the door we'd come through. "It's like magic."

Jake laughed lightly. "Our storefronts are very much for decoration and entertainment, but some of our back rooms are taller than the front rooms' short ceilings, and they're built for business. It's an illusion, and we're pretty good at illusion."

"No kidding," Esther said.

"Have a seat," Jake said as he pulled two stools out from under one side of the large worktable. "I have a file on things pertinent to the Pony Express and Broken Rope. It's not thick, but I'm pretty sure it has some information regarding your ancestor."

"Really?" Esther said.

"Jake's done an amazing job of keeping a living record of our history. He's the best," I said, though I cleared my throat immediately after — I'd sounded like I was trying to sell him. He didn't need selling. He blinked at me and then moved on.

"Let's see." He ran his fingers over some of the big archival folders, stopping at one almost directly in the middle of a set of shelves. "Here it is."

The file was neither thick nor tall, and my heart sunk a little. Jake was right, he didn't have much information.

"You know," Jake said as he reached into the folder and pulled out a short stack of items, "many people think that the Pony Express existed for a long time. Not true. In fact," he lifted a small piece of paper from the top of the stack and inspected it, "it was in existence only from 1860 to 1861. Let's see, yes, April to the following October, eighteen months. Before the telegraph was completed, the country needed a way to get communication — mostly government papers and such — across to California, so some freighting businessmen founded the Pony Express. There were stops for the riders to change horses or riders or both, drop off things, and pick up things, about every ten miles. The trail originated up in St. Joseph. The stable's still there, but I haven't been there for years."

"How long did it take them to get from Missouri to California?" I asked.

"I think they got it down to about ten days to make the trip."

"Yes, that's right," Esther said. She reached into her pocket and pulled out a small, shiny object. "I have this. I guess it was my great-great-grandfather's, but no one has been able to tell me for sure. This is the item that sparked my curiosity, and it made me want to study both my past and the history of the Pony Express. And that's why I came to Broken Rope."

"Oh, my, is that a real badge?" Jake said as he reached for the item that reminded me somewhat of his fake sheriff's badge, and unquestionably of the badge I'd seen on Joe's chest. Jake pulled his hand back, but Esther smiled and handed it to him.

"Yes, I think so. I think it's a real one," she said.

"But your great-great-grandfather disappeared. Wouldn't his badge have disappeared with him?" I said.

Esther shrugged. "He must have had more than one."

Jake held the item so I could look at it, too. An eagle rode the top of the badge, which was emblazoned with a rider on a horse and the words *Pony Express Messenger.* I was never as touched or affected by items from the past as Jake was, but I thought this was a pretty interesting artifact, and it was clear that it was working its magic on him. One side of his mouth smiled as he gently held the old, tarnished item.

"It's beautiful," he said as he handed it back to Esther. He cringed slightly when she simply put it back into her pocket. "Oh! Wait, I have something else, something other than the information in the file. I can't believe I forgot about it. Hang on a second," he added.

Esther and I watched as Jake pulled a good-sized box from a bottom shelf and placed it on the table.

"I wrapped it and then put it in this box, but it's quite valuable, and I've considered talking to a preservationist to see what else I could do to keep it as intact as possible."

He lifted the lid and pulled out the one item inside.

"I don't even think it should be out of the wrapping much, but it might be kind of fun for you to see this, Esther." Jake looked at me. "Don't tell anyone I have it."

I nodded.

It was a saddle. Kind of. It was a duplicate of the satchel I'd seen over Joe's saddle.

"This is called . . ." Jake began.

"A *mochila,*" Esther interrupted. "It's how they carried the mail."

Mochila! *That's it.*

The item looked kind of like saddlebags, but it was made to ride *over* the saddle, so it had its own formed seat cover. Its pockets weren't baglike, but more boxy and with flaps; one of the flaps was still secured with an old metal latch. The leather was mostly tan, but time had worn it darker in spots. The letters *SP CA* had been tooled into it. The other flap was decorated with *XP.* It also looked as though a number of different words had been inscribed on its surface.

"Are those names?" Esther asked as she peered closely at the *mochila.*

"I think so. I think riders signed the *mochilas.* They didn't have their own because whenever the riders changed at the stops, the *mochila* with the mail went with the new rider. It was a pretty efficient system."

"Wow, so this is an original?" I asked.

"I think so," Jake said as he nodded.

"May I touch it?" Esther asked.

"Sure. Gently."

"Of course."

Esther inspected every inch of the *mochila*. Once she'd memorized one side, she turned it over and did the same on the other side.

"Wait. What do you suppose this is?" she asked.

Jake and I leaned in to look at letters, which were small and had become dark with time and air and simple grime.

"Well, I think . . ." Jake began. He stood straight and raised his eyebrows. "Esther, I can't be completely sure, but look closely. Tell me if you don't think that says Astin Reag. I can't make out the other letters, but I wouldn't be surprised if they were *A–L*. We might be just wishing. But how amazing would that be?"

Esther blinked and then bent to look again. She gasped as she re-straightened.

"Oh, my," she said. "I . . . I don't feel so well."

Somehow, an instant later, both Jake and I were holding on to Esther's slack body.

"Did she faint?" I asked.

"I hope it's nothing more serious."

"You have quite an effect on women, my friend," I said.

"History — it'll take you to your knees if you ever start to really pay attention to it, Betts."

"Right."

"For now, lean her on me, and grab a glass of water."

I did as Jake asked, and we hoped it wouldn't take more than that to revive our visitor.

CHAPTER 6

"Oh, my, I am so embarrassed," Esther said as she sat up straight on the stool. Jake and I were on either side of her, at the ready in case she went down again. "I don't think I've ever fainted. Ever. It was just so strange to maybe suddenly be connected to a family member, someone dead for so long but whose existence was partially responsible for mine. It was like . . . well, like his ghost was in the room with us for a minute."

Jake looked at me with raised eyebrows. I shook my head. No, the ghost of Astin Reagal wasn't in the vicinity, but I was really beginning to think he'd ridden into town earlier. I wanted to confirm before I got Jake's hopes up too high, though. Disappointment flickered over his face, but he normalized quickly. He loved the entire idea of our historical ghosts, and he knew about their visits with me and Gram. Much to his chagrin, he wasn't able to see them — well, he'd had a brief glimpse of Sally Swarthmore, but that was a planned and rare moment.

"It's okay," I said to Esther, "if you're okay."

She waved away my concern. "Fine." She blinked and then looked at Jake. "May I look closely at the *mochila* again?"

"Of course," Jake said hesitantly.

Esther laughed. "I'm so sorry, Jake. I won't faint again, I promise. I was just momentarily overwhelmed."

If I wasn't mistaken, Esther batted her eyelashes at him.

"Sure. I know," Jake said as the two of them smiled at each other a beat too long.

Esther looked away first and then sat even straighter.

I relaxed back onto my own stool, and Jake scooted the *mochila* closer to Esther.

"Go ahead, touch it all you want," he said. "I keep it wrapped up most of the time; but if anyone has the right to look it over closely, it's you."

"Well, if that really is Astin's signature, I guess."

"Let's go with that being the truth. If we need to rethink later, we can."

"Thank you." Esther smiled at him again.

"For a minute I thought it was truly amazing that Jake might have a *mochila* with Astin Reagal's signature, but it kind of makes sense, too," I said, interrupting all the smiling and reminding them I was there. "Since Astin was from Broken Rope, and historical items tend to be left in attics and closets around here for a long time, maybe it's not so strange after all."

Esther nodded. "You know," her fingers rode over the tooled letters of, presumably, her ancestor's name, "apparently his disappearance was a huge mystery, and it broke up his family."

"Hang on," Jake said. "I'd love to hear everything you have to say, but would you mind if I recorded it?"

"As I mentioned earlier, Jake keeps track of our history better than anyone," I said. "He likes to make sure he's as accurate as possible."

Jake laughed. "Truthfully, accuracy isn't always the point. Stories are passed down and passed around. I just like to make sure I have as many versions of the stories as possible. I suspect there is some truth, some fabrication, in them all, but I think it's important. History is important. If I record, I'll transcribe what you say and make a file. I hope to open a museum someday. I would use your story — and make sure everyone knew that it came from you — for some sort of display."

Esther thought a second, and then said, "Certainly."

Jake pulled out his phone and moved his finger over the screen a couple times. "This is Esther Reagal, great-great-granddaughter of Astin Reagal. She's visiting Broken Rope and is looking at the *mochila* that I had in storage. There is evidence in the form of a partial tooled name that Astin might have used it when he was a Pony Express rider. He died on the trail and his body was never found. Go ahead, Esther, tell us whatever you'd like to share."

Esther cleared her throat. "Well, Astin was young, only eighteen when he signed on with the Express. I think eighteen was the oldest they'd consider for riders. It was a job meant for young bodies. It was an exciting time, and the riders were young men who loved what they did, loved the adventure of it all. They'd ride like the wind for about ten miles, and then change horses."

"Or change riders, too? Like if their — what — shift was over?" I said.

"Yes," Jake said.

Esther bit her bottom lip and looked off into the imagined distance before she continued. "It was about the riders *and* the

67

horses. The riders were amazing, but so were the horses. They were fast and apparently very smart. They were chosen for their speed and endurance. It's said that the one that Astin was on when he was on his way to Broken Rope and disappeared tried to lead my great-great-grandmother back to Astin, but no one ever found him. My great-great-grandmother searched and searched for him, for years, even abandoning her own son because of her heartbreak. They were young; so young. I think she was only seventeen, and with a new baby."

"What was her name?" Jake asked.

"Amelia Reagal."

Stepping around the table and Esther, Jake moved to his computer and started typing.

"I can't find her," he said. "I have a database of Broken Rope cemetery residents. She's not listed."

"That part of the story is vague, but we think she left town after years of searching."

"Do you know where she went?"

Esther shook her head. "Their son, my great-grandfather, stayed here. Amelia just stopped being a mom. She stopped everything except searching for her husband. It's not known where she ended up, but it's been speculated that Springfied, Jefferson

City, or Rolla were all possible places."

"What was their son's name?" Jake asked.

"Charlie Reagal."

Jake typed more. "There he is. He's buried in the cemetery next to where Betts works. She and her Gram run a cooking school."

"That cemetery's yours? I drove by it, and I wondered about the school. What a great building."

"The school is ours; the cemetery is just part of the scenery," I said. "It isn't under our care, but it is right next to the school." I hadn't noticed Esther visiting the cemetery, but I hadn't been there very often over the last few days. My duties away from the school had consisted of sewing a few ripped costume seams; fishing, of course; helping Orly with a number of little things that no one else would attend to; prepping for our fish-frying and Dutch-oven-cooking lessons; and other glamorous chores that had kept me on the move. Orly and I had hit it off, and I remembered that I hadn't been able to find him earlier. I silently noted to myself that I needed to track him down. Along with Teddy, Gram, Jerome, and the new ghost, Joe.

"It's a charming cemetery," Esther said.

"I agree." The name Charlie Reagal was familiar, but I couldn't place exactly where he was buried. I'd ask Gram if Charlie had ever visited her in his ghostly form. If so, we might end up with an even bigger chunk of Esther's history to share with her. I liked the idea of the shortcut.

"What family did Charlie stay with?" Jake asked.

"I don't know," Esther said. "That part of the story is missing. I was hoping you might be able to help."

Jake typed again. "Well, I can't be completely sure, but I think he owned the general store. Someone by that name owned it, but I'd have to look a little deeper to confirm that this Charlie Reagal was your Charlie Reagal. If it is, then he was successful. I know I've got some stuff on the old general store, but I haven't digitized the information yet. I'll find it, hopefully today sometime. Maybe it'll tell us more."

"That's . . . wow, that's so much more than I thought I'd be able to learn. Thank you."

"Trust me, my pleasure." Jake stood and moved back to the table. "May I ask you some more questions?"

"Sure."

"What else do you know — I mean, are there any other stories about the Pony Express riders that were passed down to you? There are legends and there are facts, and sometimes those stories tend to melt together a little, but can you remember anything else that your family discussed?"

Esther thought a moment. "No, not really. I wish I could."

"Believe it or not, I've actually heard an Express story," I said. Jake and Esther nodded me on. "Well, they weren't supposed to carry heavy weapons, no shotguns, but a rider did, and I'm not sure if I believe this, but the story is that halfway through his first ride, he threw the rifle off the horse mid-stride and it fired, scaring both the rider and the horse, but the noise also sped the horse up. They arrived at the next post in record time. The rider was a company star on his first ride, because he shot at himself."

"That's a good one," Jake said, but I could see the uncertainty in his eyes. He wouldn't want to make me feel uncomfortable, but I understood his doubt regarding the validity of the story.

"They *needed* weapons — though not shotguns — to protect themselves from, among other things, Native American attacks — at that time they were Indians. This doesn't really have anything to do with Astin, but in Nevada, four Express men were killed and a station was burned by Paiutes in retribution for the rape of some young Paiute girls," Jake added. "History isn't always pretty and romantic, but I think it's important to acknowledge the bad stuff with the good stuff."

"Oh, Astin helped deliver a baby once," Esther said.

"Really?" I said.

"Yes, he came upon a stalled stagecoach, and though it was against policy to ever stop, the riders were clearly in distress, so he broke policy, stopped, and helped deliver the baby. The woman who gave birth was the only female on board; she was traveling with her husband and the stagecoach driver. Apparently, neither of the men were up for the challenge. Astin had helped with Charlie's birth — they lived out in the woods; everybody lived out in the woods at the time — so he had some idea of what to do. The baby was a healthy girl."

"That's wonderful," Jake said, but he doubted her story, too, I could hear it in his voice, though he hid it better with her story than with mine.

Esther blinked and then fell into thought. "Yes, it's a wonderful story." She ran her finger over the letters on the *mochila* again. "This is more than I could have ever expected. Thank you," she said. It seemed she was suddenly tired.

"It's meant a lot to me, too, truly. Thank you for sharing," Jake said.

"I'm a bit overwhelmed. I'm not going to faint again, and you've both been so kind, but I think I'd better head back to the campsite and rest a little."

"Certainly." Jake touched the phone to end the recording.

Before the faint, Esther hadn't struck me as delicate or frail, but now I wondered if she'd be okay. I debated taking her back to the campsite myself as we stood and moved toward the door, but she seemed fine.

Esther turned and looked at us both. "It was terrible what happened out there today. I feel a little guilty for enjoying all this, but as long as I'm in town, I'll let you know if something else comes to mind."

"That would be great, and I'll let you know what else, if anything, I find," Jake said.

"I wish your museum was set up."

"Someday," Jake said.

"I don't suppose . . . Well, I don't know if this is inappropriate or not, but I'd love to take you to dinner, perhaps this evening?"

There was nowhere for me to go. I could open the door and go into the front room or all the way out the front door, but not without Esther having to move a little, which would interrupt the moment. The idea of hiding under the table ran through my mind briefly, but thankfully I realized that would have been ridiculous. I simply looked away — at the ceiling, then over toward the files. On second thought, the ceiling was better, because it had the interesting chandelier. Yes, I could inspect the chandelier parts.

"I . . ." Jake began.

Come on, Jake, do NOT say no. I almost shot him a stern look, but I just squinted as I continued to inspect the light fixture.

Jake had never had much of a personal life. He'd dated, and even had a girlfriend or two since high school, but nothing had stuck. He never seemed particularly lonely, but there were times when I thought he might appreciate some female company other than me and Gram.

"Actually, I'd love to. May I pick you up?" Jake said.

I held back a fist pump, but the pull of a smile was too strong to ignore, so I gave into it. I smiled at the chandelier, and then at Jake.

"I'm at the campsite. I'll meet you in front of the high school at seven o'clock?" Esther said.

I liked her style.

"That's perfect. I look forward to it."

"Great." Esther glanced at me shyly, her cheeks blushing like any good redhead's.

I just smiled at everyone as I opened the door and let Esther go through first.

Of course, Jake rolled his eyes at my grin.

CHAPTER 7

Though I was becoming anxious to find Gram again, and Joe, and change out of my overalls, my plans were diverted, but at least it was by someone I wanted to talk to. Orly signaled to me as he steered his big old pickup truck down a side street at the end of the boardwalk.

"Miss Winston," he said after he stopped the truck and reached over to open the passenger door with a push on some extra squeaky hinges. "You have a minute?"

I'd only known Orly for a few days, but our relationship had been built on things that either bring people together quickly or not. We'd chatted as we were setting up a mess hall of sorts, while unfolding some cots and transporting cooking utensils. I'd learned that he was born in Hutchinson, Kansas, and had lived there all his life, minus a brief time in Tennessee and a "little-more-than-brief" stint in Georgia.

His love of Kansas, specifically the small town of Hutchinson, was, frankly, kind of cute. There were a lot of small towns in the Midwest, and most of them were populated with a healthy number of people whose goal was to leave small-town life behind and move to a big city. Not Orly, though. He was, in his own words, "as deep into Kansas dirt as all that wheat."

He'd been married once, but his wife had died about ten years earlier. He had two daughters, only one of whom, so far, had given him a grandson to dote on. He said he'd be happy with a whole herd of grandbabies to spoil rotten. His use of the word "herd" could probably be attributed to the fact that he was also a cattleman back in Hutchinson, with a "smallish" ranch. I hadn't been privileged to hear one of his poems yet, but he told me that his cattle and the cattleman's life were his biggest writing inspirations.

I'd liked him immediately, even though I'd sensed that he wasn't comfortable with welcoming new friends into his life. Despite the fact that he was the president of the International Cowboy Poetry Association and had been involved with it for twenty-five years, in positions that required a multitude of communication skills, it was evident that he purposefully kept things close to the vest. Scratch that — close to the very Western-style vest. He was silent and observant much more than he was talkative. He also gave the impression that he was efficient in everything he did. No matter what task he was attending to, there were no wasted movements, no backtracking, no repeating. He was one of those people who probably *was* good at everything.

And he and I had not only hit it off well, but quickly, too. We'd been able to work together without needing to discuss much — we knew what had to be done and somehow we both knew what abilities we could each contribute, so we made a good team. This had begun the day before the poets even came to town. Since our initial connection, Orly had sought me out when something needed doing. I'd become his sidekick of sorts, and though I hadn't expected such responsibility, I had enjoyed it.

However, I didn't really know him. And there'd been a murder. And he was asking me to get into his truck.

"Sure, but Gram is probably wondering where I am. Let me text her that I'll be with you for the next little bit."

"Thanks."

The truck's engine revved a little rich as Orly waited patiently. I sensed that I was overreacting and being silly, but sending the text seemed like a smart and harmless move.

"Okay, what's up?" I asked after I hit send, and then hoisted myself onto the passenger side of the bench seat.

"I want to show you something at the campsite."

"Okay."

"Good."

Both my parents work at Broken Rope High School. My dad is the principal and my mom is the auto shop teacher, so even long after finishing high school I still spent plenty of time in the building, where the typical scents of floor cleaner and Tater Tots greeted visitors each time they walked through the front doors.

The high school had been built in the late 1800s, but the powers that had been had decided to forgo the typical brick building design of most American high schools of the time. Instead, Broken Rope High School resembled the Alamo. Jake knew the whole story much better than I did, but someone on the town's planning commission thought Spanish baroque would be an interesting design for the building that sat on the edge of town and served not only residents of Broken Rope but also those from other small towns throughout the county. It was wide, one story, the front facade rising with an ornate rounded peak in the middle above the front doors. The front lawn was also wide, and mostly tree-filled, giving the entire setting some terrific curb appeal.

The timing of spring break had been helpful when it came to scheduling the convention. Gram had always scheduled the cooking school's break at the same time as the rest of the area schools', so fortunately we'd both been available to help, and the high school was also void of students, who couldn't wait to get as far away from there as they could for a week. School staff were still working if they wanted to; very few wanted to, though, so there was little traffic to be disturbed by the influx of visitors who camped in the big field behind the school.

The field had been deemed a perfect setup for the poets. It sat beyond the school building, a soccer field, and a football stadium. Another structure stood at one far corner of the field; a big shed had been constructed and placed there only a couple months earlier for the school district to use as a storage facility. Though the walls of the shed were made of aluminum, my dad had asked for a design that wasn't as cold and utilitarian as a typical storage shed. The district had built a big red aluminum barn. It wasn't exactly what Dad had had in mind, but he'd decided to like it. It wasn't all that bad, and it sat back far enough that you could only see it once you got past the football stadium.

At the other corner of the campsite, a good fifty yards away, and across what used to be a heavily used stagecoach trail — if you looked hard or just happened to catch one with your toe, you could still find wheel ruts in the mostly overgrown ground — sat the reproduced Pony Express station. The stable in St. Joseph was different than our station; different than any of the reproduced stations through the western United States. The stable in St. Joseph was bigger and had housed more horses and men than the smaller, more simply built stations. Our station was ramped up with a little extra technology and a real door, which I'd heard wasn't typical of most of the other modern incarnations. Also, in our station, small podiums with plaques telling the story of the Pony Express lined three of the four inside walls. Electricity had been added so that track lighting attached to the wooden ceiling beams could be used to illuminate the plaques. Jake had told me that a solid door had been needed to protect the modern-day additions, but that the typical station back in the day didn't have a door, just a large opening. Behind the station was more Missouri woods — lots and lots of Missouri woods.

Orly turned the truck onto the road next to the school, steering us past the adobe structure.

"I found something, and I wanted you to see it," he said. He hadn't had much to say since we'd left Main Street, but I'd asked him if he was okay, considering the brutal turn of the morning. He assured me that he was fine, though understandably shaken up. He asked me the same question. I promised him I'd be okay, too. He also noted that no matter what the reality was, and even though the police had questioned everyone, it might not have soaked in totally with convention attendees that what they'd seen had been real and as awful as anything could be. There might be more trauma to come for some. I didn't know what I could do to help with that, but I decided I'd talk to Cliff about it later.

"What did you find?" I asked.

"I'll show you when we get there. You can tell me if you think I should show it to the police."

I blinked as the gears in my head starting spinning up to full throttle. "Wait, Orly, is this something that has to do with the murder?"

He shrugged. "Maybe."

I sat up straighter. "I think you should definitely show it to the police, then."

"I'd like you to see it first."

"Why?"

"I don't know who to trust, 'cept for you, your gram, and that Jake fella."

"You can trust the police. They're the best."

"Maybe, but this place — Broken Rope — has quite a reputation. I just dunno."

"I promise. They can be trusted. Do you want me to call them?" I fished my phone out of my overalls pocket.

"Hang on. We're almost there. You look at it first and then we'll call them if you think it's necessary. If you say it's okay to trust them, then I will, but like I said, we're almost there."

I was silent, a million questions and scary scenarios going through my mind.

Orly glanced over at me. "It's nothing to worry about. I just want you to see it."

I nodded without looking at him.

When we passed the football stadium and I could get an even better look at the campsite, my discomfort got replaced by surprise.

"More people came today?" I said, noticing the larger number of tents and campers.

"Sure. Not everybody likes all the early events, but everyone loves the late nights; the party. Lots of the new arrivals weren't even at the show this morning. I had a good chat with Jim, that police fella, about keeping things moving along. He thought the rest of the convention should be canceled, but I told him lots of people were still on their way and letting all of them know about any change of plans would be impossible. I don't think he wanted to let us go on, but he did. And here we all are."

I suspected that was why Orly didn't *trust* the police.

"Should Gram and I continue to plan on the Dutch oven and fish frying demonstrations tomorrow?"

"Absolutely."

The culmination of the cowboy poetry convention was a huge dinner, with most of the food cooked outside over campfires. The finalists for the poetry contests were announced, the poems read and voted upon (the volume of whoops and hollers was used to tally votes, Orly had told me), and prizes doled out. The rest of the evening, and most of the night (again, from what Orly had told me), was spent in celebration. A band that was heavy on fiddle and banjo music would play, and people would dance and sing and probably drink too much. No one was allowed to drive any sort of vehicle anywhere until they were cleared as ready and able and sober the next day.

I knew there were restrictions on the placement and the number of campfires that could be active at the campsite. Only two fires were allowed, and they had to be placed on opposite sides of the site, as well as a certain distance from any of the camping structures — the tents and trailers. We'd be able to do the fish fry at the campsite, but the number of fires needed for the Dutch oven demonstrations dictated that we do those somewhere else. We decided the cooking school parking lot would be perfect. It was a place that could safely handle the fire and heat of a number of cooking stations without much concern for a spark hitting the neighboring woods or school structure. Evan, the fire marshal, had assured us that representatives from the fire department would be on-site to monitor and help with any issues. The fire restrictions were obviously being respected, but I wondered if there was a law regarding restrictions on the number of campers allowed on an open field behind a high school. Even if there wasn't a law, it was clear that there were just too many people in one space, too many tents, and campers, too. I didn't know the exact dangers that went along with poor crowd management, but I was sure that Jim was losing his mind regarding the campsite, and even more so with a murder. I suspected he hadn't just shut everything down because he still wanted to investigate, and if the convention were shut down, people would just leave. He didn't want anyone to leave yet. I didn't envy the position he'd been put in.

Orly steered the truck to the far end of the field, to the back corner that was almost directly across the old stagecoach tracks from the Express station. He'd set up his tent on a corner patch, where anyone who might need him could find him easily.

He parked and said, "In my tent."

"Orly, you need to tell me what's in there. I'm concerned, and I don't know if I want to see what you think I need to see."

He chewed on the inside of his cheek a second and then said, "Well, I got you this far, so I guess it's okay to tell you now that there's a fella inside my tent. He asked me specifically to come find you and get you out here without telling you what was going on first. He thought you'd be so upset or concerned that you wouldn't come alone, and he didn't want anyone but you here."

"What fella? Who?"

"Claims to be your brother. I already told him that I'd shoot him if he's lying or tries anything funny."

I was suddenly wedged in between shock and humor; shocked that Teddy might be in Orly's tent, humor because of Orly's dry delivery of his threat; but then I realized he meant what he was saying. Teddy really was in his tent, and Orly probably truly would shoot him if he deemed it necessary.

"Oh, no," I said. "What'd he get himself into this time?"

"Your question makes me think he's exactly the type of young man I suspected him to be. Should we go see?"

I hopped out of the truck and trudged over and around camping accessories to get to Orly's tent. I was concerned about what might be going on, but I did experience a small sense of reluctant déjà vu. I'd been summoned a few times to surprising and sometimes mysterious places at often unusual hours to retrieve my brother. He was an adorable, sweet man who attracted women simply by existing, and his judgment when it came to his love life hadn't been good. Recently, the woman I thought might actually make an honest man out of him dumped him. Ophelia Buford, Opie, a lifelong thorn in my side, had claimed to be head over heels for my untamed brother and, much to my disappointment, he claimed the same for her. And then one day, she just decided that she no longer wanted to be a couple. It had broken his heart, and I'd expected his ways of coping would result in bad behavior, but so far I'd been pleasantly surprised.

Of course, our quiet and peaceful existence wasn't destined to last. It was probably almost over; it would probably end when I stepped into the tent.

Orly reached for the front flap of his very modern tent. "If he's not who he says he is or if he acts squirrelly, just give me the signal. I'll take care of him."

I nodded and he pulled back the flap.

"Teddy!" I exclaimed when I saw him. Any irritation I felt was replaced with fear and concern. I knew the man in the tent was my brother, despite the fact that he didn't much look like him at the moment.

"Betts, thanks for coming out here," he said.

He was sitting on the ground against one

of the back tent poles. I couldn't tell exactly where he was injured, but he was covered in blood. Red and brown camouflaged most of what was supposed to be a white T-shirt. His jeans weren't as bloody, but they looked too dirty and were ripped in the wrong places. He was holding a small slab of meat over half of his face; the other half was swollen and misshapen. His nose was huge, and his eye sagged. When he pulled away the meat, I saw that the other eye was swollen completely shut.

"What the hell happened, Teddy?" I said as I went down on my knees next to him.

"Don't remember, but I think I got into a fight."

"You don't remember?"

"We found him," Orly said. He nodded toward the woods that were across the trail and behind the station. "He was unconscious."

I swallowed a sudden surge of anger — why did no one think to call an ambulance or get Teddy some quick medical attention?

"Okay, I'll get the full story later, but right now I need to get you to a doctor," I said.

"No, Betts, not yet," Teddy said.

"What?"

"I wanted to take him to a doctor," Orly said, "but he wouldn't let me."

"I don't understand."

"We found him earlier and got him awake quickly. Just like now, he didn't remember much, but one of our cowgirls did — the cowgirl that found him in the woods, in fact. She said she'd seen him late yesterday evening in an argument with someone who'd been hanging around us and asking us all kinds of writing questions. I put all the pieces together and realized that the person your brother was arguing with was Norman Bytheway."

"Oh . . . he was the one who was . . ." I said.

"Yes, ma'am, he was the one killed this morning. When your brother and I got to talking, I thought maybe I should do as he asked and bring you out here before we did anything else."

I nodded at Orly and then squinted at my beaten brother. My anger and fear weren't mellowing, exactly, but I knew I needed to get a clear head, and quick.

"Oh, Teddy," I said.

"I know — what the hell happened?" he said, quoting the words I'd spoken only moments ago, and a million times before.

CHAPTER 8

"I was just hanging out, Betts, I promise," Teddy said as I inspected his face.

I looked at Orly; he shrugged. "Dunno. *I* didn't see him and Norman arguing. I don't know if anyone other than the cowgirl saw them. I can try to round up some people if you'd like me to, but I didn't want anyone to feel compelled to come forward, or worry that they should run to the police too quickly."

"Were you arguing with Norman Bytheway?" I asked Teddy.

"I don't know," he said, with hesitation. "I remember him, but I don't remember arguing."

"You said you don't remember everything clearly," Orly said.

Teddy looked at me through his one barely open eye. "That's true."

I was torn by Orly's seemingly fast loyalty to me and his protecting Teddy; I was both relieved and uncomfortable. Sure, he and I had bonded, but what he'd done could get him in trouble. Of course, I'd do what I could to make sure that didn't happen, but I knew what we should be doing. We should be — as Orly would probably put it — hightailing it to a doctor, calling the police on the way so they could meet us and get a statement from Teddy.

However, here I was, still in the tent, still trying to understand what happened before I took any steps to do what I was supposed to do.

"Teddy, who was the girl?" I asked. No one had mentioned a girl in *that* context yet, but when Teddy was involved, there was always a girl. "Was it the" — I looked at Orly — "cowgirl?"

Teddy sighed and looked away from me and to the floor of the tent.

"I'm not sure if she's the same girl that Orly is talking about, but I think I remember someone named Esther."

I looked at Orly, who shook his head. I said, "The girl who found him wasn't Esther?"

"No, ma'am," Orly said.

"Go on, Teddy," I said. I wondered how many Esthers were at the convention. I hoped that Teddy wasn't talking about the same one I'd just seen ask Jake out on a dinner date, but I was sure he was.

"I don't remember much else about her at this point. I wasn't here to meet girls, Betts, I promise. And I was minding my own business. She came on to me. I'm pretty sure. And I don't think Norman was upset by that at all, but I kind of remember him being there at the same time. I think. Shoot, I'm just not sure."

It was my turn to sigh. If he was remembering anything correctly, I doubted he was lying about the bits and pieces. He wasn't adept at lying, which was mostly a good thing.

"And you just went along with it, with her?" I said.

"Not really. I'm not . . . I'm not looking for a girl, Betts. I'm still trying to get over Opie, you know that."

In fact, I did know that, though Teddy had never needed to spend much time working to get over anyone before. He typically bounced back quickly; the fact that he hadn't this time broke my heart a little, as well as got under my skin. How could anyone ever care that much for Opie?

Nevertheless.

"Word has it that Norman was sweet on a couple girls," Orly said. "But he and Esther had been flirting, or perhaps more; at least they were seen together a lot these past couple of days. These events seem to bring that sort of thing out in some people — outside, camping, away from home, romantic poetry and singing. Well, it happens. I tend not to give much attention to those who are of age and who aren't being obnoxious."

I kept to myself that I'd met Esther — well, *an* Esther anyway. She and Vivienne had both mentioned that they had talked to the murder victim but not much more. However, she hadn't seemed particularly affected by Norman's murder, not needing extra recovery time in Stuart's shop like Vivienne had. I'd save that information for the police if I thought they needed it.

"What else do you remember?" I asked Teddy.

"I remember sitting around the fire last night. I remember a girl coming over to me. I even remember trying to let her know I wasn't interested, Betts."

"I believe you."

"Good. Then, later, I'm pretty sure it was Norman who asked me to help him with some firewood. I thought it was strange that he wanted to go *into* the woods for the wood. There were two big stacks that I helped chop last week on the edge of the field, but he said that someone had carried some logs out to the woods and someone had told them they weren't allowed to light a fire out there, which was true — fires aren't supposed to be lit out there. He wanted me to help him bring the wood back to the piles. At the time that must have made sense," Teddy said doubtfully. It didn't make any sense at all, actually, but I didn't point that out.

"Okay."

"I don't remember anything else after that."

"Not one thing?"

"Not one thing."

"You don't remember being hit?"

"No."

He'd been hit more than once, that much was clear.

The fact that my brother had been accosted — at least according to his shaky side of the story — boiled my stomach. From what I could see, it looked like he might have easily been killed. Had he been only one more blow from death? I hadn't seen Norman this morning, but had he looked beaten up? Had it been a fair fight? Had Norman even been involved at all?

Teddy's story was outrageous, but fathomable in a muddled-up-facts way, I supposed. The motivations behind the violent behavior couldn't simply have been because of a woman, though. There had to be more. I wanted to push Teddy to try to remember better, but the responsible side of me was taking over again, and he needed to see a doctor more than he needed to be pushed. Besides, maybe his memories would come back a little more as he healed.

"Orly, do you mind driving us back into town?" I said.

"Right away."

"I think I have my truck. I must have driven it here last night. And I have my keys," Teddy said as he winced and reached into his pocket.

"I think it's parked on the other side of the campsite. I'll take you two over there," Orly said.

"Thanks, Orly. I'll drive your truck, Teddy," I said as I took the keys. Orly and I helped Teddy stand. He wasn't too wobbly, and it appeared that his injuries were only on the top part of his body. His legs, ankles, and feet seemed unharmed, despite the rips in his jeans.

Instead of loading us into his truck, Orly sent a man he called Gary over to fetch Teddy's. Gary was an old, short guy with a pronounced limp, but Orly seemed to think he could handle driving. For some strange reason — perhaps because I needed something positive to think about — my mind zoned in on the fact that if Teddy had been lying unconscious in the woods last night and then some of this morning, he couldn't possibly have pulled the trigger on the gun that killed Norman Bytheway. Had Orly not put that together? He might have, but I guessed I could understand why a beaten-up guy who'd been seen arguing with a murder victim should maybe not broadcast his injuries for the world to see. However, the logistics of getting his beaten self back out into the woods to be found there after killing someone just didn't jibe.

I wished I had time to walk around the entire campsite. I wasn't sure what to look for or what questions to ask anyone, but I sensed I could figure it out as I went. Maybe I could learn something, maybe not. But, again, medical attention for Teddy was the priority.

We hoisted him up and loaded him into the passenger side of his truck. Orly shut the door with a solid thud and then tapped the door with his fingers.

"I'll ask around, Betts," he said after he perhaps read my mind about wanting to

97

search for answers. "I'll try to get some details."

"Thank you." I looked at him a long moment. "Why didn't you just tell me? I mean, let me know that Teddy was here."

Orly shrugged, which I'd already noticed a few times was an interesting maneuver for someone who was so thick in the chest. His whole torso lifted, not just his shoulders.

"He thought you might panic, or something. I understood. I know your brother needed to be checked over by a doctor, but his life was no longer in jeopardy, and it's my experience that if danger or death isn't imminent, most situations need a little time and a little thought before people such as doctors or police officers are contacted. Just the way it is."

"Makes sense," I said, and it did, to a point. "Thank you again."

"Not to worry. Drive carefully."

Doc Callahan was in his examination office and available, fully clothed, not dressed in his robe as he was when he was awakened or pulled from his house for a medical emergency. He shooed me out of the examining room, and I walked through the reception area and out the front doors. I pulled out my phone and called Cliff on his cell.

"Hey, Betts."

"Hi, Cliff, I know you're probably crazy busy." The jail wasn't far away, but I didn't want to make a big production out of what I was doing by going there to talk to him.

"Everything okay?"

"Everyone's fine, but can you meet me at Doc Callahan's?"

"Uh. Sure. Betts, are you hurt, sick?"

"No, I promise it's not serious."

"I'm on my way."

From where I stood, I could watch him exit the jail and then break into a jog as he hurried toward me.

"It's Teddy," I said as he came to a stop in front of me. "He was in a fight, or just beaten. He's conscious and going to be fine. He's being looked at by Doc Callahan. The . . . incident was last night, as far as anyone can tell."

Cliff's eyebrows came together. He was in great shape but the jog, and perhaps the request to meet at a doctor's office, had sped up his breathing slightly. "You want me to arrest the person he was fighting with?"

"You can't. At least we don't think you can."

His eyebrows rose.

"If there was a fight, chances are the other

99

person was the same person who was killed this morning. Norman Bytheway."

"I see," Cliff said after a beat. "I need to talk to him, Betts."

"I know, but can you just talk to him without Jim knowing, at least for a little while?"

"Yes."

I liked his quick response.

"Thank you. Come on."

Doc Callahan didn't question or complain about Cliff and Teddy taking up an examining room for "official" purposes. If someone had seriously needed medical attention, Doc Callahan would have kicked them out with no hesitation.

I was disappointed, however, when Cliff was firm in telling me to leave.

"Betts, we need to find a killer. I'll give every benefit of every doubt to Teddy, but he might have some answers. Go home. I'll see you later."

I left the doctor's office unwillingly, but Cliff did have a point — finding a killer was more important than my sense of big-sisterness.

As I stood outside the doctor's office and looked around Broken Rope's now-spooky, quiet downtown, I remembered everyone else I wanted to find — a couple ghosts and

Gram. The Nova wasn't far away. As I climbed into the car, I pulled out my phone to call Gram but noticed that I'd missed a text from her that said: *Joe and I will be at the school for a while. Stop by if you want to.*

I was drained, but still wired with adrenaline. I had some questions for Joe, and Gram, for that matter. Maybe putting my focus on them would help me worry less about Teddy.

Or just give me something different to worry about.

CHAPTER 9

"Joe actually was a Pony Express rider?" I
said to Gram as she, Joe, and I were gathered in the cooking school's kitchen. Joe's
horse was tethered outside. Seeing the
animal had given me a jolt when I'd pulled
into the parking lot. It was almost dark
when I'd arrived, and I learned quickly that
even ghost horses became more dimensional, more solid in the dark for both Gram
and me when I was around. I'd never seen
a horse tethered to the sign outside the
school, but I supposed many had been back
when they were the main mode of transpor-
tation and the building had been a church.

After I parked the car, the temptation to
move closer to the horse was irresistible. I
was able to pet him, though there was no
warmth or texture to the touch, and the
horse, unlike the human ghosts, had no
scent whatsoever, which I decided probably
wasn't a bad thing. But it was the horse's

eyes that garnered most of my attention anyway. With his, he looked directly into mine, blinking with an intelligence that was unsettling.

"Hey," I said softly.

The horse nudged my shoulder with his nose and then blew a breath out that was made of only sound. There was no air attached to the long-dead animal.

I inspected the *mochila* over the saddle closely for any sign of tooled letters or initials, but this one wasn't marked like the one we'd looked at in Jake's back room.

"I'll see you later," I said before I stepped inside the school. I was almost sure that the horse nodded.

A faint scent of leather hung in the air, but it was just enough that I was reminded of a fellow law school student who had always worn an old leather jacket and carried an old leather briefcase. He also drank a twelve-pack of beer almost every night and slept during most of the classes. Unlike my case, where I chose to drop out, school administrators had strongly suggested to him that failing law school wasn't the right path to becoming an attorney and had asked him to leave.

"We know exactly why Joe's here," Gram said when she saw me. "He and I have had a number of adventures together."

"Okay," I said as I looked at our new ghost. He wasn't unfriendly, necessarily, but he didn't act as though he cared much that I could see and talk to him. He was Gram's ghost, and Gram's ghost he would remain. "But I have to ask first, Joe — are you sure you aren't Astin Reagal? Or maybe Charlie Reagal, though he might have changed his last name over time?"

Joe brought his grimy face up and his eyebrows together. "No, ma'am, I'm positive. Why do you ask?"

"Yeah, Betts, why do you ask, and who is Astin Reagal?"

The situation held too many coincidences to believe that was all it really was — could it be chance that two *mochilas,* two Pony Express riders, and two badges had come into my life in one day?

"I guess it's not really important who Astin was other than the fact that he was an Express rider too," I said. "But I just learned about him today." I continued to inspect Joe and his painfully young face; young death was becoming more and more difficult for me to accept. I was looking for some sort of reaction, some telltale sign that he was lying about who he was. He seemed somewhat uncomfortable with my stare, but as I'd already noticed, he didn't seem to much care if he and I could communicate or not. Maybe he just wanted me to leave. "I don't think I've ever given Pony Express riders a second thought, and now . . ."

Gram shrugged. "It is Broken Rope."

"It is," I agreed. Sometimes that was enough to explain the string of strange occurrences in our town, but I still wondered.

"Anyway," Gram continued. "Joe does need help."

"Just a few more, Miz," Joe added, a smile lighting his face and eyes.

I hoisted myself up to a stool and said, "What do you need?"

"Joe needs to have some letters delivered. Or the essence of them delivered, at least."

"Okay," I said.

Gram joined me on a neighboring stool. "A little of Joe's story first, I suppose. He's one of our unique ghosts, Betts. He remembers what he's supposed to do every time he joins me . . . uh, us. He doesn't remember his life, just this one purpose that he and I have been working on for decades. He doesn't ever stay long; that's why it's taken us so many years. But with only three letters left, we might be able to get him taken care of on this trip."

"Taken care of? What will happen when

all the letters are delivered?"

"We don't know," Gram said.

"Not sure at all. I just know it's something I've got to do," Joe said.

"Why didn't you get the letters delivered when you were alive?" I asked. *Maybe because you are the ghost of Astin Reagal and you died on the trail, your deliveries being lost along the way?*

"That's part of what we don't know," Gram answered for Joe as she smiled at him.

I admired her attitude. Usually, Gram hadn't expressed much patience with the ghosts, but it seemed she was actually attempting to be delicate or careful with Joe, wanting to make sure his feelings weren't hurt. I wanted to know why — did she have a special fondness for this ghost, or did she just want to get rid of him as quickly as possible, and think the pleasant, polite road was the path easier traveled?

"Did you ever research his life? Is he buried in our cemetery?" I asked Gram.

Gram shook her head. "We don't know. We don't know Joe's last name, but I suspect he's buried somewhere in or around Broken Rope."

I wondered what Jake could do with the minimal information of *Joe, Pony Express rider.* Could something that vague help him find more information about our ghost? If anyone could dig up something of value, Jake could.

I also wondered if Jake or Esther might have a picture or at least a passed-down description of what Astin Reagal looked like.

"If the rest of the facts are so unclear, how can you be sure that your name is Joe?" I said.

Joe shrugged. "I don't have any idea. It's just something I know. One of the few things I am certain of."

But that didn't necessarily mean it was factual. My doubts lingered. Strongly.

"Anyway, now that you're here, Betts, I thought we could try something," Gram said. "Joe always carries his letters in the pouch contraption that's over his saddle."

"The *mochila.*"

Gram blinked. "Is that what it's called?"

"Yes," I said.

"Huh. Well, he's always had to read the letters to me because, of course, I can't touch them. I can't really read them either. I can see them, but they're blurry. I wondered if they might become solid when you're around, Betts."

I slipped off the stool. "Let's find out."

We paraded through the kitchen and the front reception area to the outside of the

107

building. The horse was still there, tethered and seemingly content, though even more dimensional. I'd never spent a lot of time around horses, but there were plenty in Broken Rope. I found them beautiful, with a wise aura, but intimidating. I'd ridden a little when I was a kid, but it had been a long time. I always kept a respectful distance, but I stepped a little closer to the ghost horse, and again it looked back into my eyes. I sensed that this creature had more answers to my questions about Joe than anyone else did. Too bad he couldn't talk.

"I told Joe about what happened when it was dark and you were around. It looks like Joe certainly has filled out," Gram said.

Just like the other ghosts, Joe *had* filled out, became less transparent, more solid, more real. I could see a straight inch-long scar on his cheek that I hadn't noticed before. He was small with delicate features. I wondered if he'd ever even grown facial hair during his living years. I remembered what Jake and Esther had said about eighteen being considered old for Pony Express riders.

"How old were you when you died?" I asked him.

"I don't know."

"We figure he might have been seventeen or eighteen, but we don't know for sure," Gram said.

"I feel like I was older than that, but I can't be certain," Joe said distractedly as he reached into a pocket on the *mochila.* "There are only three letters left in here, but I can only pull out one at a time and read one at a time. The bag will only let me do it that way."

"It's always been that way," Gram added.

"Here, can you see it?" Joe held out an envelope.

I could see it. It was as solid as Joe was and illuminated by whatever made the ghosts glow when they were in the dark. Joe still wasn't as solid as when he was alive, but the letter would seem real enough even if it wouldn't feel like paper. It was as solid as Sally Swarthmore's ax had been, as solid as the horse. I looked at Gram with my eyebrows high in question. *Should I touch it?*

She nodded, so I reached forward.

It's the absence of a noticeable change in temperature that I've found the most off-putting characteristic of the ghosts and their implements. I can feel their skin and it feels solid, but without warmth. I can sort of feel the different textures of their clothing, but there's nothing they wear or carry that is warm or cool to the touch. Until I started touching the ghosts and their items, I had no idea how important even tiny temperature differences were to the whole sensory experience.

I looked at the object in my hands; it didn't feel like much of anything.

"The outside of the envelope says *Mrs. Frederick Morrison* with an address in Broken Rope that still exists, I think," I said.

"That's sometimes helpful, though it's rare that family from back then still has descendants living in the same place. It can be a start that leads us somewhere, though," Gram said.

"Go ahead, open it," Joe said.

"Yes, do," Gram said.

Carefully, I lifted the flap on the envelope.

It opened just fine, and I was able to grasp the folded piece of paper inside and easily pull it out.

I looked at my audience of two, both of whom had big eyes full of anticipation. Actually, the horse did, as well. It was a captivated audience of three.

"I want to try to touch it, too, but I'll wait until you see if you can read it," Gram said. "I don't want it to poof away or anything."

"I doubt that'll happen, but I understand," I said.

I unfolded the letter, and it was covered top to bottom with words written in ornate, old-fashioned handwriting, but still legible.

"Read it out loud," Joe said.

"Okay." I cleared my throat; it wasn't a purposefully dramatic pause, but I sensed the audience's anticipation grow. "It's dated February 1, 1861. It says: *Dearest Elaine, I am sending you greetings from Sacramento. I know you've longed to hear from me, and I apologize for the rude delay in my communication, but I have been otherwise detained with so many distractions here and from the other side of the country.*

"*Of course, you know about the secession of our home state of Georgia and other states from the Union. This is not something I would have ever thought might happen when we moved to Broken Rope. I left Missouri a year and a half ago to fulfill my dreams in California, but the complications that have arisen through such a drastic action by our home state have filled me with concern as well as infused a surprise dose of patriotism into my soul. Though I must confess, dear sister, I'm having a hard time understanding which side I should fight for, which side to devote that patriotism to; that is, if a fight actually becomes reality. I am a Georgian at heart, but my travels have made me question many things,* including the issue that will be the cause of what might turn into a fierce battle within our own country.

"I must say that now I wish I would have listened to you. I wish I would have stayed with you and our dear parents in Broken Rope, and of course had the opportunity to meet my new niece, but I chose another path and I simply cannot ignore the inner turmoil and conflict my experiences in the world are causing me.

"Congratulations to you and Frederick on your newest daughter. Though my good wishes are delinquent, you must know that I am happy to my soul's greatest depths for our family. May your life and family continue to be so blessed. I must tell you, dear sister, that I have no plans to return to Broken Rope right away. I will either stay in California or go straight to Georgia. I'm sure everything will be solved quickly and hopefully without the need for bloodshed. I look forward to the day we meet again and peace is restored to our country. I hope to be a part of making that a reality. With deepest regards, your loving brother, Isaac."

I folded the letter and looked at Gram and Joe.

"I'm not sure how significant this is in the big historical picture, but I feel like I just

112

stepped back in time. That was amazing," I said.

"I know," Gram said. "All the letters have been interesting."

"So now what? What do we do?"

"Well, we — *you* — have to try to find someone from the family and let them know what it says," Gram said.

So the *we* was going to be *me*. Gram hadn't lost her impatience; she was just being delicate. My ability to see and talk to the ghosts had allowed Gram the luxury of tiring of them. She'd known them all her life and had mostly come to want to ignore them and their frustrating, sometimes poorly timed appearances and Swiss cheese memories. She enjoyed passing them and their burdens off to me.

"That presents a number of challenges. How do I find them? How do I tell them about a letter that they can't see? Why would they believe me?"

Gram nodded slowly. "I've handled everything differently; every time a different lie. I've even forged my own versions of the letters sometimes. I've said that my mother once told me about the letter, or that I heard a story. No one has ever questioned me. Everyone is so happy to hear what I have to share that they're just grateful for the news and don't ponder the validity — they *want* to believe. As for how to begin, you have a resource that I have never been able to use — Jake. I can't imagine a better connection for finding living descendants of those from the past."

"What kinds of letters have you delivered?" I asked.

Gram shrugged. "All kinds. One or two, I think, needed money. One had money included. Jake would have loved to be able to see that one. One was particularly sad; a girl had run away from home because she was pregnant and unmarried, which, of course, was worse than death back then. She wrote her parents to let them know she was fine but ashamed and would never return home, in order to save her family from that same shame. Turned out to be a happy story though. I tracked down her people around here and they did some research and found that missing part of their family. The girl and her baby ended up living good lives, and the family, though many generations after the letter was written, was able to reconnect. And, of course, there are extraordinarily sad ones, too." Gram paused. "Betts, I know I've told you that there's nothing to be done for these ghosts. They're dead; that's never going to change, and you simply cannot alter what happened in their lives. It's impossible. And, though we don't know what will happen to Joe when the letters are delivered, we know he won't come back to life. But for the living, perhaps there's time to make things better, or, if not better, at least give them some answers they might enjoy having. It's tricky. I've thought about this for many years. I've debated the importance of delivering these letters. I've debated whether it's ethically wrong to deliver something that perhaps wasn't — for whatever reason — supposed to be delivered. I guess that what it ultimately comes down to is this: Even answers that come late are answers, and I believe that I'd personally want to know, even if there was absolutely nothing I could do to change a situation."

"And . . ." Joe added quickly.

"What?" I said.

"It's something I *have* to do. *Have* to do. If I don't . . . well, I'm not sure, but it's something I can't ignore."

There was something *off* about this ghost. He was less aware, even while seeming to know more about his purpose for being here. The other ghosts I'd met all wanted answers to something, but there was more to them than just their ultimate goals.

Events from their lives came back to them as they visited. They seemed to blossom a little. I didn't think Joe would. I suspected his singular focus was all he could handle.

I was suddenly tired. It had been one of the most emotionally taxing days I could remember. Beyond tired — I was on sensory overload. I hadn't told Gram that Teddy was hurt or that Jerome was back, and I didn't have the energy to do so at the moment. However, I had no doubt that I would help Joe. But not right this second.

"I promise I'll work on this. Starting to-morrow."

"Thank you," Joe said.

Gram smiled.

CHAPTER 10

"The show must go on, I guess," I said as I looked out over the cooking school's parking lot. The six Dutch oven stations were perfectly spaced, and from all indications, the cooking lessons were going to be as popular as Orly had predicted. Three large busses had brought the poets to the cooking school from the campsite right after sunrise. Though I didn't think everyone who had come for the convention was attending the Dutch oven extravaganza, the vast majority certainly were.

Gram and I had thought long and hard about the six recipes to use. We hoped one wouldn't be lots more popular than the others. We wanted a fairly equal distribution of observers at each station. It looked like we'd achieved our goal with our variety of both sweet and savory options. The six recipes were monkey bread, cowboy stew, apple crisp, chili mac, breakfast cornbread, and

Dutch oven pizza. Some of the recipes required the Dutch ovens only to be set on hot coals, but others required heat from both above and below, so they would have some coals on top, too.

Orly had told us that most of the poets already knew their way around a Dutch oven, but that pretty much all of them would nevertheless be interested in demonstrations because their techniques might need tweaking, everyone enjoyed taste-testing, or you could never have too many recipes. He was right.

The stations were manned by some of our nighttime students. We offered a variety of night classes to Broken Rope locals. The Dutch oven night class had taken three weeks, and six of our students were more than happy to dress the part and show off their Gram's Country Cooking School–acquired Dutch oven skills. Gram and I would be free to roam from fire to fire and offer help or suggestions, or answer any questions that the night students couldn't answer.

"The turnout is a little surprising," Gram said. "I guess I'm glad Orly wanted to keep this on the schedule."

"I think he feels like he owes it to them, the attendees. Many traveled far to get to the convention, and some were still on their way when Norman was killed. I'm sure he's worried about anyone else getting hurt, but the police are doing a good job."

They were. No more blending with the crowd for Jim's crew. Every police officer was now dressed in his or her official uniform, and not one of them was cracking anything close to a smile. I didn't know them all; our police force just wasn't big enough to handle emergency situations that require lots of manpower. Fortunately, neighboring communities were more than willing to share some of their forces. A number of the tough-looking officers were currently roaming the parking lot and would stay through the demonstrations.

Gram sighed and glanced back toward the cemetery. Joe and the horse were weaving their way up and down it, looking at the tombstones.

"We'll get to the letter right after this," I said. The fish fry at the campsite was scheduled for late afternoon, early evening. I thought we'd have time to attend to Joe's letter in between the two cooking events, but I wasn't sure. I didn't point out the tight schedule to Gram, but she'd figure it out as we went along. My experience had been that she would never put the ghosts' needs over real-life people or commitments, but with Joe I wondered.

"Oh, I know. I just hope he sticks around. We're so close, you know."

"Speaking of sticking around, Jerome's back. Well, he was. I'm not sure if he still is, but he was."

"Why? Was your life in danger?" Gram asked.

I shrugged. "Dunno, Gram."

"So, how's it between the two of you?"

I shrugged again. "Dunno that either."

"But you're working on it?"

"Yes."

"I guess that's all any of us can ask of ourselves. I hope I get the chance to see Jerome, though he's been back so often lately that I haven't had much time to miss him."

I wished I could say the same. I just smiled.

"Come along, Betts," Gram said. "Let's get to work."

As Gram and I ventured from station to station, it was difficult not to feel extraordinarily proud of our nighttime students. They knew their stuff, and they'd all been around Broken Rope long enough to know to add some Old West oomph to their characters and teaching methods. Their demonstra-

120

tions were all peppered with just the right amount of knowledge and Old West humor and fun.

"Hi there, Betts," someone said from over my shoulder as I observed the chili mac demonstration.

"Oh, hi, Cody, how are you today?" I said.

"I'm good. I 'fessed up to my past criminal behavior, and you were right — the police couldn't have cared less. I feel much better."

"Good."

Cody was much less Western than he'd been in his costume the day before. He still wore jeans, but they were topped off by a simple green golf shirt. I hadn't noticed that his hair had been crushed by his hat yesterday, but it was full and bouncy today. He was a cute young man, and I was surprised I didn't see a gathering of cute young women around him.

"Cody, you have a minute?" I said.

"Sure. What're we going to do?" he asked.

"I just have some questions about the convention, if you wouldn't mind."

"Why not?"

We stepped back from the chili mac demonstration and moved to the far edge of the parking lot.

"I haven't been around the campsite at

night. Is it just one big party?" I asked.

"Well, not really. Oh, kind of, I suppose, but not super rowdy."

"What do you mean? Are there more private parties, in tents and campers and such?" I said, hoping he caught on to what I was saying. He did.

"There's some of that," he said without needing extra time to understand my overt code. "They're a nice group of people though. All I've really noticed is that the ones who've attended the convention for lots of years kind of hang out together, and the newbies hang out in their own group. The old-timers — that's what I call them — are more fun than the new ones. I've been lucky to get to hang out with some of the old-timers. I like the guy running the show, Orly. He's been busy, but when he's just sitting around the campfire reading a poem or listening to someone else read one, he's a very real kind of guy."

"He's been pretty involved in the poetry?"

"Sure. When he's not handling a situation, he's having fun."

"What's an example of a situation?"

"Usually it's been when someone drinks too much or something."

"I see. That happen a lot?"

Cody thought a moment. "He had to get

my wife straightened out once."

"Your wife?"

"Oh, sorry. I mean my wife in the skit. I take my roles seriously, so I call her my wife."

"Jezzie? Jezzie was drunk and disorderly?"

"Something was going on a couple nights ago. She was upset about something, and so was Orly. I just assumed that's what it was. I guess I don't know for sure."

"I see. Anyone else?"

"Yeah, some guy who'd been hanging around was a mess a couple nights ago, too. In fact, he'd been hanging around the good guy — I mean, the guy who was killed. Norman."

"Tell me more about him."

"All the girls watched this one. Good-looking fella. He wasn't a poet or an actor. He was just hanging out. He wasn't causing any problems before, but he sure had too much to drink a couple nights ago."

Teddy. I was sure he was talking about Teddy.

"What did Orly do?" I asked.

"He handled the whole thing like a pro. He grabbed the guy and escorted him to his own tent."

"Did you by chance see them go into the tent?"

"No, but that's the direction they were going."

Which was also the same direction as the woods where Teddy had been found.

"I see. Do you remember anything else about them?"

Cody's eyes focused in the distance a moment. "No, don't think so."

"Thank you, Cody," I said. If I'd had any more questions for him, I'd forgotten them now. I hadn't even intended to learn more about Orly and Teddy, and now I just wanted to talk to them.

"Welcome."

I excused myself and melted back into the crowd. I couldn't call Teddy, just in case he was sleeping, and I couldn't immediately find Orly. And I couldn't leave to search elsewhere for anyone. I needed to stay in the general area, at least until the demonstrations were over.

As I roamed and tried to tell myself that it was never a good thing to make an assumption based upon a third-party story, it was difficult to keep my focus where it needed to be. So when I saw Esther venturing through the tombstones as Joe rode his horse right behind her, it was an easy decision to join them.

I approached as she was glancing at a

tombstone on the far side of the cemetery. She either noticed me out of the corner of her eye or heard my footsteps as I got closer.

"Oh! Hi, Betts, how are you?" she asked.

"Good. You?" I wanted to ask about her date with Jake, but that seemed inappropriate. I'd ask Jake, though. I also wanted to ask her more about Teddy, but the timing didn't seem right for that either.

"I'm fine. Look who I found." She pointed at the small tombstone.

"Charlie Reagal," I said. I looked at Joe, who was also interested in the tombstone, looking at it over Esther's shoulder as the horse stood mostly still. It was a small rectangular stone that had gotten slightly off-kilter with the passing of time. The words on it were simple, stating only his name and birth and death dates. "Esther, any chance you know what Astin looked like, or maybe his son, Charlie?"

"Not at all. I've never seen pictures."

I nodded and inspected Joe again. He was very transparent in all the sunlight, but his interest in the tombstone was unmistakable, even though I wasn't sure it meant much of anything.

"No one has ever told you what Astin looked like?" I said.

"No, never."

I had no idea what my great-great-grandparents looked like either, so it was understandable. Maybe if Astin's disappearance had been bigger news, his legend and his looks would have been better passed down.

"Jake dug a little deeper and told me that Charlie definitely was successful. He and his wife, Laura, ran the general store for all their married lives."

"I bet Jake can line up your whole family tree from there if you'd like," I said.

"He offered, but I hate to ask him to do anything else."

"I wouldn't worry about that. He enjoys that kind of stuff." I paused. "You two have a good evening?" I asked as casually as possible.

Esther looked at me and laughed. "He told me that you and he were best friends and that you'd probably pump me for details if you saw me before you saw him."

"Guilty." I smiled.

"We had a great time. He's a special guy."

"Yes!" I cleared my throat. "Yes, he is."

Esther blushed, and then turned her attention back to the tombstone.

"Hey, can I ask you about something else?" I said.

"Sure."

"My brother, Teddy, was hanging out at the campsite. Do you know who he is?"

"No."

"A really good-looking guy."

Esther thought a second. "Norman's friend?"

I swallowed and then nodded. I wasn't completely sure they were friends, but I went with it.

"Okay, yeah, I know him."

"Did you talk to him?"

"I think I did. Once. Briefly."

"Can I ask what you were talking about?"

"I don't think it was more than a friendly greeting."

"Did you see what happened after you talked to him? Did you see anyone take him anywhere?"

"Betts, is your brother missing?"

"No, no, I'm just trying to figure out what happened that night. I know that sounds strange, but I'm extra protective of him."

"Oh, well, the only person I saw him with was Norman, but I spent a good chunk of time over at the Pony Express station that night. My curiosity has been recently piqued, if you know what I mean."

"I do," I said distractedly. "So, how about Norman, did you know him at all?"

"We just chatted, too."

127

"Hmm."

Esther put her hand on my arm. "You okay?"

"I'm fine. I'm sorry. I'm just trying to get some answers, but it's nothing serious." It wasn't common knowledge that Teddy had been beaten, though I wondered about the spread of gossip at the campsite. Teddy's condition was more than serious, but if Esther hadn't heard about it, I wasn't ready to disseminate the news.

"Okay." She looked at the tombstone one more time, and then at me. "I think I'll head back over to the parking lot. The cooking demonstrations are interesting. I just couldn't pass up the chance to look for Charlie. You want to come with me?"

"Go ahead. I'll be there in a minute," I said, being a less-than-perfect host.

"Sure," she said before she smiled at me again and then made her way across the cemetery.

Once she was out of earshot, I looked up at Joe. His focus was still on the tombstone.

"You're Charlie or Astin, aren't you?" I said.

"I know my name is Joe."

I looked into the horse's eyes. "You know anything else?"

The horse nodded, but unfortunately still wasn't talking.

CHAPTER 11

"You look better," I said to Teddy.

He laughed. "I look like I got the tar kicked out of me."

"Okay, you win." I smiled. I was relieved he was well enough to joke. When the Dutch oven cooking demonstrations ended, I told Gram I had to run a quick errand before we could help Joe with the letter. I could tell she wasn't pleased about the delay, but she pretended she was okay with it.

Teddy lived in a cabin right inside the perimeter of the woods that surrounded Broken Rope, the side opposite to where the high school was located. The cabin was made up of one large space on the main level; a space that was filled with a small galley kitchen, a small living room with the most comfortable couch and recliner ever mass-manufactured, and an office-type space that was home to a large, messy desk. The desk was the only part of the cabin that was messy. Teddy was naturally tidy — always had been. When we were kids, our parents had often lamented my paper-, book-, and clothes-strewn room, while holding Teddy's spotless space up as something I should strive for. I'd figured out how to hang things up and put things away sometime in my early twenties, but I still wasn't as good at neatness as Teddy was.

"I'm a little embarrassed, though," Teddy said. "I can't believe I let the guy get the best of me."

I'd lied to him. He didn't look better. In fact, he looked a little worse, with the bruises and cuts taking on a wider array of colors and the swelling still very obvious.

I hadn't seen Cliff since the day before at the doctor's office. He'd sent me a brief text last night telling me he was busy and probably wouldn't be able to get together. I hadn't been able to ask him for details about his questioning of Teddy. I was curious enough to have tried again to reach him before my morning trek to Teddy's cabin, but he hadn't answered his phone. I was sure he was busy attempting to solve a murder, though, so I was willing to cut him some slack.

"If it wasn't a fight, Teds, it was an attack, which would make the person — or persons,

I suppose — pretty sneaky," I said.

Teddy shook his head as his lips pinched. He reached up to them reflexively and then normalized. The pain had been either brief or something he wanted to hide from me.

"I was stupid, too, if I truly followed someone out to the woods. I know better than to do something like that with a relative stranger. Mom, Dad, and Gram are going to flip."

My own lips were sealed for the moment. All three of them would be upset that I didn't give them the news, but that didn't change the fact that I was currently too chicken to be the messenger on this one. Teddy would be fine; they could learn the news from him, hopefully in about ten years or so.

"Well, you're going to be okay. That's what matters."

"Yeah, I suppose," he said.

"How did it go with Cliff?"

"He didn't tell you?"

"I haven't seen him. You feel like sharing? I'm very curious."

Teddy was sitting on the couch; he shifted, but not uncomfortably so, more like a thoughtful, purposeful move, as if he was still trying to put all the pieces together in his head.

"Yeah," he said. "But I'm not sure what I remember, even now. I ended up with a concussion."

I swallowed a jolt of bitter anger. If the person who had done this to my brother was Norman Bytheway, he was now dead, but I still wanted to hurt him. I silently told myself I just needed to be grateful that Teddy was still alive; his attacker had probably wanted a different outcome. And we couldn't be sure it was Norman anyway.

"Just what you can," I said, attempting to keep my voice calm and even.

"I know I'd had a couple beers, but nothing outrageous. I wasn't drunk at all. In fact, I'd had the beers over the course of a long few hours. I was having fun, though. Those poets are a fun group. I met a couple girls, had some laughs, but nothing serious. I remember Norman sitting next to me as some of the poets were reading. He seemed like a pretty nice guy. He was kind of with that girl Esther, I think, and I don't think I noticed that she was paying me any special attention until it was kind of too late. I tried to get away, what would you call it — remove myself from the situation — but Norman laughed and said not to worry about it. He acted like it was no big deal, and Esther eventually went away on her own."

"Is Esther cute with really red short hair?" I asked.

"Yes, that's her."

"You sure it was Esther who was interested in both you guys?"

"I think so, but I also think she was more interested in Norman than in me. Or they were just talking. That might have been it."

I nodded. "How late was it when he asked you to help him with the firewood?"

"Really late — after midnight, that I know for sure."

"Who was around at the time?"

"Not as many as there were earlier, but the only person I do remember is a pretty brunette. And I only remembered her when Cliff started asking me questions. She must have overheard Norman ask me to help him, because she laughed a little and then went away. I remember her because I thought she was so pretty and I liked her laugh. I don't know, though, it's all still just flashes and partial pictures. I might not have the details right, or at least all of the details."

"Did she have a mole above her lip? Gram would call it a beauty mark."

"Maybe."

"You hadn't seen her earlier?" I said.

"No, I don't think so, but I just can't be sure."

Teddy might have been referring to Vivienne, or maybe not. There wasn't enough information to know for certain.

"Stay away from Esther, Teddy. I think Jake's interested," I interjected. Of course, I wasn't so sure I wanted Jake to get involved with Esther now. Telling Teddy to keep his distance was just a precaution.

"Got it."

"Do you remember what she said to you?"

"No."

"What about Orly? Do you remember anything about him that night?"

"No, Betts, I don't."

"Do you have any memory of anyone taking you or leading you anywhere?"

"Not really. Just Norman a little."

"What prompted you to even go over to the campsite in the first place?" I asked.

"Shoot, Betts, I've met lots of new people over the last few days. Everyone was having a good time, hanging out downtown, eating at Bunny's. It was fun to have lots of people in town in April. It's usually quiet, and after Ophelia broke up with me . . . well, never mind that. Normally, we're all just starting to plan stuff, plan skits, contests, all that stuff. This was like an early surprise party."

135

I suspected his involvement was less about the surprise party fun and more about his broken heart, but I didn't push it. And, I couldn't complain — he'd done plenty to help organize the event, too. He'd done whatever Jake had asked him to do.

"Teddy — didn't you help set up the campsite on the first day?" I asked.

"Yeah."

"Any chance you remember meeting Norman Bytheway earlier than two nights ago?"

He shifted on the couch again. "I don't know. I don't remember details if I did. Cliff asked me the same question, but nothing has come too clear yet."

"Did you help him set up a tent, a camper, something?" I nudged some more.

"Betts, I just don't know, and thinking about it hurts my head a little."

"I get that. Stop thinking. It'll come back to you, but it's not worth hurting yourself over."

Teddy's eyes unfocused and his mouth pinched. "Now, hang on, there is something there. Something about knowing him before. Something on the edge of my memory."

I held my breath as Teddy worked his bruised brain.

Finally, he shook his head. "I can't be sure of the exact details, Betts, but I think I remember an argument between Norman and Orly, the guy running the show. This was at the beginning of the convention. There weren't many people around yet. Yeah, it was when we were setting up the campsite, I'm pretty sure."

"Orly is the president of the cowboy poetry group. I can see him having heated discussions, even arguments with people. He's a very in-charge kind of guy."

Teddy nodded distractedly. "Yeah, that's true, but there's something else."

"Okay, it'll come. Concussions shouldn't be messed with. Don't force it."

"You're probably right," he said unconvincingly. "Hey, wait, it was something to do with that lady, I'm just sure of it."

"Which lady?"

"That lady that was in the skit yesterday. The one who portrayed the cheating wife."

"Cliff's cousin?"

"What? She's Cliff's cousin?"

"Yes, how did you not . . ." Teddy and I had always been close, but we'd never socialized together. He might not have met Jezzie all those years earlier, and he might not have picked up on the fact that she was Cliff's cousin. Within the Broken Rope city

137

limits, we all had a sense of who belonged to who, who was related to who, but outsiders didn't automatically get that consideration, particularly now, when so many visitors — actors and poets — were in town.

"Yes, that's Cliff's cousin, Jezzie."

"I'll be. She's funny as heck. I think Orly and Norman mentioned her name in whatever argument they were having. I think."

"Maybe both of the men liked her," I said. She was a year or two older than Cliff, which would probably make her too young, conventionally, for Orly, and too old, conventionally, for Norman. But, whatever works.

"No," Teddy said quickly. "Not that kind of argument. I've been in on plenty of those myself; I would have recognized that. It was something else, but I know she was somehow the reason for it . . . or maybe just standing close by. Dangit, Betts, this is going to drive me crazy."

"I understand. Don't fret about it, but did you, by chance, mention the argument to Cliff?"

"No, I just remembered. Good grief, how much do you suppose got knocked around in there?" He tapped his head lightly.

I smiled sympathetically. There had been more than one moment in my life when I would have joked about there not being much to be knocked around in the first place. But not now; not today.

"Hey, how about some soup? Chicken noodle?" I said as I stood and moved toward the small galley kitchen.

"That's Gram's cure for colds, not concussions," Teddy said.

"Nope, that's Gram's cure for everything," I said as I opened the cupboard above the small counter to the left of the small sink. As expected, there were a few cans of the famous soup. Of course, Gram had her own homemade recipe, but even she admitted that the healing properties of the reliable canned variety were not to be doubted.

"I'd love some soup. Thanks, Betts."

"You're welcome," I said.

I wanted Teddy to relax for a while, but that didn't stop my own mind from turning over the list of things I felt compelled to do. Of course, I'd let Cliff know what Teddy had now remembered, but I really wanted to find out more about a few women visiting Broken Rope: Esther, Vivienne, and even Jezzie. Then there was the research I needed to do to find Joe's letter recipient and more about Astin Reagal, not to mention try to figure out if Jerome had left yet. As I poured a can full of water into the pot with the soup, I realized that the best way right now to find some answers would be to talk to Jake. I'd call him as soon as I made sure Teddy was comfortable.

But first things first, I thought as I heated the soup and then poured it into a mug — because a bowl just wasn't the right way to handle the business of drinking a healing soup.

CHAPTER 12

Jake blinked and looked at the list. "Wow, Betts, you've finally taken a liking to our history."

"You're my only hope," I said with a smile.

Jake returned the smile and rolled his eyes. "Where should we begin?"

"With your date, of course. How'd it go?" I scooted up to the same stool I'd sat on the day before. Jake had been happy to hear from me, but he hadn't immediately offered any details from his dinner with Esther. Of course, I hadn't yet told him that I'd already talked to her.

"It went well, surprising even the attendees. First dates are torturous endeavors, but this was one of the easier ones I've ever participated in."

"Good. You like her?"

"Sure, but only in that way that I don't *not* like her, you know. We had a fun time and I don't think either of us repulsed the other. That's not a bad first-date report."

"Make more plans?"

"Maybe," Jake said coyly.

"Good," I said.

"All right. Next — you'd like to know what Astin Reagal looked like?" Jake said, making it clear that he'd offered all the date details he was currently willing to give.

"I would. Do you have a picture, or a description or something? Anything?"

"I'm pretty sure I don't have a picture, and, no, I've never heard details of how he looked. Why are you curious?"

"We have another ghost, who happens to have been a Pony Express rider, and who seems to not know everything that happened to him when he was alive, and who showed up about the same time that Esther showed up. His name is Joe and . . . well, I'll tell you more about why he's here in a second. It all seems so coincidental and I wondered if maybe he was really Astin showing up at the same time his great-great-granddaughter has. Or maybe it's his son, Charlie, but that seems less likely, because this ghost rides a horse, and Charlie was a general store owner. However, if you can find anything with just 'Joe, Pony Express rider,' that'd be great. Oh, and Jerome's back, too, or was." I took a breath.

"That's all truly very interesting, Betts. I'll try to get more information one way or another. It'll be difficult to work with *Joe, Pony Express Rider* but I'll try. And Astin wasn't one of our more famous legends — in fact, I'm not sure he was much of a legend; an interesting story, maybe, but not a full legend. His disappearance was an unsolved mystery that must have created some buzz, but since he wasn't famous or infamous before he disappeared, I imagine he was forgotten about fairly quickly. Remember, it was a very different time — people disappeared, people died. It's just what happened, though it happened a little more often around Broken Rope."

"I know. And thanks for checking."

"And Jerome's here?"

"Well, he was. I haven't seen him since yesterday. He thinks he now comes here to protect me. Maybe I don't need protecting any longer."

Jake nodded and remained loudly silent for a moment. Any words of advice or wisdom regarding my crush on the dead cowboy had already been said, more than once.

Ultimately — and Jake hadn't told me this part; I'd come to this conclusion myself — it was ridiculous that I harbored any sort of romantic feelings for a long-dead ghost. Jake *had* made plenty of jokes about Jerome's inability to produce pheromones, and about what a bad date he'd make to social events, since no one else could see him. Jake had played out a full scenario that included me turning into that old crazy woman who lived out in the woods and was never seen with anyone else, but was always happily talking to herself. He pointed out that that old crazy woman would also lose her teeth, which for some reason had been the bothersome picture that had stuck with me the most.

He'd been bold when talking about Cliff and the amazing possibilities I had with him. He'd firmly but kindly pointed out that I'd screwed that one up already once before and it might be good to learn from that mistake.

And then he'd made it perfectly clear that it didn't matter that no one else could see Jerome; I was simply not allowed to have strong romantic feelings for both Cliff and Jerome. It wouldn't be fair to Cliff to split my affections in any way.

I'd lied and told him I was moving quickly beyond Jerome. Okay, it wasn't a complete lie. I was working to move past him, but the work was slow and tedious. At least I was doing it. Mostly.

Besides, is it really a lie when the person you're telling it to knows you aren't being truthful in the first place?

"Well, there has to be something more about Astin somewhere. I just have to dig deep, but I can do that," Jake said.

"Thank you."

"So, what does the new ghost, Joe, want? You said you'd tell me his reason for being here."

"And that's another reason I've come to visit you today. I hope you can help me find some currently living people."

"Piece of cake."

"When Joe died, and we don't know exactly where that was or the circumstances surrounding his death, he had some mail — in a *mochila,* very similar to the one you have but with less scribbling on it — that didn't get delivered. Over the years, he and Gram have been passing along the contents of the letters to living relatives of the original intended recipients. There are three more letters, and once they're delivered, he and Gram think something will happen."

"Oh, Betts, that's probably one of the most fascinating things I've ever heard. How wonderful. What will happen to him when the letters are delivered?"

I shrugged. "No one knows, but that seems to be how the rules work with our visitors — there are no rules, or the rules get made up as we go, or the rules get constantly rewritten."

"I see," Jake said. "That bursts the intrigue bubble a little bit, but still, carry on."

"The letter I read was to Elaine and Frederick Morrison, and it was from her brother, Isaac. Here, I wrote down the address, which still exists, but Elaine and Frederick would, of course, be long gone by now."

Jake inspected the note I'd written with the date of the letter, the recipients, the sender, and the address.

"The letter was about Isaac being concerned about the state of the country — the North versus the South. The family was from Georgia but had moved to Broken Rope. Georgia had just seceded when he wrote the letter, and he wasn't sure where his loyalties were going to lie. It would be wonderful to know what happened to them all."

"Huh. Love this." Jake moved to his computer desk and started typing. Only a few seconds later, he said, "I found Elaine and Frederick."

"Already?"

"Yep, this cemetery site is amazing.

They're buried in the bigger cemetery out past that new subdivision that's being built."

"That's not a Broken Rope cemetery," I said.

"Nope," Jake said. "But it's in our county."

"I wonder why they weren't buried in Broken Rope," I said.

Jake shrugged. "They might not have lived in town their whole lives. They're pretty close by, though, so that's good. Here, let me see who's living in their house now. This isn't as easy."

I was quiet as Jake worked the keyboard again, this time with more sound effects: things like "Hmmm" and "Oh!" and "I see."

"Here we go. Do you know the Baxters? Livia and Wayne? They live at that address now."

"Not well. Can you see if they were somehow related to Elaine and Frederick?"

"Not this way, but I can try to do some genealogy to see who their descendants are and if there are any close by."

"Great."

"That'll take a little longer, though. I'll need to get back to you. Was there something else you wanted that I could look for quickly?"

"You hired the actors for all the skits, didn't you?"

"Yes."

A shadow of pain moved over Jake's eyes. Of course, he was still upset about Norman. I'd been so focused on getting the answers I needed that I hadn't asked how he was, other than his date.

"I'm sorry, Jake," I said.

"It's all right," he said. "Do you want to know something about an actor?"

"Just Norman, the victim."

"Oh, well, I told Cliff that all I really know is that Norman came from Kansas City. He called me, telling me he was hoping to come to the convention but he'd also done some acting, local television commercials, and could he help out with the skits."

"Was this his first convention?" I asked.

"Honestly, I don't know, but there was something about the way he talked that made me think it was."

"Was he easy to work with?"

"Very, but he definitely liked trying to get to know the female attendees; Jezzie, Cliff's cousin, included. I tried to explain that to Cliff."

"How did Jezzie respond to him?" I asked.

"Surprisingly, she seemed to enjoy it. She's not married, so I suppose it was no big deal. I thought maybe they were just trying to get into their characters — that happens sometimes with the actors; they get into their roles."

"Yeah, I've seen plenty summertime-character romances come and go."

"One other strange-but-maybe-only-in-hindsight thing occurred. Yesterday morning, early, before the show, right as I went out my front door to the boardwalk, Norman was muttering unhappily and typing a text or something on his phone. He apologized to me and laughed a little. Then he said, 'It's one of those last-chance days, you ever have one of those?' I wasn't sure what he meant. He waved it away and said it was nothing and we talked about other things. I didn't spend an extra second thinking about it. Until after he was killed, of course."

"I'm sure Cliff and Jim will be checking his phone."

"That's the thing. Cliff told me they couldn't find Norman's phone."

"Oh."

"I know."

We talked a little longer, but ran out of new information quickly. I thanked and hugged Jake and then left him to his genealogy search.

Just as I stepped out onto the boardwalk, I took a deep breath that was meant to be calming and cleansing. But the distinct

smell of wood smoke did not have that effect.

"Jerome?" I said quietly as I looked
around.

CHAPTER 13

"I wondered if I'd scared you away," I said.

Jerome smiled. "No, Isabelle, you can't scare me."

We were in the Nova. Originally, I'd parked on Main Street, just a few doors down from Jake's archive building, but when I spotted Jerome standing outside the Jasper Theater, I signaled for him to join me in my car. I drove us around to the back of the buildings and parked directly behind Jake's. Jake might see the car, but at least he'd know there was probably a valid explanation as to why I was sitting in it and having a discussion by myself.

"Where have you been?"

"Here and there," Jerome said as he turned his attention out the windshield and to the back of the building.

I thought he just didn't want to tell me exactly what he'd been up to. I'd already tried to touch him, feel him, but my hand went right through his well-lit ghostly figure again and again. I was beginning to doubt that I'd felt his hands on mine when we were fishing. Had I imagined the sensation, wished it were real?

"Where's here and there?" I wasn't ready to give up.

He shrugged. "Around."

I sighed. "Am I still in danger?"

"I honestly don't know, Isabelle."

"You'd be gone if I was safe, right?"

"I'm not sure. However, I don't think you're in imminent danger. Maybe I'm still here because there's a killer on the loose. Maybe I'm just here to make sure you're careful."

"Okay. I can be careful. I'm pretty careful by nature."

Jerome looked at me and gave me an honest-to-goodness smirk. I could see it clearly even though he was mostly transparent in the passenger seat next to me.

I smiled. "Come on, tell me where you've been."

He thought a moment and then said, "I've been on my property. Well, what used to be my property."

"Oh. Where is it?"

"Just outside the other end of town. You can't get there by any modern, newfangled road, but there used to be a dirt road coming in and out of it. It's all covered over with brush and weeds now."

"What made you want to see it?"

"I'm not sure," Jerome said as he looked back out through the windshield again.

I tried to inspect his profile, but between the side view, all the sunlight, the cowboy hat, and the facial hair, it became difficult to read his expression.

"Jerome?"

He seemed to try to shake himself out of whatever trance he'd fallen into. He looked at me again and smiled. "I'm sorry, Isabelle, but for some reason this time back I've been overwhelmed with a whole barn full of memories from my life. They've come at me so fast that I'm having a hard time putting them all in a respectful order in my head."

"Are they painful memories?"

"No, not like that. There are some good ones, some bad ones, too, but the good ones break my heart a little and I've never experienced that before. It's unsettling and . . ."

"And?"

"And." He paused a long moment. "It's like this, Isabelle — I can't figure out why I'm remembering. I can't understand the point of it all. I'm gone. Everyone from then

153

is gone, too. There's nothing I can do about any of it."

"Tell me a memory," I said.

He exhaled through his nose. There was no air, but the sound was distinct. "Well, all right, I will, I suppose."

I waited silently while he either sifted through the memories or worked up the guts to talk about one of them.

"Elsa."

"Your wife?"

"Well, we were never married," he said quietly, as if it was something to be ashamed of.

"That's right. I forgot. That's not as unusual nowadays as it was back then, Jerome. Lots of couples simply live together; even have kids together."

"I wish we'd married, but . . . well, the circumstances were beyond our control. Anyway, she saved me from a snake once." He laughed. "I'd been working the small herd of cattle I had and was exhausted, almost passed-out asleep in the small cabin we lived in. I was awakened by a scream and the vision of Elsa coming at me with a shovel. She brought the shovel down on a rattler that was about to bite into my foot that was hanging over the edge of the bed. I was shocked into silence as my brain figured out that she was saving my life, not killing me. I remember as clear as day — she held the shovel with one hand, wiped her forehead with the other, and said, 'Saved your hide, old man.' " He smiled into the past.

"That's not a bad memory, Jerome. That's a great memory," I said. I was touched by his story, and hearing it only made me care for him more.

"No, it's not that. It's just that seeing her so clear brings back so much."

"I understand. Some people would say that's a blessing."

Jerome looked at me. "I don't know, Isabelle. For years I'd come back to visit Miz and I'd pick up on a memory or two as time went on, but it's all so different now."

My heart sank. "I'm sorry."

"No! That's not what I meant. I don't know if I can say this right, so bear with me a minute."

"All right." I swallowed hard.

"Those memories, those feelings, I suppose, are all wonderful, but I'm afraid . . . well, I'm afraid I'm building an even bigger bank of memories with you. I cherish our strange time together, Isabelle, but someday, you'll only be a memory, too."

"Someday, when I die?" I said.

"Yes."

This conversation was not something anyone could prepare for. No matter what experiences one had already had in life, this one wasn't in manuals or books, or "Dear Abby" articles, but two things occurred to me.

"I suppose that's a risk we all take, Jerome. People we care for die. It stinks, but that's the way it is. I'd like to propose an idea, though — you come back as a ghost. Who's to say that I won't come back, too? Maybe there's a ghostly future for us after all."

Jerome blinked and half smiled.

"There's something else," I said. "Gram has a saying whenever I or Teddy get melancholy about her being so old. She says, 'Dadnabit, I'm not dead yet, so save your down-in-the-dumps attitude for later.' So, Jerome, I'm not dead yet, which frankly, might end up to be a positive or a negative. I guess we'll see — hopefully not any time soon."

"You're as right as you can be. I'm sorry for my down-in-the-dumps attitude."

I laughed. "Oh, you haven't seen down-in-the-dumps until you've seen Teddy pull it off. He's an expert."

"I'll keep that in mind."

"Good, now, speaking of Teddy, I need to tell you what happened to him."

Jerome listened intently as I told him about Teddy's beating and the fact that we thought Norman Bytheway could have been involved, but we couldn't be sure. I told him about Orly and the three women I was curious about. I described the new ghost, Joe, and how I didn't think he was who he said he was. I asked if Jerome would nose around and see what he could overhear or find out. He was more than willing to jump aboard and be the invisible cowboy detective.

"How's Teddy today?" he asked.

"Fine. Well, he still looks pretty bad, but he'll be okay."

"Something's not right, Isabelle. If a man wants to fight, he doesn't lead another man out into the woods for the battle. He fights him straight up."

I didn't know the etiquette of "man fights," but Jerome had been alive when they were all too common — and all too often solved with guns.

"I'm not sure that's the code anymore, Jerome, but do you think someone else hit him, or more than one someone elses?"

"I think it's possible, and from what you said about the state he's in, I also think they most likely wanted to kill him."

"Yeah, I thought about that. I don't think they wanted or expected him to live." I

157

shivered.

"Can you think of anyone who might have had it out for your brother?"

This list of people who had said the words "I'm going to kill you" to Teddy was long, and mostly populated by female names. But the threat had never been much more than vocalized frustration at Teddy's typical inability to care for a woman the way she wanted to be cared for.

"I'm not sure I'd know where to begin, except with women he's . . . dated."

"Cliff might already be on that trail," Jerome said.

Cliff. I still hadn't spoken to him. I really needed to track him down.

"I'll ask," I said. He was probably more interested in who killed Norman Bytheway, which was how it should be. But maybe the killer and the person or persons who beat Teddy were somehow tied together.

"Good. Now, this ghost, this Pony Express rider. You said he doesn't know what happened to him?"

"That's right."

"Believe it or not, I remember hearing a story about a missing rider who was from Broken Rope. They never found him. I can't remember his name offhand, but I remember something about his story. His wife abandoned their small family and spent the rest of her short life looking for him."

"Astin Reagal?" I said.

"Yes, I believe so," Jerome said. "You've heard of him? Is that your ghost?"

"Only recently. And he's claiming not to be the same one."

I gave Jerome more details regarding the *two* Pony Express riders who had simultaneously entered my life.

A cloud rolled over the sun as I finished sharing the information, and Jerome was momentarily shadowed in a little darkness. Even that small amount caused him to become more real and I caught an expression that surprised me: an intense focus. On me, on my words, perhaps.

"What?" I asked.

"I'm not exactly sure, but there's something more I know about Astin Reagal. I can't quite seem to remember it at the moment."

"You said memories are coming back right now. Maybe it'll become clearer."

"I hope so," Jerome said as the cloud moved on and the sun came back.

"You don't by chance know what he looked like?" I asked.

"Not at the moment."

"Let me know." My phone buzzed. "It's

Jake. He has some more information for me. He obviously doesn't know we're right outside his back door."

"I like Jake. Let's go talk to him."

"Hi, Jerome!" Jake said to the space beside me. He cleared his throat and looked at me. "Is it okay to be happy he's back?"

"Yes, of course," I said.

"I saw you," Jake said to the space. "I recorded your image."

"How's that?" Jerome asked.

"Jake has a camera that's meant to pick up ethereal signals. I thought it was a gimmick, something fake, but he got a picture of you," I said.

"That seems impossible," Jerome said.

"Maybe, but it certainly helped me," I said. "Trust me, Jerome, there are moments I feel like maybe I'm a little off my rocker because I can see you ghosts. The pictures of you confirmed for me that I'm just weird, not weird and crazy."

"I'd like to see the pictures."

"He'd like to see the pictures someday, Jake."

"I can do that," Jake said. "But for now, I have some information." He smiled coyly. "And a picture. Let's start there."

Jake's enthusiasm for his research was

contagious, and Jerome and I followed him eagerly around the table to the far corner, where a stack of files and papers sat. He lifted the top item from the pile.

"This is Astin Reagal," he said.

The picture was beyond grainy; white blobs and spaces were scattered throughout. But there was no doubt that this was not the Pony Express rider that was presumably still hanging around with Gram and waiting to deliver a letter.

The young man in this picture had a full face and distinct features; a large nose that fit well between wide-set eyes, a crooked mouth, and thick stubble while still looking very young. I was disappointed, but I moved that to the back of my mind for the time being.

"I remember this picture," Jerome said. "Jake must have found this in an article in the *Noose*. Back in my day, they did a story about the long-missing rider. Seeing this now brings back the exact moment I read the article. Another strong memory."

"Did you find this in an old *Noose*?" I asked Jake.

"I did."

"Jerome remembers this. It must have been published when he was alive."

"Hang on. Let me look." Jake rummaged

161

through the stack again. "Yes, right here's the article, which I haven't been able to clean up enough to read, but the date is pretty clear. July 9, 1918."

"I was killed a week later," Jerome said.

"He died a week later, Jake," I said.

"And another weird coincidence," Jake said.

"Not really," Jerome said.

"Why not? What's up?" I asked.

Jerome focused on the picture a long moment.

"What's going on, Betts?" Jake asked.

"I don't know yet. Jerome's remembering something."

Finally, Jerome looked up and smiled.

"Betts, I don't think I'm here for you this time," he said.

"No?"

"No. I found him. I found Astin's body — well, his skeleton at least. I think I must have been killed before I was able to tell anyone."

"Plus you were plotting a bank robbery," I said.

"Yes, that, too. But no wonder I don't have any sense that you're in big danger. That's not it at all. I'm here this time to rediscover Astin."

"Where is he?" I asked.

Jerome scratched at the side of his head, knocking his hat off-kilter. "I think somewhere close to my property, but I'm not exactly sure at the moment. I bet it comes back to me."

"I hope so."

"I wish I knew what you two were talking about," Jake said.

"Jerome discovered Astin's remains when he was alive — when Jerome was alive," I said.

Jake's eyes opened so widely and lit so brightly that I almost thought Santa himself had come into the room.

"Well," I amended, "he's not exactly sure where they are. He's trying to remember the details."

"Oh." Jake deflated.

"Excuse me, Isabelle. I need to go," Jerome said before he disappeared.

"Uh," I said, but he left so quickly. "He's gone."

"Well, I'm sure we'll get more details, but he left right before I could get to the good stuff."

"So far, you've had some pretty good stuff. I'm ready for more," I said.

"Happy to oblige. It's about the other ghost and the letter you need to deliver."

He rummaged around some more and

pulled out two small pieces of paper.

"I took some notes to better explain this," he said as he laid the papers out on the table in front of me. "It's not much, but it'll take you right to the person I think you need to see."

"Great. Show me."

"Okay, the letter was to Elaine and Frederick Morrison, from her brother, Isaac."

"Right."

"Elaine and Frederick were both killed in a house fire when they were very old — that's just an interesting tidbit and has nothing to do with the letter. Anyway, they had three children, two of whom died in childbirth."

"Good grief," I said.

"I know, but that's what people did back then — lots of dying."

I'd heard that recently.

"But one child must have lived if you have something."

"Yes, their daughter Ashley lived to be very old; died in her sleep. She had twelve children. All of them lived to be pretty old, too."

"See, not everybody died all the time."

"With those twelve, I had twelve avenues to search, but I chose to start with only a couple. Her son Elroy didn't take me anywhere; not much of a record of his life. But her daughter Jenny took me to something pretty good."

I nodded to prod him along.

"I'll skip over her kids' names and go right to her grandson. It's Jim. Jim Morrison."

"The police chief?"

"The one and only."

"Cliff's boss?"

"Yep. Why? Is that a problem?"

"I don't know. It might be. Probably not. The ghosts have caused him more trouble than he'll ever realize, of course. I'll just have to figure out how to handle it appropriately."

"You're kidding, right?"

"What do you mean?"

"You've got me." He tapped his chest. "I'll do it."

I hadn't even thought of asking Jake to be our messenger, but it made sense. Jake could say or do anything regarding a historical aspect of Broken Rope, and he'd be quickly and easily believed.

"That's a great idea. Let me call Gram," I said as I pulled out my cell and dialed.

CHAPTER 14

The crowd inside the jail was an eclectic one, though two of the members were invisible to everyone but me and Gram.

Jim and Cliff were both there, each of them seated in their own desk chairs. I didn't recognize the person who was lounging in the back cell, but a quick tête-à-tête with Cliff assured me that the old man had nothing to do with the murder.

The two police officers had been surprised to see Jake and me enter the building. They'd both been huddled over something on their desks, and seemed hesitant about a conversation regarding something other than the police matters they were investigating, but we told them we could be brief.

Gram joined us a few minutes later. So did Joe and his horse. Gram had explained to me that the two ghosts had wanted to be present when the messages were delivered, no matter how or where they were delivered.

She claimed they'd been in even more cramped locations than the jail lobby.

Of course, Jim, Cliff, and Jake couldn't see Joe and his horse, but Gram and I could. They didn't seem to bother her at all as they filled up the space in the front of the jail, the area with a wall covered in handcuffs and a cuckoo clock that chirped every fifteen minutes. They couldn't cause any trouble, but their presence made me slightly claustrophobic.

"Miz, what're you doing here?" Jim asked when she came in. "I thought this was just about something Jake found."

"I was curious." Gram shrugged. She sounded fairly convincing as she smoothed her NC State T-shirt.

"Okay," Jim said, not as convincingly.

"Thanks for taking the time," Jake said as he scooted a chair to the other side of Jim's desk.

Jim scratched his head and pasted patience onto his face.

"What do you have, Jake?"

"Well, every now and then I come across something that turns out to be such a gem. I can't help but research everything to death, you know that."

"I do."

"Well, my research led me to you this

167

time, and I thought you might want to know about it."

Jake unfolded a piece of parchment paper. He, Joe, and I had done what Gram told me that she had done — reconstructed the letter. Jake had the parchment and he was quick with calligraphy-like writing, so it was easy for him to create a quick and dirty forgery. He didn't think Jim would pay the least bit of attention to its validity. He seemed to be right. Jim sent the paper only a cursory glance. He might ask to look at it more closely after it was read, but Jake was ready with a lie if need be. He'd tell Jim that his documents were too delicate for more than him to touch them, but he'd be happy to get him a copy later.

"Oh . . ." I said as the horse's head came over the low gate that bordered the front lobby. The animal sniffed at Jim's head. I had the urge to apologize for its intrusive behavior, but of course Jim had no idea that a horse's nose was next to his ear. Could the ghost horse smell things?

"What?" everyone asked aloud — or just looked my direction with questioning eyes.

"Nothing. Sorry." I looked at Gram, who winked at me.

"Okay, well, anyway," Jake said, "I found this letter, and it led me to you, Jim."

"I got that. What's it say?"

"This is a letter written to your great-great-grandmother. It's from her brother, Isaac. I don't think she ever received it."

"How do you know that?"

"I found it with some other letters that were part of a group of letters that never got delivered. They were supposed to arrive in Broken Rope via the Pony Express, but something must have happened."

"Sounds feasible," Jim said, and true to our prediction, he didn't push for deeper answers.

Jake cleared his throat and read the letter. I watched Jim. I watched Joe and his horse. The ghosts were mostly unmoving — in the stillest way a horse could be, I supposed. But Jim's stern features surprisingly transformed. He'd been sitting back with his arms crossed in front of his chest, but he relaxed as Jake read. He sat forward and placed his arms on his desk. His crinkled forehead remained crinkled, but the crinkles became more curious than impatient.

Jake finished the letter and folded the parchment. He looked at me out of the corner of his eye. I shrugged. I didn't know what was supposed to happen next either. Nothing had changed. The ghosts were the same, and Gram had started to inspect her fingernails.

"I see," Jim finally said after a long moment. "That's very interesting, Jake."

"It is? I mean, yes, I agree that it's interesting, but I'd love to know more. Have you ever heard anything about these people?"

"I have, in fact."

That got everyone's attention, including Gram's. She looked up from her fingers.

Jim smiled and then laughed a tiny bit — nothing jovial. Ironic, maybe.

"Everyone wondered what happened to him. Isaac became the family story. No one knew that he might have traveled east to fight in the war, or even considered it. I guess if that letter had been received they would have at least known he was thinking about it, but the communication just stopped — long before that letter. He was labeled 'the coward' because he never wrote home and, as far as anyone knew, never went back to Georgia. Sadly, he became an embarrassment. Shoot, maybe he did fight in the war after all. No matter what, he must have died shortly after sending that letter."

"No one heard when he died, or where?" I said.

"Don't think so."

"I gotta say, I think it's kind of amazing that you even know about him," I said.

170

"Some stories fade but don't die, I suppose." Jim smiled. "My dad would have loved to read that letter. He spent a few years trying to track down what happened to Isaac."

"I wish I would have found it sooner," Jake said.

"It's just good to know it existed. At least he tried to let people know what he was thinking and that he might not make it home. Gosh, Jake, when you find these things, do you ever wonder how different life might be for lots of people if things never got lost or miscommunicated?"

"All the time, Jim."

"I bet."

I looked at the ghosts and at Gram. Still, nothing changed. No one behaved differently, but I didn't know if they were supposed to. We hadn't discussed it that much.

"Jim," I said because I wanted to stall a little longer, just in case. "What do you think this will mean to your family now?"

Jim blinked. "Just the knowledge changes everything a little. I doubt it will do much to transform our lives, but there's a long history of not having an answer, of being embarrassed. Answers are good. Now the stories that are passed down have more satisfaction and less negativity attached to

171

them. We didn't know what happened to him, but now we have some idea that he tried to communicate." He laughed. "It's like there's a punch line, a twist to the story, a happier ending. That'll be fun."

"I like that," I said.

Jake looked at me as if to ask what he should do next. I didn't know, so I looked at Gram. Jim decided for us.

"That all?" he said.

"I believe so," Jake said.

"Well, we need to get back to it, then," Jim said. He'd had his moment of sentiment.

"Got it." Jake stood. Gram and I followed suit, and then she and I paraded out of the jail as Jake carefully refolded the fake letter, keeping the act going. Cliff and I shared a glance, but it was clear that he didn't feel like he could take the time to talk to me privately or give me any new details. Hopefully later.

"Well, should we check out the next letter? We still have time," Gram said as she and I stood outside on the boardwalk. Joe and the horse were now in the middle of the street. "We can move to Jake's archives. Joe, come on, bring the horse."

"So, that was it?" I said. "Was something else supposed to happen?"

"Nope. Just moving on to the next letter."

"That's a bit disappointing."

"I do think we're getting closer to something happening though. Come on, let's get into Jake's."

Gram led the way across the street. Joe and the horse followed her.

Jake was the last one out of the jail, and he stopped next to me as he watched Gram.

"Did that do what it was supposed to do?" he asked.

"Nothing happened, but I think so. I think all the letters have to be delivered before the 'big thing' happens. Gram wants to read the next one. She and the ghosts are going to your archives."

"I wish I could see that horse. Come on. I'd like to hear about the next letter."

The horse's big body in the back room made me uncomfortable, so I asked if we could leave him in the front. I was certain the animal agreed with my plan as he focused his brown eyes on me. He blinked his long, mostly transparent lashes and briefly lifted one side of his mouth. Was he really trying to communicate something? Unless he started tapping Morse code with his hooves, I would probably never know. I doubted that even in their ghostly form could animals master a spoken language. I nodded at him just in case, though. At least he should know I was aware of his attempts at communication.

"Two more, Miz," Joe said with a bright smile. "Two more and I think everything will be taken care of."

Taken care of?

Joe reached into the *mochila,* but stopped cold when he saw something on Jake's table. I moved so I could see what had had such an effect. Joe was looking at Jake's picture of Astin Reagal.

"Who . . . who's this?" Joe said.

"Jake, Joe sees the picture of Astin. He'd like to know more about him. He's standing right about here." I pointed at Joe.

"There's a chance you knew him, Joe. He was a Pony Express rider, too. His name was Astin Reagal. He disappeared on the trail."

"I know," Joe said.

"He knows," I said to Jake. "How do you know? Did you know him?" I said to Joe.

Joe shook his head slowly as if to clear out some cobwebs. "I . . ." He looked up at Gram.

"What is it, Joe?" she asked.

"I knew him," Joe repeated.

"Right. How?" Gram asked as she peered at the picture through some reading glasses she'd put on.

"I don't think I should tell you," Joe said. "Not yet."

"Why not?"

Joe shook his head some more.

Gram sighed. "Okay, but when?"

"Let's get the last two letters delivered, and then I'll tell you."

Gram looked at me and Jake. "Okay."

"Jake," I said. "Joe somehow knew Astin but he doesn't think he should tell us how until we get the last two letters delivered."

Jake blinked. "Well, that's inconvenient."

That was the first I'd ever heard Jake say something less than flattering about the ghosts.

"I know, but it's how they work," I said.

I wanted to protest, I wanted to bargain; I even wanted to threaten not to look at one other letter until Joe told us how he knew Astin. But it would have done absolutely no good. I would have made a ruckus and then Gram would have calmed me down and told me to go ahead and read the next letter.

"Let's get to it, then," Jake said.

"Could we dim the light, Jake?" Gram asked.

"Certainly." Jake hurried back to the switch on the wall and dimmed the light enough that the live humans could still see each other and the ghost became dimensional enough that I thought I'd be able to hold and read the letter without too much effort.

Gram inspected Joe. He blinked away the trance that Astin's picture had put him in.

I tried not to be irritated by Joe's unwillingness to tell us how he knew Astin Reagal. I tried to look at it a little differently; before that moment, we truly didn't *know* that there was any connection between Joe and Astin. Now we knew. More would be revealed. And the coincidences actually might have more substance.

"Here," Joe said with a shaky voice as he handed me another envelope.

I took it as Gram squinted at Joe, though she didn't say anything. This letter was smaller than the first one and tinged more yellow.

"Can you see the letter in my hands?" I asked Jake.

"No."

I held it, noting its substance, though not its texture. "It doesn't have a full address, just a name — *Alicia Zavon* — and *Broken Rope*. Wait, Alicia Zavon. I know that name. Jake?"

"If it's the Alicia Zavon I'm thinking of, and I bet it is — how many could there be?

— then she's definitely one of our legends. She killed her husband."

"Even I know this one," I said. "Alicia Zavon and her husband were old — very old for the time. In their seventies, I think?"

Jake nodded.

I continued, "And one day she 'up and got teered of him hittin' on her with his fists,' so she loaded up his shotgun, put it to his back and marched him downtown, and shot him in front of everyone."

"There's more," Jake said.

We all, including Joe, looked at Jake.

"Alicia fell victim to the town's biggest legend. Her rope broke."

"Ah," Gram said. "That's such a bizarre occurrence, and it happened more frequently than I think anyone would have imagined. I don't know if our ropes were poorly made or if we were just cursed to fail at hanging criminals."

"It's said that Alicia roams the streets every Valentine's Day, the day she was hung. Twice." Jake said. He looked at Gram.

"Oh. No, I've never met Alicia. I'd like to, though. I bet she was something else," Gram said.

"Let's see what her letter says," I said.

I pulled the paper out of the envelope, unfolded it and read: *"Dearest Mother, I just* received your letter today and I must say that it has left me terribly frightened and concerned. Please don't do anything rash. I know all about Daddy, but I also believe his cruelty is tied to his liquor. We knew to run away when he'd been drinking. Give me a chance to come home and see what I can do to help fix things. Please leave him if you need to, but please don't do the dreadful thing you said you're thinking of doing. You would break my heart and the hearts of my brother and sister. I'll be there no later than February 16. I just need to get a few things put in order and make sure Harold and the girls can fend for themselves for a few weeks. All my love, Elizabeth."

For a long moment, we were all silent. The letter required some digestion.

"Well, that *was* interesting," Jake said.

"Considering what happened, it's probably not good that letter wasn't delivered, but I suppose that's one way legends are made," Gram finally said.

"True," Jake said.

"So what do we do with this one?" I asked. "I can't imagine giving this information to anyone."

"It's been a long time, Betts," Gram said. "And we have to deliver it; there's no question."

"Yes. Thank you, Miz," Joe said.

"I'll be able to find a descendant easily. If I remember the story correctly, Elizabeth did come back to town, too late of course. But I don't ever remember the stories mentioning that she sent a letter that her mother never received. Of course, like people dying or disappearing, that just happened back then. Letters didn't always get delivered, or sometimes they were delayed by weather, illness, whatever. It wasn't too much of a big deal."

"But Elizabeth probably went back to her family — Harold and the girls."

"No, she didn't; that I know, too," Jake said. "I don't think they ever joined her in Broken Rope. I think she abandoned them."

"Like Astin Reagal's wife?" I said. The story was still fresh in my mind.

"No!" Joe exclaimed. "Astin's wife didn't leave him, did she?"

"Not really — she abandoned her son to look for him, though," I said.

"I see." Confusion rolled over Joe's face, but only for an instant.

"What is it, Joe?" Gram asked.

"Nothing, I'm sorry. I'm . . . I'm not sure. Maybe we're just getting closer to the end of the letters. It seems like I'm remembering things. But not big things — just little unimportant things that bother me. I'm fine. Ignore me."

I turned to Jake. "How quickly can you find a descendant? I'm sensing that it would be good to find one as fast as possible."

"Why don't you and Miz run down to Bunny's for lunch and I'll see what I can put together. I'll call or join you. The ghosts are welcome to stay, of course."

No one stayed with Jake as he got to work with his fast fingers over his computer keyboard. Gram led the way to Bunny's, which was located at the end of the main thoroughfare. I followed her, and then Joe and his horse trotted behind.

Gram and I didn't notice it until we arrived at Bunny's and his wood smoke scent became strong, but Jerome had joined us, too. He had followed behind the horse.

"Hello, Jerome," Gram said when he moved to the front of the line. She looked at me, and then at him again.

"Miz, always good to see you."

"You, too, but you sure do seem to be visiting a lot."

"I'm working on it," I interjected, answering Gram's tone and unspoken words about both Jerome's and my behavior during those visits. Gram and Jerome both knew that I was working on figuring out how to keep

180

my friendship with Jerome strictly friendly, not romantic. I didn't sense that Jerome wanted to work on the same issues from his end, but he didn't have another significant other to think about. How we managed whatever relationship we were destined to have, the details would be up to me.

"Well, that's a good start." Gram sighed and pulled the door open. "Shall we go in?"

CHAPTER 15

"Joe's sticking close by," I said as I looked out Bunny's Restaurant's large front window. Joe was pacing. The horse was still, almost eerily so. Earlier, I'd felt a slight breeze, but the horse's tail and mane were motionless. Every now and then I saw his eyes blink, but his head didn't move much.

"He's in a hurry to get the letters delivered," Gram said as she looked out, too.

"I can only imagine what it would be like to know that your task list — potentially your last task list — is almost done. He seems to think the outcome will be something positive. I hope so."

"I hope so, too. I really do, Betts. But it won't be terrible if you and I don't have to figure out what to do about the letters anymore. So far you might have found it interesting, but it does get a little tiresome."

"You like him, though, don't you?"

"To be honest, I don't know if I like him

as much as I think he's just a kid, and one who's alone. Gent had his family. There aren't many younger ghosts. I don't mind the adults being confused and alone so much. Joe has always seemed so . . . lost."

I should have figured that out. Gram was great at being a grandmother.

"He was pretty adamant about not coming inside," Jerome said.

At first, Bunny had sat Gram and me in a small two-person booth, but we'd asked for something bigger. Bunny had pinched her lips — making her mustache bristle — and then showed us to a bigger booth. I sat on one side of the booth and Jerome and Gram sat on the other.

"I know," Gram said. "He seemed like he didn't like you, Jerome. You lived long after his time. He couldn't have known you. Maybe you just rubbed him the wrong way. Ghost envy."

"I've never met him before. Didn't get a good look at him this time. He didn't look at me. Never trust a man who won't look you in the eye," Jerome said.

I twisted slightly and looked out the front windows again. Jerome was right; for whatever reason, Joe hadn't wanted to look him in the eye. Even I'd noticed. "Gram, are you sure Joe has never been able to recall his last name?"

"No. He doesn't know. Or, I suppose, he has never wanted to tell me. I guess I don't know which."

I wondered again if Jake had a way of looking up all the Pony Express riders who had, in fact, gone missing, and if there was one with the first name of Joe, or Joseph or Joey, on the list. Something wasn't right about Joe, although — and I had to remember this — they were ghosts, and the biggest thing that wasn't right about all of them was that they were dead. Presumably, this symptom could cause a number of other strange, potentially unexplainable occurrences. I shook off the wonky feeling and decided to think about it later.

"Gram," I said as I turned around. "Jerome found Astin Reagal's remains, back when Jerome was alive."

"Really? That's pretty big news, I would think. Where are his remains?"

"I'm not sure. I've been searching, but it's been a long time."

"Where were you searching?"

"Out by what used to be my property, on the way to Rolla, about a mile or two out of Broken Rope. At least, I'm almost certain that's the area where I found his skeleton before."

"Did you tell anyone about it?"

"I believe so. I think I told Elsa."

"Your lady?" Gram asked easily, as if asking about someone's "lady" was a common question.

"Yes."

"Jerome's been remembering her this trip."

Gram's head cocked slightly, and her mouth straightened into a tight line. "You've always had some memories of Elsa."

"It's that I'm remembering . . ."

"He's remembering their connection better this time," I continued for him.

"Interesting. Perhaps it's meant to be. You and Betts have been too squirrelly-eyed for each other. Maybe Jerome remembering how he felt about Elsa is good."

Jerome and I smiled at each other, more to share our humor over Gram's observations than to flirt, but the gesture could have been misinterpreted.

"Oh, for heaven's sake," Gram said at our continued "connection." "Jerome, tell me more about Astin Reagal's remains, if you remember the details."

"I think that's why I came back this time — to help you all find them."

"Really? Okay, I guess I won't analyze that idea too much but just go with it. So, how are you going to find him?"

"Keep looking, I guess."

"Why didn't you tell anyone besides Elsa?"

"I can't remember exactly. I died a week later, so that could have played a big part in my secrecy. I think that at that time she was the only person I trusted. I don't think I was well thought of by then," Jerome said as he scratched a spot above his ear, tilting his hat sideways again. "But I sense that there was a good reason. I remember a couple things from back then — there was the newspaper article that talked about Astin and how he'd been lost. I think Jake found that same article. Then, I remember having a strange sense of where he might be. What's missing is the part that explains why or how I knew."

"You sensed it, like psychic-ly? Had impressions or something?" I said.

The hat settled back into position as Jerome stopped scratching. "I don't know what you mean, Isabelle."

I was about to offer a quick explanation, but Gram interrupted. "Isn't that Orly coming in?

I turned to see Orly push through the front door. He saw me immediately and waved, so I returned the greeting and he moved quickly toward us. Though I had questions for him and hadn't been able to find him during the Dutch oven demonstrations, I kind of hoped he wouldn't join us. I still hadn't told Gram about Teddy, and my lie by omission was only going to seem bigger if he was the first one she heard the news from. However, some of the questions I had for Orly were specific to Teddy. Maybe I'd be okay if he did join us, but I'd have to do a quick job of giving Gram at least a heads-up about Teddy.

"Looks like we're going to have some company," Gram said.

"Should I leave?" Jerome said.

"No, it's fine, but . . ." I hesitated, but I didn't see any other way around it. "Gram, there's something you should know. Teddy got into a fight and Orly helped him." I didn't need hindsight to know that the way I'd just handled giving her the news was cowardly and badly done.

"Uh," Gram said.

"Betts, Missouri," Orly said as he approached the table. "How are you lovely ladies? I must tell you that the Dutch oven event was a huge success. Everyone is buzzing about it."

"That's great to hear. We're fine, Orly," I said as Gram continued to digest the news. "Would you like to join us?" I scooted over so he wouldn't try to sit on Jerome.

"Oh, I don't want to intrude," he said.

"Not at all," I said. "We'd love for you to join us."

"I can't imagine better company. Thank you."

Orly sat next to me, which meant he was catty-corner from Jerome and directly across from Gram. We were two Winston women and two cowboys. Despite the slight transparency and different time periods, it was difficult not to notice the similarities between Jerome and Orly. The obvious one, of course, was that they were both cowboys, which I suspected made them somehow soul-brothers of sorts. The cowboy lifestyle had modernized over the years between their two lives, but nonetheless, they were the stuff of ruggedness, the type of people who lived outside more than inside. Ruddy skin and big shoulders were more their trademarks than mere aspects of their physical descriptions.

Orly was older than Jerome had been when he'd died, but there was a congruity in the set of their jaws and — I peered at the table to confirm — strong similarities in their calloused hands and marred fingers — none were perfectly straight. I'd liked Orly immediately, but now I hoped my initial

188

instincts hadn't been off.

"How's everything at camp?" I asked Orly.

"All right. A little subdued, but the Dutch oven cooking demonstrations were enjoyed by everyone. Thank you both for your kind hospitality this morning."

I nodded. "Our pleasure."

Gram kind of nodded, too, but I could tell she wished for a chance to talk to me without Orly present.

Orly cleared his throat. "We're trying to continue on without being disrespectful. It's a difficult balance."

"Did you know the man who was killed?" Gram asked.

"Just from the convention this year," Orly said. "But I'm learning more and more about him every minute."

"Like what?" I asked.

"He was interesting. He asked a lot about writing poetry. And, apparently, he asked a lot of questions about me, even though the two of us only had a couple brief conversations that were so unimportant I don't remember them at all."

"Did you have any arguments or discussions with him?"

"Not that I remember."

"You might need to be careful, Orly," Gram said. "Remember, the killer hasn't been found yet."

"Certainly, Missouri, but I'm pretty convinced that the killer was only planning on killing one person. I've been thinking about it. Almost everyone who was at the convention was there and watching the skit. The killer could have killed anyone, or more than just one person. None of us were prepared to shoot back, defend ourselves. I know that eventually the police would have figured out what was going on, but even a few moments of chaos . . . well, I don't even want to think about it."

"So, what if we try to figure out who wasn't there; someone who stayed back from the crowd maybe, someone who seemed to disappear. Maybe that would help the police find the killer," Gram said.

"My thinking exactly, Missouri," Orly said. "That's what I've been doing, talking to people to see if they noticed anyone go missing suddenly. It's a backwards sort of task, but at least I feel like I'm doing something."

"Found anything?" Gram said.

Orly laughed. "Well, it seems lots of people noticed that someone or a few someones were missing, but then when I look closer, ask more questions, I find that those people were actually there. I don't think I'm very good at asking the right questions."

"Or maybe you could just use some help," I said. "Gram and I will be there later this afternoon. After she fries up some catfish, the frying duty is going to go to some of your poets. We'll stick around and snoop."

"Well, young lady, your grandmother's words of warning apply to you, too. There's a killer on the loose. You don't need to put yourself on any potentially harmful path."

I thought a minute. "I think we can all be casual. I'll get Jake there, too, and I'm sure Cliff was already planning on going." I wasn't *sure* he was, but I thought it was a good possibility. "We'll blend in. Believe it or not, even if Jake's the only one who plays a part during the tourist season, we all have a healthy supply of Western wear," I said.

"Alrighty. Same words of caution still apply, though." Orly paused. "How's your brother?"

I gulped and kept my eyes away from Gram. "I think he's better."

"We're going to check on him after we eat," Gram said.

I sent out a silent wish that his face would miraculously look a million times better by the time we were done with lunch.

"Oh, good. He's up and around, then?"

191

"Yes," I said. "Mostly."

"Despite how he turns the girls' heads, he is a nice young man," Orly said.

"His way with girls is more a curse than a blessing, believe me," I said.

Orly laughed. "I suspect that's true."

"Orly, I need to ask you something specific about my brother," I said. "And it's going to sound like I'm accusing you of something."

"Oh. Well, goodness, then, accuse away. I think it's always best to get to the meat of the nut. Don't mince words, Betts."

"I was talking to Cody this morning at the cooking demonstration."

"Cody?"

"Cody was the bad guy in the skit that Norman was in."

"That Cody. Yes, ma'am, I know who you're speaking of."

"He mentioned that he saw you the night Teddy was beaten," I said. I thought I heard Gram sigh heavily, but I didn't look at her.

"I'm sure he did. I'm all around that campsite."

"He said he saw you escorting Teddy back toward your tent." I didn't think I needed to add that the tent was the same direction as the woods where Teddy was found.

Orly looked up toward the ceiling and

thought hard. He looked down and at me a moment later. "Betts, my dear, I'm not sure you have any reason to believe me or believe anyone else at this point. You don't really know any of us. But I can assure you that I didn't escort Teddy anywhere. I have no recollection of seeing him that night. I wish I would have. Maybe I could have prevented what ultimately transpired."

"He doesn't sound like he's lying, Isabelle," Jerome said.

He didn't. At all.

"However," Orly continued, "and I'm not trying to throw you off your game or anything, but I will tell you this: That young man Cody is an interesting fella. I've seen him lose his temper a time or two in just the past couple of days. Out of the blue—like, for no real reason at all."

I hadn't seen Cody lose his temper during any of the rehearsals I'd watched, but I certainly hadn't seen them all. Jake had seen many. I'd have to ask him if he observed any irrational behavior from the "bad guy."

"Thanks for telling me that, Orly."

"My pleasure."

"What can I get for y'all?" Bunny asked as she approached. She seemed less baffled by our bigger table request since Orly had joined us.

We ordered and tried to talk about more pleasant things as we ate. I didn't ask any other questions. I'd look for the opportunity to find some answers this evening.

Shortly after our food was delivered, Jerome disappeared, saying that he was going to go look for Astin's remains before meeting us that evening at the campsite. After he left, it was difficult not to see myself as the third wheel, because I had a distinct feeling that Orly became extra attentive to Gram, and it seemed she was okay with it. I wished I could squeeze in a question about Jezzie, but not only did it seem inappropriate but I might actually ruin Gram's mood. I figured I'd done that enough for one meal, so I kept the question filed away for later.

"Theodore William Winston, how in tarnation are you not in the hospital?" Gram said as she leaned down and placed her finger gently under his chin.

"I'm okay, Gram," he said, but his eyes shifted in my direction. He wanted my help, but I figured we were now way beyond getting out of this unscathed.

Gram stood and looked at me. "I can't believe you didn't tell me. Do your parents know?"

I looked at Teddy. He shook his head.

"No, Gram, but it looks much worse than it is," I lied. "Teddy's fine." He was, but it was still bad. "We thought that if the bruises and swelling could go down first, you and Mom and Dad wouldn't have to worry."

"Oh, Betts, cut the crap. You just didn't want to be the one to tell us that Teddy was hurt."

I sat on the couch next to my brother. "Yeah, well, there is that."

Gram sat on Teddy's other side and sighed.

"Oh, hell, I wouldn't want to be the one to tell anyone about this. I understand, but I'm just worried, that's all. Are you sure you shouldn't be being monitored or something?" Gram said.

"Doc said I'd be fine recovering at home. I'm feeling better, really. I know I still look bad, but my headache is mostly gone and I'm not dizzy anymore. Man, was I dizzy."

I hoped he'd stop there.

"The man who was killed was the person who did this to you?" Gram said, asking the question based upon the bits of information I'd given her on the way over to Teddy's.

"I'm not sure . . . I think so. My last memory is that I was going with him, but some other things are coming back to me."

"What?" I said.

"Noises . . . no, *sounds* are coming back, not *noises*. Actually, to be more specific, I think other voices are coming back. I think that while I was being beaten, I heard other voices. Guys and girls."

"Anything more than that, like who the voices belonged to?" I asked.

"I'm just not sure. I think that the guy sounded familiar, but I can't place how."

"What about Orly? Did the guy sound like him?"

"No, Betts, I don't think so. This was a younger voice, someone more my age."

"So, the voice might have belonged to Norman?" I said.

"No, *another* male voice besides his," Teddy said. "I think there were two male voices."

"What about the girl or girls?"

Teddy shook his head. "I just can't be sure. Maybe if I go hang out at the campsite again, I'll hear something that clicks."

"No!" Gram and I said together.

"I'm afraid you're not going anywhere quite yet," I said, though I wished it was a feasible idea for Teddy to come with us later that evening. It simply wasn't, and it would be foolish for him to even try. He still needed rest.

"Well, I'm making you some homemade chicken soup," Gram said as she stood.

"I'm not sick, Gram," Teddy said.

"No? Well, you're not well either, and chicken soup cures just about everything." She walked around the couch and moved to the small galley area.

"I don't know if I have all the ingredients," Teddy said.

"I'll figure it out," Gram said.

Both Teddy and I knew not to mention that I'd already warmed up a can of chicken soup. Gram was going to make the soup no matter what.

Once she was mostly out of earshot, Teddy leaned toward me and said, "I remember a little of the argument I heard between Orly and Jezzie."

I nodded surreptitiously.

"I'm pretty sure I heard Orly tell Jezzie that she'd 'never get away with it.' And then, Betts, I'm also pretty sure he said something about Norman. At least I think I heard Norman's name. Would you go ahead and tell Cliff?"

"Sure," I said. He wasn't going to be happy that his cousin might have been involved in anything shady — a fight, a murder, whatever — but he needed to know.

"Thanks." Teddy relaxed and closed his eyes.

My phone dinged quietly, announcing a text. I looked at the text as I stood and joined Gram in the galley.

"Jake has our contact for the new letter," I said.

"Oh, good," Gram said as she looked at the concoction in the pot on the stove. No matter what she'd put in it, I was sure its healing properties were stronger than the canned version I'd used. "I'll have this done in a jiffy. Tell Jake we'll be there soon."

I nodded. I didn't tell Gram the most interesting part of the text. Jake had said: *You won't believe this one, Betts, and you won't want to follow through and talk with the descendant, I promise.*

CHAPTER 16

"Opie! Opie's a direct descendant of Alicia Zavon?" I said.

"Very direct," Jake said. "It's kind of amazing we didn't know about it before, but I've never paid much attention to Alicia's family tree."

"But Opie lives for this kind of stuff. If she knew she was related to an infamous Broken Rope legend, she would have been shouting it from the treetops."

"I guess she doesn't know, then." Jake shrugged. "Look, there's the glitch of her daughter Elizabeth coming back to town. That's where the error probably occurred. Elizabeth's lineage just kind of got forgotten because she left her family back in California; a family of which one daughter was named Ophelia, by the way."

"Oh, no, Opie was named after one of Alicia Zavon's granddaughters?" I said.

"Seems that way," Jake said.

"But then she should know already."

"Maybe not. Maybe her parents only knew that Ophelia was a family name, even if they didn't quite grasp the entirety of the true story of their ancestors."

"Ugh. If she doesn't know about all of this, her world is going to be rocked, and then she'll be beyond impossible to be around. She'll want to be crowned queen of all Broken Rope legends."

Jake shrugged again. "Oh, she won't be any more bothersome to you than she already is. As for the rest of us, I suppose we'll adjust."

"I've never quite disliked her the way you have, Betts," Gram said, "but, yes, she will want some sort of accolade. Maybe a parade." Gram scooted off the stool. "But nevertheless, we've got to get this letter delivered. Right away would be better than later." She glanced at her watch. We still had time, if our visit was brief.

I tried to come up with a good case for not going out to Opie's house and telling her about a non-delivered letter that would surely be the highlight of her life, or at least her week, but I couldn't formulate one solid excuse. Even the fact that she recently broke up with Teddy wasn't good enough. Teddy broke up with lots of girls, and lots of girls broke up with him.

"Oh, criminy," I said, using one of Gram's favorite terms. "Let's go get it over with. We need to get back for everything this evening."

After Jake outlined the details, we left for Opie's, and we made quite the group. I gave Gram a lift in the Nova, and Joe and the horse followed behind, trotting so quickly that the horse's hooves would have stirred up dirt if they'd been attached to an animal that was alive and it was back when all roads were unpaved.

Ophelia Buford lived in a mansion — well, a mansion by Broken Rope standards — on the edge of town. She and I had grown up together, enemies since we were young, enemies squared when we were in high school and Cliff broke up with her and started dating me shortly thereafter. No matter how he'd tried to make her understand that he hadn't broken up with her just so that he could date me, that his feelings for me had been a surprise, she had never forgiven me for luring him away from her. Our relationship had been quite antagonistic toward each other. She was openly rude to me and I was openly rude to her. However, when she was dating Teddy, we'd both tried to mellow our bad feelings for each other.

We'd become more passive-aggressive than just plain aggressive.

I didn't know the details behind their breakup, but when Teddy told me that Opie had ended the relationship, I hadn't felt the pure glee I'd anticipated when daydreaming of the day the happy event would occur. Instead, I was sorry for my brother's broken heart. I didn't understand Teddy and his Lothario ways, but he was my brother, and he didn't attempt to hide the pain he felt over losing Opie. I also didn't understand Opie, but the fact that she dumped my kid brother — no matter how much he might have deserved it, and he just might have — my feelings for her fell comfortably back to irritated dislike. For years I'd called her my personal Nellie Oleson, and now as far as I was concerned, it was really on. No more passive with my aggressive.

"Just be nice," Gram said as we pulled onto the long birch tree–lined driveway. "We don't know what happened. Teddy . . . well, he doesn't have a great track record, Betts. As much as we love him, maybe Opie was right to dump him, though it bothers me, too. Just remember who we're dealing with and that neither of them is all that talented with personal relationships."

I made a noncommittal noise as I glanced

in the rearview mirror at the horse and rider. Joe was bent over, the flap of his hat blowing somehow backward with the horse's forward progression. How their movements were separate from the current-day movement of air around them baffled me. They didn't stir up present-day dust, and the present-day dust and wind around them had no effect on their state of being. Two separate worlds, but taking up the same space.

As I looked back toward the driveway in front of us, something caused me to do a double take in the mirror. What had I seen on Joe's face? For a fast and brief instant, it was as if something happened, transformed slightly, maybe, but my mind hadn't picked up on it quickly enough to understand exactly what I'd seen. Had his face become less grimy for just a split second? Possibly. But why would it do that?

"What?" Gram asked as she twisted and looked out the back windshield.

"I'm not sure. I think I saw . . . I'm not sure what I saw."

"I don't see anything unusual. Well, unexpected," she said before she turned around again.

I shook it off and turned my attention fully toward the front of Opie's family's mansion. The white, stately manor was wide and intimidating. Four thick columns punctuated the front, and the windows were perfectly placed and reminded me of a friendly jack-o'-lantern. The wide double front doors, each with a large brass knocker, gave the whole place more of an Oz castle aura than a country home feel.

Opie had never moved out of her parents' house. She hadn't ever behaved as if she'd even considered the idea. Her parents traveled frequently, so she often had the whole place to herself. And it was a big place; ten thousand square feet of living space with a huge pool and some horse acreage extending from the back.

During the moments I wasn't irritated by her, I had to give her at least a little credit. She was as unfriendly as she could be to me, but she'd never flaunted her family's fortune. Well, at least not in a snobbish way. I'd seen her pull out her checkbook and throw lots of money at Broken Rope issues with no request for anonymity, but she'd never done it to prove herself better than anyone; she'd just known what needed to be done, and she knew she had the funds to take care of the problem. She'd never asked for any sort of thank-you in return.

I also had to give Teddy a little credit. He

hadn't fallen for Opie's money — I knew him well enough to know that he wasn't lying to me when he said he couldn't have cared if she was poor. Teddy wasn't all that into money himself. He lived simply, making more than enough money to pay his bills and still have the type of fun he liked to have.

I hadn't brought it up with him, but I suspected that his less-than-über-ambitious nature might have been at least part of the reason Opie had thought to end the relationship. Despite her humble behavior when it came to income, I couldn't see her living in his cabin, and he'd never consider living in her family's house.

"I'll be nice. Or as nice as she allows me to be," I said after I parked in the driveway and we got out of the car.

"No, you have to be nicer than that. Just ignore her if she tries to get you riled, Betts. We just need to deliver this letter."

"I wish we'd let Jake do this one, too."

"No, I want to do this one. We're getting close to the end with Joe — whatever that might be. I feel I owe it to him. I wished I'd been the one to talk to Jim. Afterward, it bothered me, and I'm not going to make that mistake again."

I was surprised to hear that she was

regretful, but I said, "I understand."

"Ready?" Gram said as she looked at me.

"Yes."

"Ready?" Gram said to Joe, who'd dismounted and was standing behind us.

He rubbed his finger under his nose and then scratched his ear. His face was as dirty as it had been when I first met him. I still didn't understand what I'd seen a moment earlier. "Yes, ma'am."

We walked up to the front doors. Gram lifted one of the heavy knockers and tapped lightly. We could hear the sound echo through the cavernous house. Opie's BMW was parked around the side of the garage, out of sight from anyone who didn't take the time to take a quick look. I suspected her parents were traveling again.

It was a long moment before a slight shuffle of footsteps moved toward the door. The hesitation after they stopped made me think that Opie was considering her visitors through the peephole long and hard. I tried to keep my expression neutral.

The door finally opened.

"Miz, Betts, what's up?" Opie asked.

She looked terrible. Normally, when she wasn't in costume as a local historical character, she was done up. She wasn't shy with makeup, and her bleached blond hair

206

was always a little bigger than it seemed it should be. She wore her clothes tight — and it truly got under my skin that she looked good in things a size or two smaller than what she should be wearing.

But today, she was different. I wondered why she'd opened the door. There was not a stitch of makeup on her face, and her hair was pulled back into a tight ponytail. She wore sweats that were perhaps older than my own favorite pair.

"Uhm, everything okay with Teddy?" she asked, before we could answer her first question.

So that's why she opened the door. A part of me wanted to understand what had gone on between her and my brother. A bigger part still didn't want the details.

Gram looked at me and then back at Opie.

"He's fine, Ophelia. We're just here to share some information with you. We found out something we thought you might find fun and interesting," Gram said.

"What's it about?" Opie said.

"We came upon some evidence that you are related to one of our more infamous citizens," Gram said with a fake smile. This wasn't any easier on her than it was me; she just wanted to be more mature.

Opie's eyes lit brighter. "Who?"

"Can we come in, Ophelia? There's a letter attached to our discovery and we'd like to read it to you."

"Sure," she said, no hesitation.

I recognized that a part of me kind of liked that we might be telling her something to bring her out of whatever funk she was in. What was wrong with me? I had no doubt that at any minute she might say or do something that would insult me directly. Why would I be happy to make her feel better about anything?

Gram led the way inside. I followed her, and Joe followed me; the horse remained outside this time. Joe whistled when we were in the entryway; it was decorated with a large round table adorned with a vase of fresh flowers. A crystal chandelier hung above the table, and even though it wasn't lit, the sun, coming in from a window above the front doors, made all the small crystal pieces shimmer.

"These folks are richer than everyone I knew combined," Joe said.

Evidence of the Buford fortune continued as Opie led us out of the entryway and into a library next to it. The room wasn't small, but it wasn't so big that it took away its cozy feel. One red velvet chaise took up the space beside the front window, and four high-back leather chairs filled the middle, facing each other in pairs; tall Tiffany lamps were placed in between each pair.

The walls were, of course, filled with hardback books, probably many of them first editions, though I doubted Opie cared much about the books. She wasn't ever much of a reader, or a student. She didn't have to get the grades to put her in the running for college scholarship money. She hadn't had the ambition I'd been required to have to maintain a 4.0 in high school, finish college at the top of my class, and then jump into law school. I did drop out of law school a year and a half in, which was a humiliation she hadn't had to face. And, other than the fact that Cliff had broken up with her and then started dating me, she'd probably had lots more fun than I did when we were younger. And we'd both ended up in pretty much the same place: Broken Rope, either working or living with our families. I tried not to dwell on the irony.

We each sat in one of the leather chairs as Joe perused the books on the shelves. He seemed much more interested in those than in our sharing of the letter.

"Ophelia, it's a long complicated story of how we came upon the letter I want to read to you. And the hows and whys won't make a lot of sense anyway, so would you mind if we just skipped over that part? Jake authenticated it and then researched how you were related. Can you just trust me on that?" Gram said.

Opie sent a quick but unmistakable glance of doubt in my direction but gave Gram a fully agreeable nod. "Of course, Miz."

"Good. Well, here it is."

Gram put on her reading glasses and then read the reproduced letter, written by Jake on parchment, just like the first letter, from Elizabeth to her mother, Alicia Zavon.

Opie was enthralled, literally on the edge of her seat through the entire reading. I don't think she breathed or blinked until after Gram was done.

"I . . . I know who you mean. Alicia Zavon killed her husband, right?" she said when Gram refolded the letter.

"Yes, that's the one, but there's a little more," Gram said.

"Okay," Opie said, her eyes now fully bright and alert, still not blinking.

"Elizabeth did come to Broken Rope. She was too late, because the letter never reached Alicia."

"Oh, my! So if the letter had arrived or if Elizabeth had arrived a little earlier, then maybe Alicia wouldn't have killed her husband?"

"It's possible, but then other things might not have occurred either," Gram said. "And Elizabeth never went back to her family, so it seems that the lineage was all but forgotten. Jake is working to figure out if the rest of the family eventually came to Broken Rope or not, but one of Elizabeth's abandoned daughters was named Ophelia. It seems that you are a part of Alicia's family tree."

Opie stood, gasped, and put her hand to her chest.

I forced myself not to roll my eyes.

"I'm related to Alicia Zavon and I'm named after one of her granddaughters!?" Opie said, almost breathless.

"It appears so," Gram said.

"This . . . this . . . well, it changes everything, doesn't it?" Opie said as she moved to the space behind her two chairs and began to pace.

"Well, I don't know," Gram said, "but it's very interesting."

"No, Miz, you don't understand." After a couple back and forth jaunts, Opie returned to the chair and sat. She leaned forward and rested her elbows on her knees as she continued, "I've always known I was somehow special to this town. I've always known! Now, this proves it."

"Opie, I think you've always been special, too. I didn't need this letter to prove it," Gram said.

I held back a myriad of protests, including incredulous noises and doubtful commentary.

"Oh, Miz, you're so sweet," Opie said. And then she actually took the next half second to send me a disgusted and disappointed look before turning her gleeful aura back to Gram.

"It's true, my dear," Gram said.

I looked at Gram. Okay, maybe this wasn't too hard on her. Maybe she was being sincere to Opie. I sure hoped I was more like her when I grew up.

"Oh my, oh my, oh my, this is such a wonderfully tragic story," Opie said.

"Yes, it is, but it is also the distant past," Gram said, bringing at least a little present-time reality back to the moment. "This happened a long time ago, Ophelia, and there's nothing to be done to change it. It's good that you know though, I think." Gram looked quickly at Joe, who'd moved to a spot beside the lamp in between me and Gram.

I looked at him, too, and there *was* something different about him, but again I couldn't put my finger on what it was. Was he more solid? No, not really. But I could still somehow *see* him better even with all the bright light. Was that it? I couldn't be sure.

"Oh, yes, Miz, it's very good that I know. I think I shall have to do something to honor the memory. No, that doesn't sound right. Murder was involved. I think I shall have to do something to document . . . yes, that's the word, *document,* the entire tragedy of the situation. Perhaps a statue or something. Maybe something right in the middle of town. I could stand next to it for a couple hours every day during the summer and let the tourists take pictures. I'm sure Jake can help me figure it out."

"I'm sure he can," Gram said.

Suddenly, whatever it was about Joe that had seemed momentarily different was gone. I couldn't distinguish what had disappeared, making me think I'd imagined it. Maybe I was just trying too hard to see something, see apparent changes with the reading of the letters. Maybe I had also just hoped that I could feel Jerome's touch in bright daylight.

"Oh, Miz" — Opie looked at me again, this time with less disdain — "and Betts,

213

you two have brightened one of my darkest times. I'm ever so grateful. Thank you."

"You're welcome," Gram said.

"Ya, uhm, yes, you're welcome, Opie," I added.

Gram stood, and I followed suit.

"We'll be on our way, then," Gram said as she stepped around me and exited the library. She was done.

"Betts," Opie said as she grabbed my arm.

"Yes?" I looked at her hand on my arm.

"How's Teddy?" she asked.

"I think he's okay." I squinted as I tried to read her pretty blue eyes. Did I see sincerity there? Did she really care about him? Would she be upset if she heard about the fight and the condition he was genuinely in? My hard heart softened a little, and even though I thought I'd probably regret it, I said, "Actually, Opie, he was in a fight and, well, he's fine, and he's going to be fine, but he got a little beat up."

"What happened?"

"He's still sorting out the details."

"Oh, dear, should I . . . Oh, Betts, I want to see him, I miss him. Should I?"

I shrugged. "I don't know, Opie. Teddy doesn't share his personal goings-on with me. I don't know what happened between the two of you."

"I'm too old for him, Betts. I knew he wouldn't remain interested in me long-term. I thought it was best to break us up before I got too deep."

Judging from the condition she was in and the mood Teddy had been in, I suspected they'd both already fallen too deep. I wanted to tell Opie to quit being so stupid. Though Teddy had a reputation, he also knew how to care about people; he truly did have feelings, too. But I didn't think I should advise either of them regarding anything.

"I don't know what to tell you, Opie, but he has seemed a little down in the dumps since you two broke up."

"He has?"

"Yes," I said. I had the urge to run. I could tell she was about to ruin our moment.

"I will call him today," she said, as if assuring me.

I smiled as I nodded and turned to leave.

"Betts, wait," she said as she took the steps to catch up with me.

"Yes."

"Thank you." She smiled sincerely. "And, well, never mind." She put a few stray pieces of my hair behind my ear. She wanted to insult my hair, but she held back.

It was the nicest she'd ever been about my hair.

I sighed deeply.

"See you later, Opie," I said before joining Gram and Joe and the horse outside. If she only knew that she'd had a ghost from Broken Rope's past right in her house.

At least I had that on her.

CHAPTER 17

After our visit with Opie, Gram insisted on us all going back to the school. I asked her why we just couldn't back out of Opie's driveway, find a quiet spot, pull out the last letter, read it, and call Jake for help. Or better yet, just call him first and set up a quick meeting. Surely he would have to be of assistance again, and we still had a little prep to do at the campsite.

Gram said, "No, this is important, Betts; the culmination of so many years of Joe's and my search, or *mission,* maybe. This all began back at the cemetery outside the cooking school; it needs to end there, too."

"Okay," I said, hoping she didn't catch the forced enthusiasm in my voice.

So Gram rode with me in the Nova, Joe and the horse again following behind as we left the country, drove through Broken Rope's small downtown, exited on the other side of town back into the country, took that curve in the state highway, and returned to the cooking school.

I had, however, called Jake over to join us. Though Gram had wanted to read the last letter in the cemetery, I knew I wouldn't be able to clearly see it in the bright outside light so I had to ask for a small change of venue. We sat inside the school at a corner of one of the large center butcher blocks. Joe and Gram on one side. Jake and I on the other. We'd closed the blinds and turned off all the lights. I pointed out to Jake where Joe was sitting.

"How was Opie?" Jake asked.

"As expected. There might be some statue planning in your near future," I said.

Jake thought a moment and said, "I can handle that."

He could.

"This will be a very heady experience for Ophelia, but she'll be all right, and even though she'll find a way to make it all about her, the town will somehow benefit, too. She's good at making sure everyone gets included. Eventually," Gram said. She turned to Joe. "Are you ready for the last letter?"

"I am," Joe said as he nodded.

"You're completely sure?" Gram said.

"Yes."

The shoe was most definitely on the other foot with this ghost. It took almost all I had to hold back a sigh of impatience or tell him and Gram to hurry up. Normally, I was the patient, curious, and sympathetic one, and Gram was telling the ghosts to move it along, or perhaps to just go away for a while.

It was more than plain impatience for me, though I wasn't sure if I didn't like Joe or didn't trust him or didn't . . . something. I had been sensing something was off from the beginning, but I couldn't pinpoint anything, exactly. Whatever it was, it made me wary and suspicious and drove me a little crazy. I was usually on top of my instincts, and I didn't like not understanding what I was feeling.

"Shall we?" Jake prompted.

"Okay, Joe, go ahead. We're ready," Gram said.

"Miz, whatever it is, I just want to thank you for everything. All these years . . . thank you," Joe said.

"You, too. You've been a delight."

I blinked.

"Here goes." Joe lifted a flap on the side of the *mochila*.

"He's reaching in the *mochila* now," I told Jake.

"Excellent. I'm ready." He held a pen

poised over a brand-new, small notebook.

Joe reached in and pulled out a folded piece of paper. This one was off-white. But it also had dark edges, as if . . .

"Oh, no," I said.

"What?" Jake said.

Gram had also said something similar to my "oh, no."

"There might be something wrong with the letter," I said to Jake. "It looks like it's been burned, around the edges at least, and the burns seem to be spreading as we're looking at it."

"Not good," Jake said.

If the piece of paper had been real, not something from the world of the dead, or the unknown, or wherever it came from, I doubted that it could be unfolded without falling apart. Not only did it look like it was burned; it was thin and flimsy. I didn't know whether to attribute its condition to its afterlife existence or if it had simply been delicate when it was real. The blackened marks extended toward the center — more of the letter had been burned than not burned.

Joe did manage to unfold it, though he was slow, carefully holding the edges by his fingertips.

Once it was open, he placed it on the table

and carefully smoothed it mostly flat. He spent a long moment looking at the paper, his concentrated focus not giving away much of anything.

I was peering at the letter, hoping something would become clear, but nothing happened quickly. I scooted off the stool and moved closer, to the spot behind Joe. He looked up and directly at Gram. I touched the paper just to see if I could feel it; I could.

"It has only a few words," he said.

"I see the same thing," I said, when I finally did.

"Okay, what are they?" Gram asked.

"Sure to die," Joe said.

"The paper only says: *Sure to die,*" I said to Jake.

"Well, that's interesting, in a scary way," Jake said.

"That's all it says?" Gram moved next to me.

"That's all I can see," Joe said.

"Me too. That's all I see," I said. "No, wait, what's down at the bottom? It looks like the letters . . . *S-T-I-N.*"

"Is that in the signature spot?" Jake asked. "The spot where you'd sign off?"

"It looks like it," I said.

"Could that be the last part of Astin's first name?" Jake said.

"I suppose it's very possible. You think he wrote this letter?"

"I don't know, but it would fit with whatever seems to be going on."

I put the letter down and looked at Joe. "Seriously, it seems more and more like you are, in fact, Astin Reagal."

"Why? Because he might have been the person who signed this letter?" Gram said.

"Something like that," I said.

"No, Betts, I am not Astin Reagal. I am certain of that. I am certain that my name is Joe."

"Jake, what was Astin's middle name?"

"I have no idea, but I can try to find it."

"Please do. Something tells me it will be some form of Joe."

"But didn't you say that Joe doesn't look a thing like Astin's picture?" Jake said.

"I know, but there's something about that, too. His face does strange things, like changes just a little bit for an instant and then changes back."

"Changes enough that it could look like Astin's if it changed only a little more?"

"Well, no, not really."

"Betts, I am not Astin Reagal, but I bet this letter was from him," Joe said.

"Why is it incomplete?" I asked.

"The letter?" Jake asked. "Why is the letter incomplete?"

"Yes," I said.

"I have a hunch. Maybe we have to find Astin's remains first, before the letter will be able to be read all the way through," Jake said.

"Really?" I said, but then suddenly that idea somehow felt right.

"It's not an easy search," Gram said, "but maybe Jerome did come back for that purpose. I hope he finds Astin soon."

Jake cocked his head as he fell into thought. "You know, maybe you're doing exactly what you should be doing and you don't even know it. Maybe those words wouldn't have even appeared if Esther and Jerome hadn't come to town. Or maybe I just need to keep researching and Jerome needs to remember where Astin's remains are? How's this — maybe the words on the paper will help Jerome in some weird way."

"I suppose that's possible," I said. "Anything is."

"I think we need to go with Jerome. Or you do, or Miz does, or even Joe does. I know Jerome is searching but even he might need some help. Yes, I think this is unlike any letter you've dealt with before, and it is the last one. There are so many other strange things happening that perhaps the

223

letter has to behave differently this time. Perhaps it can't tell us everything because it's important that other things happen first. Make sense?"

I looked at Gram. "What do you think?"

"I have absolutely no idea what to think," Gram said. "But I suppose Jake might be on to something. Searching for Astin Reagal's remains can't hurt, I suppose. It's worth a shot."

"Okay, I guess we'll talk to Jerome next time we see him. I know he's somewhere between here and Rolla, but I'm not sure exactly where. You know, Gram?"

"I don't think Jerome and I ever once talked about where his property was, but I know the general area. We can look." She checked her watch. "Not today, though. Tomorrow maybe. We've got fish to fry today, but tomorrow for sure." She smiled sympathetically at Joe.

"It's okay, Miz. It's been a long time. I can wait a little longer."

I wondered if he could, though. The ghosts' visits had expiration dates. Was Joe's visit truly destined to be short? Was he going to get so close and yet not be able to finish what he and Gram had started all those years ago? The singed and incomplete letter made me think that Joe *might* not be destined to have all the answers. But I didn't vocalize that thought. It wouldn't have gone over well.

CHAPTER 18

I'd grown up in a family of fishermen. Both of my parents had instilled the ritual of waking me and Teddy up long before the crack of dawn to gather poles and worms — never anything but worms, back then, but I'd never tell Jerome that part — to take us out to a nearby crick, not creek, not pond, not lake, but crick. I'd never been all that thrilled to be awakened that early and dragged out of my comfortable bed for some family time, but I'd enjoyed it once we got there and dropped the lines. We'd always fished for catfish, and it was always an adventure.

There were giant catfish in the waters of Missouri. Some were hundreds of pounds. Literally. But we never went for that variety. We just fished for some good-sized "catters" that we could fry up at home.

This tradition had, however, begun with Gram when my dad was younger. Apparently, they spent many a morning drowning worms and catching those catters.

But the best part of fishing for catfish is, without a doubt, eating them. According to Gram, there was truly only one real way to cook catters: Fry them up in a cast-iron skillet over an open flame. It isn't a difficult process, but it does take a little practice to get it right. Gram has had plenty of practice.

"Yeah, that's the part I don't like, the cleaning." A gentleman in jeans, an embroidered red Western shirt, and an out-of-place light blue Bermuda hat stood closest to Gram, but the crowd was pretty big.

There was no doubt that the cowboy poetry convention's party atmosphere probably wasn't up to par with the celebration-filled bash it had been in years past, but Orly and his crew had found a way to infuse some lively spirit that wasn't disrespectful to the murder victim.

One of the ways that he'd done this was to continue to spread excitement about Gram's cooking demonstrations, about both the Dutch oven dishes and the frying demonstration. When the poets first heard that Gram was going to offer cooking lessons during the convention, enthusiasm built quickly. And after the success of the morning event, even if people weren't interested in learning the techniques for frying the fish over a campfire, people were interested in seeing Missouri Anna in action, and they had gathered in appreciation.

I was always a little surprised by her still-rising celebrity. It caught me off guard when a fan asked for her autograph or for a photograph with her. Her cooking school's reputation had only grown. The building itself and the cemetery next to it (if only the tourists really knew what was going on there) had become bona fide Broken Rope attractions.

"I agree. Tell me your name," Gram said.

"Jed," he said.

"I agree, Jed, but you get used to it after a while. And you get quick, too. You can clean and fillet a catter lickety-split, and you learn not to even pay attention to the cleaning part," Gram said as she flung the catfish's guts into a pail next to the small portable table and chair she was using.

"Oh," Jed said. He attempted to smile.

"And then you slice here. Like that. And then here. Like that. And voilà, you have fish ready to fry."

"Can this apply to any fish, Missouri?" Esther asked. She was on the other side of the crowd, and I'd seen her there but hadn't had a chance to talk to her. I thought Jake

228

would be happy to see her when he arrived.

I was again surprised by how the cowboy poetry crowd had continued to grow. Jim and Cliff had thought about not allowing any more visitors, but the logistics of such a ban were too difficult to seriously consider. They'd had Orly and a few of his crew keep track of names of new arrivals, and they checked with him constantly, apparently running names in their criminal databases to see if anyone suspicious joined the activities, or could no longer be found. It had to be a difficult task, added to all the other difficult tasks Orly was handling.

"Sure, you can fry any fish, but it's hard to beat a fried catfish. Its flavor works perfectly with the breading and the spices. Speaking of which, the breading is made up of buttermilk, and then cornmeal, corn flour, garlic powder, some peppers and a dash of hot sauce."

"Sounds too spicy," Jed added.

"Try it. If it's too much, you can always mellow the hot stuff, but I don't recommend it. A little kick to your catter is the only way to go."

"I see."

Esther caught my eye and smiled and waved. I waved back.

"So there I've whisked together your buttermilk and hot sauce. That's what's in this bowl." Gram pointed.

Gram was set up pretty close to the west campfire, which blazed hot but still under control. Orly had lit the fire according to Gram's specific directions. A grill had been placed above the flames, and a skillet with about a quarter inch of oil filling its bottom sat on the grill. Gram had fried catfish so many times in her life that she knew about how high the flames needed to be to keep the oil at the right temperature. I'd never attempted to fry anything outside, but I knew that the oil would be about 350 degrees, and would remain close to that as long as Gram was in charge of the show.

Along with the small folding table in front of her where she'd displayed the proper way to clean and fillet the fish, there was also a cooler full of more fish being kept on ice. There'd be lots of fish fried this evening, but the duties would be turned over to a couple of the poets after Gram was done with her part of the demonstration. She'd watch everything else closely, though. If catfish were going to be fried by someone other than Gram, the cooks would at least be supervised by Ms. Missouri, Anna Winston, herself.

She took the fillet she was working with

and slapped it down on a couple paper towels.

"You have to make sure the fillets are dry before you work with them," she said as she wrapped and patted the fish. "And then drag the fillets through the buttermilk, and then the cornmeal and spices." She dunked and then pulled the fillet through the buttermilk, lifting it when it was well covered and giving it a small shake to get rid of the excess, and then she dipped it in the cornmeal and spices, making sure both sides were coated. "Place it in the oil. Take care not to burn yourself. The oil can pop up and get you."

Somehow Gram never burned herself.

"Hi," a quiet voice said from behind me.

"Hi, Esther," I said as I turned. She'd snuck around the crowd. "How are you?"

"I'm fine. You have a minute?" she said.

"Sure."

So we wouldn't disturb Gram's demonstration, we moved away from the crowd. We stood next to a tent that had peace sign patches sewn into it and had probably been made in the 1960s.

"Everything okay?" I asked.

"Sure, everything's fine," she said. "I just wanted to . . . gosh, I have no idea how I managed to maybe get in the middle of

231

something, but I might have, and I wanted to tell someone. Honestly, Betts, this has been a strange and kind of awful trip, but kind of good, too. I've appreciated Jake's research, and he's such a sweetie, but the murder has made everything so scary, and I just heard that your brother was the one who got beaten up and I wanted to talk to you about that."

I was glad to be getting the information without having to be the one to ask the questions first. "Yes, his name is Teddy. Did you see what happened?"

"Not really. No, not when he was being beaten, but I saw some other stuff before that that I've been thinking I should tell the police, but I'm kind of scared."

"Are you scared of the police?" I asked. "You don't need to be."

"No, I'm scared of what might happen to me if I talk to the police about what I saw. I was hoping to tell you and between the two of us we can figure out how to get the information to them."

I nodded. "Certainly."

"The night that your brother was beaten — as I already told you, I did see him. I'd seen him around for a couple days. He seemed to be having a good time. He's quite adorable." Esther smiled and blushed a little. I wanted to remind her of Jake, but again I just nodded. "Anyway, he obviously likes to have a good time, too, though I don't think he was drinking much, just having fun. He seemed to enjoy the poetry and the music."

"Are you sure he wasn't drinking, or acting drunk?"

"Not when I saw him, no."

"Okay."

"Right. Well, there was a woman who seemed very interested in both him and Norman, and I feel kind of rotten for not telling you about her earlier, but she seemed pretty upset when neither of them returned the interest. I didn't want to tell anyone about her anger that night after Norman was killed because I didn't want to be the one to make someone else maybe look guilty of something so horrible, but then I heard about your brother and her anger at both of them suddenly seemed even worse than her anger with just one of them. Gosh, I'm not sure that makes any sense at all."

I'd had plenty of moments when something had suddenly become clear after only receiving a little more information. I got what she was saying. "Who?" Though I was pretty sure I knew who she was talking about.

Esther looked around and then whispered, "Vivienne."

"I see."

Esther was claiming that Vivienne was doing what Teddy had claimed that Esther had done. Was Esther lying or was Teddy misremembering?

"However, Betts, the thing about Vivienne that I think is more important than the fact that she hit on your brother and Norman is the fact that she's been hitting on lots of guys. She's pretty, but mostly she seems like she's glad to be on vacation or something. You know, like what happens at the poetry convention stays at the poetry convention."

"I get that." Orly had mentioned some people having that attitude earlier.

"But she was more upset by being pushed away from Norman and your brother than by anyone else. And she was extremely upset right after the murder — you know, when you found us in the shoe repair shop — but other than that, she seems to be almost unaffected by it all. And . . ."

"Go on."

"And, well, her behavior and reactions seem inconsistent, and her anger over your brother and Norman was so off the charts. Rage, maybe."

"That's never fun to see. Who else? Who

else has she . . . well, seemed to be interested in?"

"One of the other guys I've seen her talking to a lot is Orly."

"I don't understand. You think she's interested in Orly?"

"I don't know. I don't think so. I just saw them arguing and I wonder what he was so angry with her about."

"When was this argument?"

"The night before Norman's murder."

"Maybe he was just telling her to cut it out," I said.

"Maybe."

"Do you know where she is right now?"

Esther nodded. "That's why I came over to talk to you. I think I know exactly where she is. Come over here."

Esther led us to a spot on the other side of the patchwork tent. We now stood next to a tent that must have been close to brand-new, and she nodded to the right.

"See her?" Esther asked.

I did, and surprisingly, while I was watching her, she suddenly became very animated and loud. My attention was solely on her, so to me she was the one who seemed the loudest.

But, actually, lots of people were screaming right along with her.

CHAPTER 19

"Gram?" I said before I bolted away from Esther and pushed through the crowd.

The reactions and emotions from everyone were too big for something simple to have occurred, something like a mean snap of oil.

Fortunately, Gram was fine; scared almost as witless as everyone else, but fine. So far.

She'd jumped up from the chair, displacing both it and the table with the fish. In my lifetime, I didn't think I'd ever heard Gram scream, but she probably had.

"Gram, you okay?" I asked as I found myself next to her.

"Fine. Scared the rotten right out of me, but I'm fine. We need to get this thing killed though."

The "thing" she was referring to was a snake. It was not coiled, which meant it could move quickly and bite if it was so inclined. Though it was currently facing the other direction, it was only a few feet away.

"Move away a little more, Gram," I said as I grabbed her arm. "Is that a cotton?"

"I think so," Gram said.

The snake was mostly brown, which made it difficult to distinguish from other, less wicked snakes, but this guy's or girl's head was also triangular, which was a characteristic I'd been taught to look for and then run from. Cottonmouths are one of Missouri's most deadly snakes; they're one of many states' most deadly snakes. They're usually found in water or very close to it, so it was strange to see it writhe on the dirt around the campfire, far from any water source.

"Step back," I said to Gram, pulling her another step backward, but she pulled her arm from my grip.

"Someone got a gun? Or a shovel?" she said.

"Gram, come on! You're not going to kill that snake. Just get back."

"I got this, Missouri." Orly appeared from the crowd, carrying a shovel and a shotgun — they'd apparently both learned about the same sorts of snake-killing weapons. I hoped Orly would use the shovel, but cottonmouths are so dangerous that I probably shouldn't have worried about the weapon as much as just hoped for a good aim.

Cliff was planning on joining us later, but I knew there were other officers roaming the campsite. I wondered where they were and how they'd feel about someone waving and then potentially discharging a firearm. If I'd had my wits about me a little more, I would have been concerned that Orly even had any sort of firearm. Hadn't all weapons been confiscated by the police?

"Come on, everybody, get back a little," Orly said when the crowd suddenly turned more curious than cautious.

The bowl of batter had somehow been propelled into the flames. As it burned, it sizzled and sent up small puffs of dirty smoke.

Only one of the coolers of fish had been overturned, blazing a scaled trail of dead catfish that spread from the cooler and out about six feet. Based upon what I saw, I thought that the snake must have come from the cooler, although that didn't make a lot of sense. I couldn't understand how it got in there in the first place. Sure, it had probably resided by or in the river where the fish had been caught, but I didn't think it was capable of slithering its way into a cooler, nor would it want to. I didn't understand the behavioral motivations for cottonmouths, but I knew they were mostly afraid of humans, their fear causing them to react violently when they were bothered by any.

I also couldn't imagine that someone would actually find a cottonmouth and touch it long enough to put it anywhere, including in a cooler. They are fierce and deadly in the most lethal ways possible. They like their own space, and I believe Teddy once told me that if a cottonmouth is disturbed, it will "chase you down just to make sure you never come back again." Everyone knows that they aren't to be toyed with. No one in their right mind would do anything short of run away from a cottonmouth.

This snake was probably four feet long when stretched straight. From my vantage point, it looked huge, but I didn't know if it truly was big for its breed. Orly was probably a very capable snake killer, but I wished for a law officer with some ace gun skills.

"Okay, fella, or little lady, who knows, I'm not going to hurt you," Orly said.

I didn't think snakes could hear, but I didn't like what Orly said. *Not going to hurt it?* Was he really not going to kill it? Gram was still close enough to the action that if something went wrong, she could be bitten. I stepped forward next to her. I'd yank her back hard if need be.

"What can I do, Orly?" I said as I put my hand on Gram's arm.

"Nothing, Betts, just give us room. I'm going to get him out of here." Orly took the shovel and, with one quick swipe, uprighted the cooler that had previously held the fish. It was a pretty skillful move.

"Just shoot it!" someone from the crowd exclaimed.

I was now leaning that way myself, but I didn't join in.

"Nah, he's got a right to live just as much as anyone else," Orly said.

I wanted to beg to differ, but I still kept quiet, because he was the one holding the shovel and shotgun.

In movements that were almost too fast to follow, Orly used his shotgun and the shovel for scoop and carry maneuvers, kind of like awkwardly shaped, giant chopsticks. Seconds later, the snake was somehow placed in the cooler and the lid was down. Gram was just as quick as Orly had been when she leapt to the closed cooler and sat on it.

She peered up at Orly and said, "Got a rope?"

"I believe I do, little lady," Orly said.

I'd seen plenty of gentlemen become smitten with my grandmother. She was amazing and still had whatever it took that seemed to draw men right to her. I didn't mind the flirtation, but understanding what had been going on between Orly and Vivienne moved up a notch on my priority list. Gram could take care of herself, but she didn't need to be just another notch in Orly's convention cowboy belt. Unless she wanted to be, I suppose.

Relief spread through the crowd in the form of some nervous laugher, a little conversation, and a smattering of applause. I took a deep breath and released it.

"Look over there." Esther had appeared by my side. She was nodding across the crowd.

Vivienne was the subject of the nod. Her arms were crossed in front of herself. She was glaring directly at Gram.

"Uh-oh," I said involuntarily.

"I know. She might have something for Orly, and we all saw his and your grandmother's snake-wrangling teamwork. They seemed to enjoy it."

Truthfully, Orly's, Vivienne's, and, for the most part, Gram's love lives were none of my business, and I typically wouldn't be interested in any details or gossip, but between the murder and Teddy's beating, I was intrigued. Though it felt a little high school-ish, maybe knowing more about who had the hots for who might tell me about who'd also been acting with violence.

"You think Orly has something for Vivienne, or Vivienne for him?" I asked.

"I don't know if that was it. Not sure. They were arguing, and I'm sure I heard Norman's name, that's all I know. And then she seemed interested in your brother and in Norman, and seemed so upset when they didn't respond. I'm sorry, Betts, I don't know the details, but I know something was going on and I just can't help but think . . ." Esther said, her words trailing off. No one wanted to accuse anyone of anything violent.

I needed to talk to Vivienne, or at least find out more about her. And about Esther, too, for that matter.

Predictably, Gram was no worse for the wear. In fact, since no one got hurt, the moments with the snake somehow infused her with an extra dose of adrenaline. There were plenty more catfish that had been caught and stored in coolers that hadn't been upturned, and hadn't been invaded by snakes — we checked. The two poets who'd claimed to have some experience with both campfires and catfish jumped in to take care of the rest of the fry as Gram supervised.

I helped, too, and lost track of Vivienne. Finally, I found a moment when I thought I could step away from the frying activities, and I was pleasantly surprised to see Jezzie and Cody sitting side-by-side on a couple camp chairs. As I approached, I thought I heard Jezzie say Norman's name.

"Hi," I said.

They both looked up. Neither of them was happy to see me, or maybe it was just that neither of them was plain happy.

"What's up?" I asked.

"Hey, Betts. We were just talking about Norman and who would have killed that poor man. I'm more and more distraught the more I think about it," Jezzie said.

She was pale and looked very tired.

"I'm so sorry, Jezzie. This has to be hard on you."

"It is. I didn't know him all that well, but I sure liked what little I knew. He seemed like a sweet guy."

I nodded.

Jezzie rubbed her knuckles together. "That morning — that morning before he was killed, he told me he'd made an important decision *not* to do something. He was a little upset, but mostly relieved. I was all about getting into my character so I only briefly asked for more details, but he could tell I was distracted so he didn't tell me more. If only I knew more. I've been asking Cody here if he knew anything."

I looked at Cody. He shook his head and shrugged at the same time.

"Did you tell Cliff about that?" I asked Jezzie.

"Of course, but I don't think it did much good. I feel like I let him down."

"You didn't," I said. "He and my brother Teddy were kind of friends, too."

"Yeah, I know. Does he know anything?"

"No, not at the moment," I said. Maybe the news hadn't made it to Jezzie yet. Cody just looked at me with wide, unsure eyes. "Teddy was hurt, Jezzie. He was beaten up the night before Norman was killed."

"No! That's terrible. Is he okay?"

"He'll be fine."

"Oh my gracious, I'm so glad to hear that."

"I heard he'd been drinking quite a bit earlier that night." I looked at Cody to see if he would waver from his earlier comments. I didn't want to believe that he had been correct about Teddy's behavior, but Cody gave no sign that he wanted to change his story. I turned my attention back to Jezzie. "Teddy doesn't remember much. Any chance you saw anything suspicious?"

"No, and when I saw him he certainly wasn't acting like he was too drunk, but I left early in the evening so I could get some rest. I'm not as old as the old ones around here, and not as young as the young-uns. I'm right in the middle group who likes a good night of sleep more than not." There was no humor in her words, but if she'd been in a better mood, I might have laughed.

Instead, I hesitated to respond, which caused both her and Cody to look up at me.

"Jezzie, were you upset with Orly that night?" I finally asked.

"I don't . . . oh, yes, I was. Well, not really, but we were having a discussion."

"May I ask what it was about?"

"It wasn't much of anything, just rehearsal schedules and such. Nothing important."

"That was it?"

"That was it."

"Oh."

I looked back and forth at Jezzie and Cody, and I couldn't help but wonder what they were hiding, or just keeping to themselves, maybe. They both now had that forced, wide-eyed innocence that pretty much always indicates some sort of guilt.

But any more questions I might come up

with would have to wait to be asked. I saw Cliff's car moving along the road at the edge of the campsite. I excused myself and hurried to greet him.

The snake story had made it back to the police station, and Cliff's first item of duty was to tell Orly that the snake would be disposed of by the police, and that waving a shotgun in public, even if a murder hadn't recently occurred, was a bad idea. In fact, I'd been correct — no one was supposed to have a firearm in the first place. The police had taken possession of all weapons. Or so they thought. The shotgun was now also in the possession of one of the other officers.

I didn't think Orly cared much that the police weren't happy with him, but he was dutifully obedient with Cliff, apologizing and promising to never to do such a thing again.

"How are you?" I said to Cliff after he took the tied-shut cooler and placed it in his police car. He'd driven his official vehicle, though he had changed out of his official uniform into some jeans and an appropriate Western shirt. I didn't know if he'd decided to be more casual since we'd be together this evening or if he didn't want to look so much like a cop. Jim must have given the okay on the clothes.

"I'm fine. How about you?" he said. "I've been a little busy the last few days, haven't I?"

I shrugged. "Goes with the job."

"It does. Seriously, you doing all right?"

"Yep. I'd like to find out who killed Norman and who beat up Teddy. I've been trying to ask some questions. You and Jim find out anything more about either of those crimes, though I realize the murder is much more important? Maybe you'd like to share the details with me?"

"You're much more curious than you used to be in high school."

"Not really. You just weren't a police officer when we were in high school. If you had been, I'd have been extra curious. If I remember correctly, I paid very close attention to all your football stuff. I even learned some of the plays."

"Yes, you did." Cliff half smiled. He took a deep breath and then surveyed the campsite. Any reminiscing would have to take place later.

As the sun was low on the horizon, some people were eating, some were chatting, some were reading to each other, and some were writing their poetry as they sat in camp chairs and scribbled on notepads. Cliff was probably building a mental grid, separating the groups with his cop eyes.

"We'd like to have some answers, too. Other than determining that the weapon used to kill Norman was a .38 Special, we don't have anything new, Betts. We're trying to get more information on everyone here, but particularly Norman Bytheway, and we're having a hard time finding much at all about him."

"No family in Kansas City?" I said.

"Nope. We can't find any family anywhere. His last name is unusual, but there are a few Bytheways in Missouri. We've got calls in to the ones we could find. But Norman might not have even been from Missouri. It could be a dead end."

"So, whoever his family is, they don't know he's dead yet?"

Cliff shook his head. "Unless they killed him or they're secretly here, part of the poetry group, or have paid attention to the news reports — but we expected a call or something after we released his name; got nothing. So as far as we know, none of his family knows anything."

"I think I remember Jake telling me that he was a part-time actor in Kansas City. He must have had another job, one that paid the bills."

"He must have, but we have yet to figure

out where. There were no credit cards or checks in his possession. His driver's license expired over a year ago and the address listed wasn't current, or at least that's what the people who answered the door there said."

"I can see letting a license expire. Those things get forgotten sometimes."

"They do, but the fact that we can't find anything more about him is, of course, strange. Pretty much everybody leaves a trail these days."

"He wasn't who he said he was?" I said.

"That's one thought, but even though the license expired, it did have his picture on it. We do think he was using his real name."

"I *might* have something helpful."

"That'd be great. I hope so."

I told him about Vivienne and about the supposed argument between her and Orly. I also went over everything Teddy had told me. I told him what Esther and Teddy had noticed about Vivienne and Teddy and Norman, and what Cody had observed. I even mentioned that Esther had commented about Jezzie and Orly arguing, and the reason Jezzie had just given me for the argument — or, as she put it, "discussion."

"That's good stuff, Betts. I'll find and talk to them all again."

I didn't think it really was good stuff. I thought it was a bunch of different stuff that wasn't fitting together and didn't have much backing it up, but maybe it would lead to something.

It looked like Cliff wouldn't have to go far to talk to Jezzie. In tandem, we both noticed her hurrying in our direction. We were beside Cliff's car, so we were back from the crowd. Jezzie kept looking behind her as she moved toward us.

"Jez, you okay?" Cliff asked as he stepped protectively toward her.

"I'm fine, Cliffy, but I saw you two over here and I wanted to talk to you and Betts without Cody around, so I hurried over. Y'all don't see him coming this way, do you?"

We surveyed the area, but neither of us saw him anywhere.

"You want to go someplace else?" Cliff asked.

"No, no, I just want you both to know that Orly and I *were* having a discussion the other night, and it was only partially about rehearsals. It was about Cody. I'd heard he had a criminal record and I was worried. Orly assured me that all would be fine. Now, let me say that I don't think that Cody killed anyone, but I just didn't want him to

250

know that that's what Orly and I were discussing. You understand, Betts?"

"Of course."

"And I didn't even think about mentioning it to you until Betts asked me about it only a little bit ago," she said to Cliff. "I'm sorry."

"It's okay. We know about his record, and it was nothing violent, so we aren't concerned. Frankly, there are quite a few people in town who have some sort of arrest record, and we're looking at them all. I appreciate the update, though," Cliff said.

"Oh, good. Well, I'm going to go back into that party for a little longer, but I'll be going home soon. I'll stay in touch, Cliffy. We still need a family dinner while I'm in town. Gracious, I never meant to get this involved in things. I was just coming out for a visit."

"We will definitely get together for dinner, Jez," Cliff said.

"Jezzie," I said before she could get away. "I have a horrible question for you."

"Have at it," she said, though she blinked uncertainly.

"Have you had any romantic interest in anyone around here, maybe Orly — or even Cody?"

I thought Cliff might hate me forever for asking his cousin such a question, but he gave no indication that he was bothered by my boldness.

"Oh, my! No, not even a little bit, my dear. Why in the world would you ask?"

"I don't know. Conventions and things, and camping under the stars, with the romantic cowboy poetry adding to the ambience."

Jezzie laughed. "No, my dear, I have no interest in those boys. I have me a good old-fashioned boyfriend back home that I would never even consider cheating on, even if whatever happened in Broken Rope stayed in Broken Rope. I'm sorry if I've given anyone a different impression, especially you."

"No, I was truly just wondering. That's all."

"No problem." Jezzie sighed. "I'm going back in there, but I bet I don't last long."

"We'll see you later, Jezzie," Cliff said as she turned and hurried away.

"Sorry, Cliff," I said.

"No need to be. I don't know why you were curious, but if you needed to know, you needed to know. I think she sounded like she was being honest."

"I do, too."

"Howdy!" another voice greeted us.

Cliff and I turned to the person attached

252

to the happy greeting. If I remembered correctly, his name was Gary. He'd been the one to fetch Teddy's truck.

"Hello," Cliff and I said.

"You're one of those police officer fellas, arn't cha?" The man was short, but that was only the beginning of his unique looks. He wore a very old cowboy hat; I'd yet to notice many new ones. Strands of thick, short gray hair stuck out from under the rim and framed a sunken and wrinkled face. He didn't have many teeth — I saw only one in front — and his tongue seemed to move around constantly. He dressed the part, but something told me that he always wore stained Western shirts and faded jeans; this wasn't a costume for the convention.

"I am," Cliff said. "What can I do for you?"

"I'd like to tell you a story."

"All right. My name's Cliff Sebastian. This is Betts Winston. What's your name?"

"That's part of the story." The man winked.

"Go on."

The man cleared his throat and straightened the knot of an invisible tie.

"Sometimes Gary's not seen, it's the one way I can hide. Sometimes I can hear but no one thinks I understand. But that Norman fella, I saws how he was. And what happened next wasn't just because."

Cliff and I were silent a moment.

Though Gary's poem was somewhat ominous, I couldn't translate it at all.

"Tell me if I'm wrong, but I think you're trying to tell me you think that Norman Bytheway might have gotten what he deserved? Is that correct?" Cliff said.

"No, sir, that's not what I'm trying to tell you. I just want you to know that mehbe that Norman fella wouldn't do what someone ask-ted him to do."

"I see. Gary, I appreciate knowing that, but I could sure use some more information. Can you tell me what he was asked to do, or who asked him to do it?"

"I wishes I could, but even though sometimes I see, sometimes I don't see what I'm looking at, too."

"Oh," Cliff said. "Would you just let me know if something else comes back to you, if you remember more?"

Cliff handed Gary a card. Even though I doubted that Gary had a cell phone, he carefully put the card in his back pocket and then turned and walked away. He moved as though he had a catch in his hip, though not a full-on limp.

"That was interesting. And kind of sad," I said.

"Yeah." Cliff squinted and ran his tongue over his bottom lip. "Yeah. Come on, let's go find some other people to talk to."

"Sounds good to me."

CHAPTER 20

The rising of the clear, bright quarter moon was idyllic. It was difficult to see many stars because of the artificial light poles around the campsite, but as the moon rode along the top of the forest of trees that bordered the site, it seemed to watch protectively over the convention. It looked like it had been hung there on purpose, just for the poets.

The daytime and early evening convention events, like the catfish fry and the Dutch oven demonstrations, were about fun and frivolity. The evening activities were still all about fun, but a blanket of reverence also fell over the crowd once the sun set. Perhaps some of the atmosphere had to do with the murder, but I suspected that the music played and the poetry read were both so well respected that rowdy and out-of-control behavior wasn't typically accepted until later, when all the performances had been accomplished.

Burly cowboys who weren't imbibing stood stoically guarding the two campfires, resembling the way some of our summer bouncers posed. I admired Orly's attention to that detail, but I spent a moment wishing that at least one of the campfire guards had been aware enough to protect my brother a couple nights earlier.

At the far end of the space was a stage. It wasn't fancy or very high up off the ground. But it was wide and made of strong metal that held the weight of many people at once. Orly had been either on the stage or close by it for most of the evening. A small sound system with one microphone and one amplifier was used so that everyone gathered around could hear the poets and singers. Most of the men and women, but mostly men, who took the microphone and recited or sang something they'd written were blessed with booming voices and didn't need the sound system's assistance, but it helped with some of the quieter types.

Though Cliff had said we could question people together, ultimately, he and I had gone different directions with plans to meet up later, compare notes, and maybe revisit people. First I found Gram. She wasn't surrounded by poets with catfish frying questions by that time, and I was able to ask her how she thought the snake had made its way into the cooler. She said she couldn't be sure, but she was certain that since no harm had come to anyone, including the snake, that there was no need to give the situation any more thought. I decided not to argue.

After I spoke to Gram, I was surprised to see Teddy's truck make its way down the path next to the campsite. Joe and the horse trailed behind, but I didn't think they were following Teddy on purpose. I'd wondered where the ghosts had been; their sudden appearance at the same time as Teddy's was somewhat curious, but I'd need to find out more to know if it meant anything.

After Teddy parked the truck, Joe continued to steer the horse past it, past the campsite, and toward the Pony Express station. It would be interesting to look at the attraction with someone who'd actually spent some time in a few of the real ones, but finding out why Teddy left the comfort of his couch or bed to come back out to the convention took precedence.

The truck stopped close to the stage. Though I shouldn't have been, I was totally surprised to see not only my brother exit the vehicle, but Opie, too. And she'd been the one to come out of the driver's side.

She'd fixed herself up, Opie-style, but Teddy still looked rough.

They both sent me looks of impatience as I approached.

"I know, I'm not supposed to be out, Betts, but I was going a little stir-crazy and Opie offered to drive us here. Also, my memory might come back to me a little better if I'm around where it all happened."

"Hi, Betts," Opie said.

I took the folding lawn chair that Teddy had lifted out of the bed of the truck and smiled at them both.

"How are you doing, Teddy?"

"Well, I'm a little better," he said.

"Good. How are you, Opie?"

"I'm great, Betts, really glad you and Miz stopped by earlier. I'm so thrilled about what you told me. I'm a real part of our history. I told Teddy all about it, and he's excited, too," she said as we all made our way to an area in front of the corner of the stage.

I nodded. Opie was not a part of "our" history, all of ours, but just a small part of Broken Rope's history. But that was okay.

Evidently, they thought I'd be upset that Teddy was out and about. I wasn't happy, but I also wasn't upset. They also probably thought I'd comment on what seemed like their suddenly reignited relationship, but I didn't have anything to say. Teddy was over twenty-one. I'd realized a long time ago that he was going to do whatever he wanted to do no matter the repercussions. It wasn't ideal, but it was truly none of my business.

"He's great, isn't he?" Teddy nodded toward the stage as I unfolded his chair and Opie unfolded one for herself.

I looked toward the cowboy on the stage. A tree stump, or perhaps it was a plastic fake tree stump, had been placed stage left and gave the poet a "rugged" place to sit. His arms were heavy over the guitar on his lap. He wasn't singing or reciting a poem as much as doing a little of both. His old brown hat was blackened in the spots that had been often touched by his fingers. He was lit by a small spotlight off to his side, but I noticed that he must always use his left hand to remove the hat. A trail of worn finger marks on the left side of the brim seemed to dance in the light with every little movement.

He said/sang words about a cowboy lost in a sea of tumbleweeds. The cowboy searched and searched for a landmark — a butte that would point him toward home. Considering the tone, I thought that maybe the cowboy in the story never would find the butte, that he'd be destined to die among the tumbleweeds under a "diamond sky."

The song was melancholy but not unpleasant.

"Talented," I said.

"Most of them are," Teddy said. "It's why I was hanging out with them all. They're a fun group, sure, but I love what they do with words."

I nodded. "Anything coming back to you?"

"Yeah." Teddy looked at Opie, who smiled stiffly. He turned back to me. "I told Opie I might have been talking to a girl or two, Betts, so no need to hold back. She understands we were broken up."

Were?

"Okay," I said. "How about the details with the girls? Can you remember anything specific?"

"Yes, there's one thing. The women named Vivienne and Esther were definitely in the area, and there was some flirty stuff going on, but there was something else, too. I'm now sure there was an argument, though the people who were arguing keep changing in my memory. But now I have no doubt that the ruckus was over a letter, and Norman was trying to calm everyone down. So I don't think the evening had as much to do with flirting or who liked who after all." Teddy, his face still horribly swollen and bruised, looked at Opie, who gave him a more genuine smile this time.

"A letter? What kind of a letter?" I said.

"Either I don't remember, or I never knew in the first place. That part's not fuzzy; that part seems to be gone all the way." He tapped lightly on the side of his head. "So maybe I never knew."

"That's definitely more than we had before. Thanks, Teddy," I said. And I couldn't help myself; I added, "You shouldn't be out here, you know that don't you? You should be home resting."

"I had to get out of the house, Betts," he repeated.

He and Opie could have just gone to Bunny's if he needed to get out. The cowboy poets were an interesting crowd, but either they'd captured Teddy's limited attention span in a way few other things could or there was another reason.

"Teddy, you're not here to pick a fight, are you?" I said.

"Of course not. I couldn't fight in this shape anyway," he said.

No, he couldn't, but he wouldn't always be this messed up. He'd heal and be almost as good as new faster than it might take other, less stubborn people to heal. He'd always been physically resilient. In time, he'd be able to retaliate. Searching for the person or persons who'd hurt him might be why he'd come out this evening, even more than his newfound love of cowboy poetry.

I looked around a little, but the state of Teddy's bruised face didn't appear to faze anyone. It seemed that no one was paying attention to my brother or Opie. I'd try to keep a watch as the evening wore on.

He wasn't in the mood for a lecture from anyone, his big sister included. For now, he'd be safe in his lawn chair. Opie could be pretty ferocious if she was pushed. She wouldn't let anyone touch him.

"I'll be back by to check on you. Call me if you need anything," I said.

Teddy and Opie gave me quick nods.

As I walked away, I was torn between wishing I hadn't talked to Opie earlier and being glad that Teddy seemed to be happy that they might be back together. The torment.

I wove my way through the crowd. As I walked past people, some in small groups, some just standing by themselves with their attention toward the stage, I inspected faces and tried to listen in on conversations. And I learned nothing. No one looked or talked like they were a killer or someone who'd wanted to beat up my brother. Too bad it wasn't that easy.

Toward the edge of the activity, I saw Joe and the horse again. It was dark enough that they were very filled out and dimensional. The campsite lights were bright but they didn't illuminate the space that stretched over the old stagecoach tracks and to the station. The outside of the station was lit by one weak light above its front door, and a little inside light escaped out of the small windows, but none of it was enough to lessen Joe and the horse's three-dimensional forms. Had someone — Jake maybe — decided to leave the station open and lit during the evenings through the convention? There was also someone else walking toward the station. It took only a second for me to recognize Esther. I watched to see if she somehow acknowledged the ghosts, but she didn't. They watched her, though, intently.

I looked around but didn't immediately see Gram, Jake, or Cliff — or Jerome, for that matter. The station was set back enough that I would have liked to take someone with me to see what Esther was up to, but no matter how mixed up everyone's stories were, I truly didn't sense that she was dangerous. She went through the front doorway as Joe dismounted. He didn't follow her, but went to one of the small windows, pulled himself up, and peered inside.

"Curious," I said. I hurried across to the station.

"Joe?" I said quietly as I got closer.

He turned and looked at me. Did I see tears in his eyes?

"You okay?" I said.

"Betts. I'm fine. Just wondering what the young woman is up to."

I inspected him and decided that he probably hadn't been tearing up, but I couldn't be sure. I lifted myself up on my toes to see inside the window, just like Joe had done. Back when the station was a true station, it was mostly empty, except for the things that the station keepers needed to care for the horses and riders. In its replica state, the informational plaques told a condensed yet historic version of the Pony Express story and were fascinating even to me. Esther's interest in the story made sense.

"Why?" I asked Joe. "Why were you curious what she was doing?"

He looked away from me and then back inside the building, up on his toes again. The way his eyes landed on Esther and then seemed to pinch with some sort of longing sat funny and, frankly, was a little creepy.

"I remember her from the cemetery," he said. "And she was talking to your friend Jake in his big room. When she left him I wondered where she was going."

Had Joe been tailing Esther?

"I'll go in and talk to her. You want to come and listen?" I said.

"I do," he said, but his words were threaded with pain.

I blinked and inspected his face again.

"You okay, Joe?"

"Fine, fine. Let's go."

What was it about his face that I couldn't distinguish? My lack of sight bothered me. Why couldn't I understand or process exactly what happening? Or was nothing happening and I was imagining things? It felt like my perceptive abilities were set to slow motion when his face did what it did, and they never caught up to the answer.

"All right," I said. "Follow me."

The door's noisy hinges prevented me from entering covertly. At the squeaks, Esther turned and smiled.

"Hi, Betts."

"Hi," I said as Joe and I came through and joined her at the back corner of the space. It wasn't huge, only about twenty by thirty feet. "How's it going?"

"Great," she said, but much less enthusiastically than if she meant it.

"Needed a break from the crowd?" I fished.

"Something like that." She shrugged. "This seemed like a good place to get away for a second."

"And learn something about what one of your ancestors was a part of."

"Uh-huh," she said absently.

"Esther, is something wrong? Is there something I can help with?" I asked, wondering if the station itself had been the cause of her melancholy. Maybe Joe's too?

I sensed him standing behind me. He sniffed. There was something off-putting about the sound. It wasn't the sniff so much as its tone, if such a thing was possible. I pretended to itch my earlobe so I could turn to see him. He was very transparent as he stood directly in the glow of a small ceiling spotlight. He seemed curious but not bothered.

"No, I'm really fine," Esther said, again not convincingly. She forced a brief smile. "I hope it was okay to tell you the things I told you earlier."

"Yes, it was, Esther. You don't need to worry about that."

She nodded and smiled briefly again. "You know, I have enjoyed getting to know your friend Jake over these last few days. He's a sweetheart."

"Yes, he is." I smiled. "I think he's enjoying getting to know you, too."

"They'd be a perfect couple, Betts," Joe said. "Her, being a descendant of Astin Reagal, and him all about the history. They'd be perfect. Tell her."

I itched my earlobe again, this time as I furrowed my eyebrows. I wasn't going to say any such thing. Usually as time went on, I began to understand the ghosts better and better. My understanding of Joe was going the other direction. He was just becoming more of a mystery. I wanted to know why he thought they'd be so perfect together and why he cared, why he'd even paid attention to Jake and Esther, but I'd have to save that question for later.

Joe saw my disagreement and frowned.

"I'm glad, but you know our friendship won't have much opportunity to blossom," Esther said.

"Kansas City isn't far. At least it's in the same state." I shrugged.

"Probably too far to really have much of a relationship," she said.

Was she sad about the lack of a real future

268

with Jake, or was there something else going on?

"Forgive me, Esther, but I sense that there's something else wrong. Can I help?"

I was sure she wasn't aware of the fact that she patted one of the front pockets of her jeans. It was a quick maneuver. I thought it might be the pocket with the badge.

"I'm fine, Betts. I don't know. I guess that thinking about my ancestor has brought a lot of family stuff to the front of my mind. The thoughts require some attention." She smiled at me.

"I understand." I didn't; it just seemed like the right thing to say.

"Betts, ask her if she's found out more about Astin," Joe said. "Maybe your friend Jake has found some information that you haven't heard yet. Ask, please."

I couldn't think of a reason why not. I said, "Have you and Jake found more about Astin?"

"No, nothing new about Astin, but about some other family members, maybe."

"Oh?" I said.

Unfortunately, my question didn't get explored further. From inside the station, we could hear the crowd outside, but it was a muffled version. It still wasn't a rowdy group, as the volume of laughter and conversation continually rose and fell. But there was suddenly one distinct sound that stood out from the crowd noise and made us all jump and gasp. A gunshot cracked and boomed.

"Was that . . . ?" Esther asked.

"I think so," I said. "Listen, Esther, stay here a minute."

I hoped she'd do as I asked but I didn't stick around long enough to find out. I wasn't about to follow my own advice. I hurried around the ghost and then threw myself out the door.

And someone lots stronger than me stopped me in my tracks.

CHAPTER 21

"Hang on, Isabelle," Jerome said as his arm barricaded me from moving forward.

The air released from my lungs with an *oomph* sound. If it hadn't been so dark, I didn't think he would have been solid enough to stop me. But considering what I thought had happened by the river, maybe he would have.

"Jerome," I said with the breath I had left. "What's going on? Was someone shot?"

It was difficult to understand what we were seeing over at the campsite. Tents and trailers and the stage blocked most of the activity; so did small groups of people. But almost everyone was looking only one direction — toward the center of the site.

"I don't know. Let me find out. I just got here," Jerome said as he released my arm. When he was certain I wasn't going to run away, he said, "I was out searching for Astin. It was as if I heard a gunshot from far away and then I was suddenly here. I had no idea what happened, but when you came out the door I figured I was supposed to stop you from rushing over there."

"Maybe you really are here to protect me." I didn't point out that showing up after the gunshot and not before might have meant he needed to take his job a little more seriously.

"Maybe. Just stay put a second. Let me find out. I'll be right back," he said before he disappeared.

I looked inside the station. Even with the commotion, Joe hadn't left Esther's side. She was leaning against an informational podium and biting worriedly at a fingernail.

I took a deep breath to hide my own concern and opened the door.

"Come on out if you want to," I said. "I don't know what happened yet, but I think we're okay if we stay by the station until we get some details." If a gun or something else was aimed my direction, Jerome would appear again and throw me to the ground. Hopefully. And I'd pull Esther with me. I looked back to the campsite and told myself to stay aware.

Esther joined me outside, and Joe followed behind. He came through the door and then strode to the horse, who'd been standing by the side of the building. I hadn't looked closely at the horse yet tonight, but I did now. Its brown eyes locked on mine. We stared at each other a moment, but I still had no idea what it was trying to tell me.

"Was a gun fired?" Esther said.

"Sounded like it, but you have to understand, that noise happens lots around Broken Rope." Though I'd heard fake shots, blanks, so many times over the years, I thought I recognized their pops over the louder, real gunshots. What we'd heard sounded more like a real gun.

"Oh, that makes sense," Esther said, though she didn't seem much less concerned. "But after what happened to Norman, at the show. Well, *boom*s or *pop*s or whatever might scare me forever now."

"That's to be expected."

"It was horrible," she continued. "Really, really terrible."

"I'm sure."

Esther closed her eyes for a second and then shivered off a chill.

"You truly didn't know Norman before the convention?"

"No," she said. "I just met him here."

"Esther, I was talking to my brother tonight. He's over there." I pointed with my head and tried not to think about the fact

273

that he, Cliff, and Gram (and Opie, I supposed) might have all been in the middle of
a group where a gun had just been fired.
"He mentioned something about you and
Vivienne arguing over a letter. Do you
remember that?"

In fact, he couldn't remember who had
been arguing about the letter, but if I had
the wrong people, Esther might see a chance
to correct me and then give me even more
information.

"Oh. Your brother remembered that?" she
said.

"Yes."

"Well, I'm not sure that's exactly what was
happening," she said.

"So, what really was happening, then?"

"Wait!" Joe said.

I looked at him and shook my head. Of
course, Esther couldn't hear his plea, but if
she saw me shake my head, she'd wonder
why.

"It started that very first evening," she
began.

"No, Betts! Ask her to wait a minute."

I wanted to tell Joe to go away, but I just
glared at him.

Esther spoke again, but I couldn't understand her words because Joe was almost
yelling, demanding that I ask Esther to stop.

I thought as quickly as I could.

"Hang on, Esther. I'm sorry, but my phone is buzzing." I reached into my pocket and pulled out my completely silent and inactive phone and looked at the screen. "Oh, I've been waiting for a call from this student. I know this is rude. Could you give me a second?"

"Sure," she said hesitantly.

I walked toward the side of the building where the horse patiently stood. I turned the corner enough so that Esther wouldn't hear me, but not so far that she'd think I'd abandoned her. Joe joined me.

I held the phone to my ear.

"Joe, what's the problem?" I said quietly.

"I don't want her to tell you about the letter. Not yet."

"That makes no sense at all. Why?"

"Because it's going to make the wrong person look guilty."

"So? Why does it matter to you?"

"It matters."

"I couldn't care less what you want or don't want me to do."

"No, Betts, please just wait. Once the last letter is finished, things will be different."

"Different how?"

"I'm not exactly sure."

"Then how do you know?"

"I do."

"What's the connection?" I glanced back at Esther, smiled, and waved. "Unless you're Astin Reagal and you are her ancestor. You *are* Astin Reagal, aren't you? You're some weird incarnation. You don't look like you looked when you were alive. These ghost rules keep changing. That could be it, couldn't it?" I was talking to both Joe and myself. I was rambling.

"No, Betts, I'm not Astin Reagal, I promise. My real name is Joe, but there is more to who I really am. It will be solved when we finish the last letter. That's the only way to understand anything. For any of us to understand anything at all."

"Is that the only way to understand what happened to my brother? Is that the only way to understand who killed Norman Bytheway?"

Joe nodded, but I could tell he wasn't completely sure.

"How in the world are we supposed to finish the last letter?"

"I think that we need to find Astin's remains, that's all."

"That's all?"

"I know. It sounds next to impossible, but I think we're getting closer. I think your friend Jerome is getting closer."

"And yet, you don't like him? Why?"

"I don't know him, and I'm uncomfortable around those I don't know."

What a strange comment for a ghost to make.

"Joe — that makes no sense. I'm having a hard time coming up with a logical response to anything you're saying."

Joe shrugged.

I wanted to question Esther. At that point, I wasn't even quite sure how to get out of it. *Thanks for your willingness to share, but I'm not interested anymore* wasn't going to work. And I really, really wanted to know what she had to say. It didn't seem right not to find out what she knew. I looked hard at Joe, but I didn't sense anything. And then the horse nudged my shoulder with his nose. It was when I looked at its brown eyes that I somehow understood the need to wait until the last letter was finished. It was something I'd never comprehend or be able to explain, but those big brown glimmering eyes did me in, and I suddenly got it, whatever "it" was. Or had I been covertly hypnotized?

"Okay," I mumbled.

I was grateful to see Cliff at the edge of the campsite. He waved before he jogged across the path. I put the silent phone back into my pocket and went to join Esther.

"We'll talk later," I said conspiratorially to her.

"Sounds good," she said with a note of relief.

"Hi," Cliff said as he joined us. "Cliff Sebastian." He extended his hand to Esther. If she'd talked to any of the police officers before, it must not have been him.

"Esther Reagal."

"You two hear the commotion?" Cliff asked.

"Yes, is everyone okay?" I asked.

"Fine. Thankfully, no one was hurt. A real gun with a real bullet was fired, but it didn't hit anyone."

"Whose gun?"

Cliff shrugged. If he knew, he'd tell me later, when we didn't have an audience.

"It's all taken care of," he said. "You're welcome to come on over there if you'd like."

Cliff might have thought that Esther and I had run away from the noise. Neither of us offered up that we'd been at the station the whole time.

"Thank you, and excuse me. I think I will go over and see what's going on," Esther said before she scurried off as though she decided she actually didn't want to tell me

278

about the letter and was glad for the chance to get away.

"I'll find you later," Joe said before he turned to follow Esther. The horse glanced at me with what I interpreted as gratitude and then followed behind its rider.

"Cliff, what happened?" I asked as they all disappeared into the crowd.

"One of the convention attendees had a firearm in the glove box of their truck. They claim that they remembered it when they saw one of the police officers tonight. We'd asked everyone to turn in their firearms, of course. The gentleman gathered the gun and was bringing it to the officer. He dropped it accidentally and it fired."

"That's terrible. Disgracefully reckless. Someone else could have easily been hurt or killed."

"We know. But we're grateful that didn't happen."

The chances of another tragedy had been high, too high. I shivered and then shook off some goose bumps.

"Everyone's okay, Betts. Let's go back over," Cliff said.

I nodded, and together we followed along the path Esther, Joe, and the horse had just taken.

All activities had resumed after the interruption, but the first thing I noticed was that Teddy and Opie were still on their lawn chairs and looking toward the stage. If the gunshot had disturbed them, they'd recovered quickly.

"Those two mend whatever their disagreements were?" Cliff said as he looked their direction too.

"I don't know," I said.

"He can make these sorts of decisions without his big sister's help." Cliff smiled.

"Well, his judgment is still up for debate, but you're probably right."

"She's not so bad. She just doesn't like you."

"That's your fault, if you remember correctly. If you'd only stayed with her she might not dislike me with so much vehemence."

Cliff laughed. "Let's go see how he's doing."

As we wove our way toward Teddy and Opie, the lighting changed. Someone switched on a stronger spotlight and aimed it at the stage. I looked toward the middle of the crowd and saw Orly on a platform, crouched down on one knee and directing the big light. With his hat pushed back, he again reminded me of Jerome, and I scanned the crowd for the now-missing cowboy, but couldn't find him.

"Let's just sit next to them and watch the show," Cliff said. "This must be a big one. I told Orly to do something spectacular to take everyone's minds off the wayward gunshot."

Teddy and Opie smiled briefly in our direction as we walked toward them. As we sat on the ground next to them, I noticed that we had a perfect view of the Express station across the way, and I wondered how I hadn't noticed that the light on the corner of the building had also been illuminated. I remembered the front light, but not that one. I mentally shrugged it off as the show on the stage began. I hadn't seen this skit, but I'd heard about it. It was politically incorrect, in that it was a battle between cowboys and Indians. Jake had been hesitant to allow the skit to play, but he'd told me that Orly had convinced him that all would be fine. I hoped so.

But I didn't get to see enough of the show to judge the crowd's reaction.

A *snap* sounded from toward the station, and my attention swung quickly away from the skit.

The corner light *hadn't* been on, I hadn't misremembered. There was now illumination, though, but not from a modern light.

Lit torches hung high on each corner of the building. I glanced over at Cliff and up at Teddy sitting in the lawn chair to confirm that they couldn't see the torches. They would have both noticed the fire if it was something real happening in present time. They were both still focused on the show.

"Cliff, I'll be right back. Gotta find the lady's room," I said quietly.

"Want me to come with you?" Cliff asked.

"No, I'm good," I said. "I'll be right back."

"Okay. I'll come searching if you're not back in a few minutes," he said.

I kissed him quickly and stood. He smiled and winked at me before I turned and pretended to make a path toward the football stadium and the doors that had been left unlocked for access to the bathrooms.

Once I knew I'd wound around enough to be out of his sight, I turned and hurried to the edge of the campsite. I couldn't go directly to the station because Cliff would see me if he happened to look over. He'd wonder what I was up to.

But I thought I'd be okay watching whatever happened from this distance. Suddenly, Joe rode his horse at lightning speed out of the campsite crowd and toward the station. I was still okay staying put, but when another ghost rider appeared, from the path on the side of the station, it was all I could do not to run across and join them.

I'd only quickly inspected the picture Jake had found, but I knew the figure whose features were dancing in the torchlight from a hundred and fifty or so years ago was someone Esther would love to talk to. If only she could talk to ghosts.

It seemed that Astin Reagal was in the house.

CHAPTER 22

"Uh-oh," Gram said as she appeared next to me. "What do you suppose this is all about?"

"Not sure exactly, but that looks like Astin Reagal."

The man on horseback was smaller than I thought he'd be; skinnier, with narrow shoulders. But Jake and Esther both had told me the riders were on the smaller side, so the horses could travel faster with the lighter load. Astin sat as high on his horse as his short stature would allow as the horse stepped in place, waiting for a command from its rider. But Astin looked around as though he wasn't sure where he was.

"We should probably go talk to him. This might be his first time back as a ghost. His memory is probably all screwy. They're so terribly confused on their first trip back to Broken Rope," Gram said.

I glanced back at Cliff. Along with everyone else in the crowd, his attention was on the skit being performed on the stage. He smiled the direction of the skit, and I could see the shadow formed by his dimple.

"Let's go around to the left a little so we won't be noticed right away," I said.

Gram nodded and then led the way.

Astin's smell was distinctly horsey. It wasn't a pleasant scent, but it wasn't plug-your-nose awful either. Its pungency sharpened the closer we got.

"Astin?" Gram said as we looked up at the young man on the horse.

"I'm Astin Reagel," he said, though he sounded uncertain. "Who are you?" The horse turned in an impatient circle.

"Hi, Astin, I'm Missouri Anna Winston, and this is my granddaughter Isabelle. You're at the Broken Rope Pony Express station, but things are different than what you remember."

"Different how?"

"You're not in your time. You died a long time ago. You're just back visiting."

This was the first time I'd met a ghost who was on their first trip back. I hadn't thought about how such a moment should be handled, but I marveled at Gram's calm words. Surely it was more difficult than that to keep them from freaking out.

Astin's face scrunched up as he thought for a long moment. The horse mellowed, and though it wasn't completely still, it wasn't jittery nervous.

"You say your name's Missouri?" he asked.

"Yes."

"And what are all those folks doing over there?" He nodded toward the campsite.

"It's a long story, but none of them can see you. You will only be able to talk to me and Betts, and perhaps any other ghosts that might be around."

Astin blinked rapidly. I looked at Gram — was he going to faint or something? But she stood patiently with her hands on her hips. She didn't seem to be concerned, so I didn't think I needed to be either.

"Well, I'll be," Astin said. "This is as strange as a purple lightning bug."

"And it'll probably get even stranger," Gram said with a smile, "but I'm glad you understand what I'm saying."

"I do. I really do." He scratched his head. "I sure wish I could remember something other than my name. Anything would be good."

"That's normal," Gram said. "You'll remember a few things the longer you're here. You won't stay forever, though. If you're like the others, you'll come and go."

"That right?" Astin sniffed.

"Yes, that's right," Gram said.

"What do I do now?"

"Anything you want. You can go pretty much anywhere around Broken Rope. Lots of you go back to the places you lived. Or died. Or were killed. After you remember things, of course."

"There's lots of us?"

"Yes." Gram and I both looked at Joe. Astin didn't seem to care much about the other ghosts in the vicinity, but Joe was certainly taken by Astin. He and his horse were stone still as they stared at our new visitor.

"I'll be," Astin said again. "Maybe I'll go out by where my house was."

"That's a good idea." Gram looked at me and shrugged. "But you might want to know that there's a mystery around your death. Any chance you want to try to remember some of those details and clear that up for us?"

"I don't understand."

"You disappeared. Out on the trail. You up and disappeared," Gram said.

"I disappeared? Did I have any kin?"

"Yes, you were married and had a baby, a son."

"That's terrible that I left them."

"Not the best way to leave this world, but it was a long time ago. The pain that your demise caused is long dead, too, Astin. It's been well over a hundred years."

Astin whistled. "This shouldn't be happening, should it?"

"No, it shouldn't, but it does, and we deal with it."

"Why can you two see me?"

"We have no idea."

"Wait, a name just came to me. Was my son's name Charlie?"

Gram looked at me.

"Yes," I said. I leaned over and spoke quietly in Gram's ear. "Can I tell him what his son did when he grew up?"

"Sure."

"Astin, your son grew up and ran the general store. He was successful."

"That's good news."

"You just never know," Gram said. "You can't spend a lot of time worrying about how things were. They won't change and there's always some good. However, it's interesting to see if any of the mysteries can be solved. Like where your remains are located," Gram said.

Astin looked down at us for a long time before he said, "I only remember this: I took a shortcut. I remember I wanted to hurry home. I took a shortcut. No, it turned out not to be a shortcut. I just thought it was one."

"Do you remember where?" Gram asked.

"Sort of." Astin looked toward the crowd watching the skit.

"Tell us," Gram said.

He shook his head slowly. "I was almost home. I was almost home. That's all I know right now."

"I see." Gram didn't hide the disappointment in her tone.

"Astin!" Joe suddenly said.

"Yes, sir. Who are you? I thought only those two ladies could see me," Astin said.

"Joe's a ghost, too, another rider. Remember him?" I said.

Astin squinted and stared. "No, not at all."

"Are you sure?" I said. "I think there's some sort of connection between the two of you."

"I don't remember any connection at all."

"Astin, Astin," Joe said.

"That is my name," Astin said as he inspected Joe again.

"You don't remember me?"

"No, sir."

"I didn't think you would, but that's not important anyway," Joe said with disappointment lining his voice.

"What's important is finding where you died. Were you killed, Astin? Did someone kill you?" Gram said.

"I don't know. I'll have to think on it."

"Yes, think, Astin, think," Joe said.

I looked back toward the campsite. The skit was still being performed. Even from where I stood, the stick horses didn't seem hokey or contrived. Teddy and Opie were still sitting in the folding chairs, but Cliff was no longer in the spot by them. He must have gone to look for me, but just hadn't made it this direction again.

"Gram, have you seen Jerome?" I said.

"Earlier, yes. Why?"

"He might be able to help Astin and Joe. He's been looking for Astin's remains. He might have a better idea. I think I'll go look for him. You okay here?"

"I'm fine."

I hurried back to the campsite.

As interesting as it would have been to watch and listen to Joe and Astin, I did think that Jerome might be able to help them. And I didn't think Cliff needed to find me by the station again.

Unfortunately, I couldn't immediately find either the ghost or Cliff, but I finally found Jake. He and Esther were sitting together

290

on a long bench that was made out of a fallen tree trunk. They weren't watching the skit. The bench was back from the main crowd and gave them enough quiet to talk about whatever they were talking about. I didn't want to interrupt and I did want to interrupt. It was only a short time earlier that Esther had mentioned how unfeasible a long-distance relationship between the two of them would be. As close as they sat and as attentive as they were to each other, it didn't look like she was sharing the same thoughts with him.

"Hi," I said as I chose to approach.

"Betts, how's your evening? Here, sit." Jake patted the trunk on his open side.

"No, thanks, I'm looking for Cliff. Have you seen him?"

"The policeman who found us by the station? You lost him already?" Esther smiled.

"I did."

"Haven't seen him, Betts." Jake squinted and then turned to Esther. "Could you excuse me a minute? I'm going to help Betts track down Cliff."

"No . . ." I protested.

Jake stood. "It's fine. I'll be right back, Esther."

Jake led the way away from the pretty redhead sitting on the tree trunk. We snaked around two small groups of poets. I hadn't noticed that the skit had ended until I realized no one was looking toward the stage any longer. One of the groups we'd approached was listening to a woman read a poem; the other was laughing about a shared joke.

"Jake, I didn't want to take you away." In fact, I thought his exit from the tree truck was awkward and impolite.

"Betts, what's up? You look frazzled. Can I help?"

"I look frazzled?" I said.

"Yes."

"Oh. I didn't know I looked frazzled." I took a deep breath and swiped my hand over my hair to try to smooth the pieces that must have come out of my ponytail. "Well, we've got a number of ghosts, and I can't seem to find the one who might be able to give me some answers or help the others."

Jake blinked. "So you're not looking for Cliff?"

"No, I am."

"Why?"

"Because I think he's looking for me."

"Oh, okay. There are new ghosts?"

"One. Astin Reagal."

"Really? Does he know where he died,

what happened to him?"

"Not quite yet."

"That would be valuable information."

"I know. It might take a little time. Their memories and all."

A low-level commotion seemed to build around us. For a moment I didn't know what was happening. It took Jake and I both a second to realize that the crowd was all being drawn toward the stage.

"The skit's over, right?" I said.

"Yeah."

"Something else must be going on," I said before I fell in step with everyone else.

The skit was, in fact, over, but there was another show being played out in front of the stage. The actors were Teddy, Opie, and Vivienne.

Vivienne was yelling at my brother. Teddy was standing and holding Opie behind him, though I could tell Opie wanted to be part of whatever battle was ensuing. Even injured, Teddy would never let a girl fight his battles, though he might have no choice with me. I continued to move toward them.

"You're such a jerk. You totally deserved what you got," Vivienne said.

"Back off," Teddy said. "Just back off."

"I will not. I have every right to be **angry** at you. You led me on."

"No, I didn't. I remember that part. I didn't lead anyone on. I was just having a good time with everyone. I never led anyone on."

I cringed. There was a pretty good chance that he had led someone on. He didn't even realize he did what he did; his flirtatious nature was simply just him. But still.

"You're not the brightest bulb in the pack, are you?" Vivienne said.

"Hey!" Opie said, but Teddy continued to hold her securely behind him.

"Maybe not," Teddy said, "but I'm smart enough to figure out what's going on here, and it needs to stop. You're partially responsible for this." Teddy pointed to his face.

What did he remember? I wanted to jump in to defend his honor, but I didn't want to interrupt if we were about to learn more about the beating.

"Hey, folks, what's the problem?" Cliff said as he appeared from the crowd. I wanted to cheer at his arrival, but I didn't.

"This guy's a jerk," Vivienne said as she pointed at Teddy.

"And that's reason enough to cause such a scene?" Cliff asked. "Let's calm down and we can chat amongst ourselves about the problem."

Vivienne grimaced at Cliff. He wasn't

wearing his uniform, but he'd been around enough that she should have known he was a police officer. He caught the grimace and sent her back an authoritative glare. It worked. She either finally recognized him or decided he was probably right. She nodded and then stepped around Cliff and seemed to be leaving the campsite. Cliff nodded at Teddy and Opie, and then he spotted me and sent me a look that said "Take care of these two," and then turned to follow Vivienne.

I followed up on that unspoken request immediately and hurried to Teddy.

"I leave you two alone for just a few minutes and look what happens," I half-joked.

"She came out of nowhere," Teddy said.

"What did she say — I mean, at first? How did all of that start?" I asked.

"She called him some horrible names," Opie interjected.

"S'okay, Ophelia. I can take it." Teddy smiled at her. She calmed and looked away where she could pretend to focus on something else. "Almost the second she stopped to say something to us, I remembered more about her involvement in this." Teddy pointed at his face. "I think she was the one who lured me out into the woods."

"For the firewood? She's the one who hit you?" I said.

"No, I don't think so. I mean, I think she got me out into the woods, but not for firewood. I do think there was a guy involved, and I'm not just saying that because I'd be embarrassed that a girl might have done this to me. I would be, but I know we need to get the story straight."

"Remember what you said about getting the firewood? Remember that Norman wanted you to get firewood with him?"

"I do." Teddy sighed. "I'm beginning to think that he didn't want me to go out into the woods with him, though. I think maybe he just wanted me to help him get some firewood. I think there was a separate incident with Vivienne." He scrunched up his forehead and reached to his blackened eye. "I'm sorry, but my memory still isn't a hundred percent. But I'm almost certain she's the one who got me into the woods. Her or the redhead, the one named Esther."

It was my turn to sigh. Between the ghosts and Teddy, the reliability of memory recall was currently at nil to negative-nil.

"Teddy, you need to relax and quit trying so hard," I said. "When you were talking to Vivienne just now, did you accuse her of luring you into the woods?"

Teddy nodded his head slowly. "I think I did."

I looked at Opie, who was still looking at something else.

Finally, I turned my attention to Cliff and Vivienne. They were speaking calmly, with no flailing arms or adamant stomps. I'd have to grab Cliff and tell him that Teddy still wasn't putting all the pieces together correctly and he might have said something to Vivienne to set her off, but it wouldn't hurt for him to see what he could get from her, so I didn't rush over.

I'd practically forgotten about Gram and all the ghosts, but I remembered them again as I saw Gram trudge through the grassy patch and make her way toward me. I was on the other side of the stage, so I couldn't see the station, but there didn't seem to be much light coming from that direction.

"Teddy . . ." Gram began.

"I'm okay, Gram."

"Opie, he shouldn't be out yet. Get him home, make him rest," she said.

"I think that's a good idea," Opie said as she settled her eyes on Gram's.

"They're gone," Gram said when Teddy and Opie were out of earshot.

"All of them?" I said.

"Every last one of them, unless you found

Jerome," she said.

"No."

"Astin was on the verge of remembering what happened to him and then suddenly, *poof,* they were all gone. The torches were gone and the electric lights came back."

"Just like that?" I said.

"Just like that."

"Does it usually happen that way?"

"No, but there was such a strange high energy to these current visits, Betts. I wonder if they didn't all just use up their juice so quickly that they had to go."

"*Gone*-gone?"

Gram shrugged. "I've never had a ghost leave so abruptly unless they were going to be gone for a while. Of course, I can't remember such a short visit as Astin's either, but maybe I've forgotten."

Forgetfulness: the theme of the evening.

"The letter adventure will have to be completed at another time?"

"Looks that way."

"We'll never know what happened to Astin, or how Joe knew him? And Jerome is gone, too?"

Gram shrugged again. "I think so. Maybe they'll be back someday."

She patted my arm and then set out to do something other than deal with her grandchildren or the ghosts. She was probably glad to rid herself of us. At least temporarily.

I might have been content to mull over what Gram had said as I waited for Cliff to finish with Vivienne, but Jake interrupted my frustrated thoughts.

"Betts, did I just hear Teddy say something about Esther?" he asked.

I wasn't fond of these sorts of conversations, but I supposed I owed it to Jake to tell him what I'd heard about Esther. It felt gossipy and unfair, but I didn't see that I had much of a choice.

"Come on, Jake, let's head back to that bench," I said.

CHAPTER 23

"Yes, she claimed to have been interested in Teddy, and she said that he was just as guilty," Cliff said.

"I can see them flirting, but could that have been what led to Teddy getting beaten or them yelling at each other tonight?"

"I think that tonight Vivienne was irritated when she saw your brother with Opie, and she probably said something snippy to him. He probably said something equally snippy. Perhaps Teddy led her on a little. Just perhaps, though. I can't tell you if there was more than that going on — but I'll work on it. None of the people attending the convention are safe from being under suspicion, for either the murder or the beating. I still don't know if the two incidents are tied together, but we'll get it figured out."

Cliff sat up and reached for the pitcher of iced tea that was behind us. It was late, but we were sitting on the steps of my small back porch, decompressing from the evening of cowboys, poets, actors, and ghosts. My conversation with Jake had been brief. I told him the details of what I'd heard and he listened. Then he excused himself, saying he was tired and wanted to go home. I offered to drive him but he declined.

I had taken a moment to be sad that Jerome might really be gone, but I knew he'd be back again someday, and I thought that someday might be soon. I figured I could always step in front of a bus and see if he appeared to save the day, but considering that tonight he showed up *after* the gun was fired — well, I might not want to test my luck.

The mysteries of Astin Reagal and Joe and his letters gnawed at me, but if I'd learned anything from Gram, it was that I should never, ever, ever count on the ghosts. Maybe their disappearance was just a lesson I needed to learn the hard way.

Still, I didn't like having more questions than answers.

"Refill?" Cliff asked as the pitcher hovered above my glass.

I nodded.

"So, no more ideas at all about who killed Norman Bytheway?" I asked.

"No. Jim called me earlier with a little more information about our victim, though. He was living in Kansas City. He was on his own. No wife, no ex-wife, no kids, no pets. Jim found his parents — or the police up there found them. They saw a news report and finally called. They were devastated, as expected, but apparently they hadn't seen him in over a year. They didn't go into detail as to the reasons why."

"Where are they living?"

"In Kansas City."

"I can't imagine living in the same town as my parents and not seeing them for that long. There must have been a problem."

Cliff nodded, and I noticed the light from the quarter moon move over his face. "There might have been. Jim got a hold of a detective in Kansas City who will work on getting the full story. Hopefully, we'll know more soon."

"Does Jim think that knowing the reasons for Norman and his parents not talking might lead to his killer?" I said.

"Anything's possible at this point. We don't have much else to work with right now."

"Norman had no past connections to anyone at the convention?" I said.

"Not that we can find, but sometimes

people don't share the truth that easily. Unfortunately, these things don't always move as quickly as you'd like them to move."

"Don't Teddy's beating and Norman's murder have to be tied together somehow?"

"No, not really. There are a lot of people in town, Betts. Lots can happen and none of it be related to anything else. We're much more prepared for a crowd in the summer, and Jim thinks we didn't staff up well enough for this group. None of us thought it would be this big. When you get a crowd like this you just never know. Jim admits we should have had a twenty-four-hour presence at the campsite from the beginning. We didn't. If an officer had been around, perhaps whatever happened to Teddy wouldn't have happened."

I grimaced. Hindsight and all.

"Teddy will be fine, though. Unlike Norman," I said.

"True."

Cliff swirled his glass, causing the ice to clink as it cooled his tea.

"Betts, I have to ask you a question," he said after a pause I deemed way too dramatic.

"That doesn't sound good," I said.

Cliff laughed, but not with humor.

"It's not bad."

"Ask away."

"There's something going on in your life that I don't understand. Something I would like to have some details about."

"What do you mean?" I swallowed hard.

Cliff looked at the glass in his hands before he turned his full attention in my direction. His face was in moon shadows, but I still knew his features were intense. I knew serious Cliff as well as I knew funny Cliff, playful Cliff, and even silly Cliff.

"Betts, there's a piece missing. From us. I'm either not picking up on something or you're purposefully keeping something from me. I wish I could pinpoint what it is, but I can't. I need you to tell me, Betts. If it's me, I'm willing to fix it. If it's you, I need to know if you're willing to fix it. It's important."

I sighed. "Cliff . . ."

"One second, Betts. Let me finish. Tonight, I saw you and Miz over by the Express station after you told me you were running to the ladies' room. You were standing side by side and looking at . . . well, it looked like you were both staring at something, but there was nothing there. When I saw you two, I was struck by how many moments since we've been back together that I feel

304

like there's something or someone in the room that I'm not seeing. That sounds crazy, I know, but it's what I'm getting. Can you help me understand what's going on? Maybe just tell me what was going on tonight."

I wanted to tell him about the ghosts. Frankly, I felt like I owed him that much. But more important than that, I was suddenly devastated that he thought we had a missing piece — and I knew I was the one responsible. I thought I'd been so smooth. I thought it had been okay to have a crush on a dead ghost, because how harmful could that possibly be?

I was so stupid. Just because Jerome was dead didn't mean it was okay to have a crush on him. Because any crush I had on anyone, dead or alive, diluted my feelings for Cliff, even if I hadn't meant for it to. If I wasn't willing to give him my one hundred percent, I didn't deserve his one hundred percent. Jake's voice sounded in my head as I thought those thoughts.

I was so, so stupid. (That might have been Gram's voice).

Now was the moment to spill the beans. It was late. It was a beautiful night. It was dark; I could use the darkness to hide and he could use the darkness to process the

305

wild and weird story I wanted to tell.

There was only one thing holding me back. It was Cliff. He was solid, logical, real. He'd never even liked to read books that had a tinge of something otherworldly or fanciful. It was one of the reasons I loved him so much.

I thought hard about the words I wanted to say.

"Cliff, there is something, but it's not something that can ever come between us. It's been a distraction for me, but I'm ready to work through it and do better. The missing piece is all on me. It's something that's hard to believe and at first had more to do with Gram than with me. But I'm involved now, too. It's nothing bad. It's just very weird."

"Weird how?"

"Weird, unreal. I have an idea. Before you ask any more questions, take a day, a few days, and think about whether or not you want to know." My mouth was so dry. I took another drink. "Cliff, I'll tell you if you really want to know, but you need to trust me on this part — you might not want to. Honestly."

Cliff looked up absently to the sky. I watched his profile as he considered my warning. For an instant I thought I saw the

306

boy he'd been in high school, and my heart mushed a little. Oh, geez, I was so stupid. I saw his signature half smile, the shadow of his dimple pulling, before he turned and looked at me.

"Really weird?" he asked.

"The weirdest," I said.

"I'll think about it."

If nothing else, maybe now he could be relieved that whatever he'd been picking up on wasn't a product of his imagination. I knew the feeling.

"I'm crazy about you, you know," I said.

"I know," Cliff said. "You'd better be. We've got lots ahead of us, Betts. Lots."

"I'm glad to hear that," I said.

And I truly was.

CHAPTER 24

The next morning, right before six, I was awakened by a text. Cliff, still feeling like he needed to stop by the jail and confirm there was nothing he was missing regarding the cases he and the other officers were working on, didn't stay the night. He hadn't left because I hadn't told him about my distraction; just the fact that I confirmed there was one was enough to ease the waters. If he truly wanted me to share the ghostly details, there might be other issues ahead, but I decided I could only worry about that when and if it happened.

The early text I received from him said: *Crime scene tech from St. Louis here. Do you want to come watch her work?*

I texted him back that I'd be there quickly. I remembered Cliff mentioning that Jim had planned on calling in someone from St. Louis, but I was surprised that I'd been invited to attend.

I hurried out the door without even one longing glance at my coffee machine. I'd stop by Bunny's later.

It didn't take long to return to the scene of the crime. My drive to downtown could be as short as three minutes or as long as about four and a half; today, it was on the shorter side.

I parked on a side street and walked quickly to the end of Main. I easily spotted Jim, Cliff, a couple other officers, the fire marshal, Evan, and a group of four people I didn't know. The group was made up of three men and one woman, all of whom wore matching blue zip-up jackets. The woman was undeniably in charge — of everyone and everything. I didn't think anyone noticed my arrival, and I decided it was best that I stay back and out of the way, so I skirted around the edge of the activity and then stopped close enough to hear what was going on but hopefully still be unobtrusive. Evan, who'd been back a bit from the group, stepped back farther and stood next to me. We smiled and mouthed quick and silent hellos to each other. The woman held on to the arms of one man and moved him to the place where I knew Norman had been standing when he was shot.

"Okay, Cliff, sweetie," she said. "This is

where I believe the victim went down, is that correct?"

I took a double-take at her deeply Southern and extra friendly tone. Even though she wore jeans and the drab blue zip-up jacket, she was very pretty. And also young. She might have been my age, but I guessed a couple years younger. Her black, chin-length hair was held back by a bright pink headband and her big blue eyes were both lovely and intelligent.

Cliff looked at some notes and pictures he held. "Yes. That's the spot, Amy."

"Good. Okay, lie down. No, about three feet back," she said to the man whose arms she held. "Good. Now, I'm going to put you into the position that the victim was found in." She pulled a picture out of her own pocket and showed it to the young man on the ground.

He maneuvered his body to look like the one in the picture, who I assumed was Norman. I hoped I wouldn't ever see the picture.

"That's right," Amy said as she crouched. "Now, just move your leg a teensy bit this way. Good."

Amy stood and then plopped one hand on her hip as she confirmed that the man in the picture and the man on the ground were both in identical poses.

"Now, Cliffy, when I looked at the body this morning, your ME and I did some trajectory calculations. Grant is the victim after he was shot. Billy," she grabbed another man, "is the victim before he was shot," Amy said.

Cliffy? I crossed my arms in front of myself and brought my eyebrows together.

"Okay," Cliff said. He saw me out of the corner of his eye as he looked up from the papers in his hand. He smiled briefly and then turned his attention back to Amy.

"Billy, I need you to stand right here. Yes, your feet will be away from Grant's a bit." Amy pulled out a tape measure and crouched again. She placed the bright yellow strip on the ground as Billy did exactly as she asked and Grant stayed in an uncomfortable, twisted position on the ground.

Once again, Amy righted herself.

"Now," she said a little more loudly as she looked at the small crowd watching her every move, "this is where the bullet went into the body." She placed her fingertip on Billy's chest. "Based upon the calculations that we made this morning, we can assume — almost completely safely — that the shooter was no more than fifty yards back and was no more than five feet five inches high."

I leaned over and said to Evan, "Really? She can know that much?"

"I think so," Evan said, a little awe lining his voice.

Amy pulled her hand away from Billy's chest. "That puts your fairly short shooter back over there, in the spot in the street, in between that cookie place and the saloon."

"If I remember correctly, that's the spot where the hanging platform sits for the cook-off, right?" Evan said to me.

"One and the same. It's where the town's real hanging platform did its work back in the day. We do try to keep it authentic," I said.

"You think the killer was someone from Broken Rope and their location was somehow symbolic?" Evan said.

"No, I don't. Well, I hope not, Evan."

"Knowing the shooter's size does narrow the suspect list," Evan said. "I mean, of course there are men that height, but I imagine that Jim and Cliff will start to focus on more women, which would be a much easier task if we didn't have so many visitors."

"True."

Jake was five feet six inches, but I hoped

that his height challenge didn't put him close to being on the suspect list.

"Amy, how sure are you of all this?" Jim asked. He looked tired, but I'd seen him in worse condition. Still, I hoped the solution to the murder was close at hand.

"Jim, I'm the best you can get. Isn't that right, Cliff?" She smiled and winked at him.

I didn't even like thinking I *might* be jealous, so I decided to call what I was feeling curiosity. How did they know each other? How long had they known each other?

"Amy's the absolute best," Cliff said sincerely.

My lips twisted involuntarily.

"It's all based on measurements, Jim, you know that," Amy said. "I just happen to be extra good at measuring." She winked again, right at Cliff.

Jim scratched his bald head and pushed up his glasses. He'd been a police officer long enough to both respect Amy's abilities and remember to question everything, remember that even with measurements and precise crime scene investigations, anything at all is possible until you knew the exact truth and specifics.

"It'll be difficult to question everyone that's close to five feet five inches tall, Amy. We have a bushel of visitors in town. Is there

313

anything more you can tell us?" Jim asked.

Amy tapped a finger on her pursed lips. She looked at Jim, at Cliff, and back at Jim.

"Well, this isn't based on a measurement, Jim. Not really. But given the distance and the method, I'm guessing the killer didn't know the victim very well, but wanted them dead enough that when they saw a gun, they picked it up and shot it because they were a good shot. Or they were shooting at someone else and missed, or they fired the gun accidentally. Find the gun, and I imagine you'll figure out the other partics quickly."

I guessed that "partics" meant particulars.

"Wait. You're saying you think the killer found a gun somewhere? Just found one and used it?" Jim said.

Amy shrugged. "I kind of do. If the crime was premeditated, it wasn't 'pre' by much. Too risky. It's kind of amazing the killer didn't get caught considering everyone that was around. No one would plan to kill someone with such a large group of onlookers. I'm taking into consideration the spot from where the shot was fired. I don't think the shooter was hiding, or even trying to hide. That's a pretty telling fact. I think it was an impulse, or maybe even an accident."

Jim blinked and didn't hide his doubt.

"We don't just leave guns lying around; real or fake. It's something we pay pretty close attention to," Jim said.

Amy shrugged again. I was beginning to dislike the smug maneuver.

"You said you have a lot of people in town. Maybe one of your visitors lost a weapon. You might want to check. Or, like I said, maybe it was just an accident and the shooter is scared witless — who wouldn't be? In fact, as I'm sure you know, there's a big chance that the killer isn't still around." She looked down toward the intersection where the hanging platform would sit in only a few months. "Look at all those woods back behind everything. They weren't in the woods when they shot, I'm sure of it, but I wouldn't be surprised if they just ran off into them. You should check everything."

Jim blinked and set his jaw firmly. "We do. We will."

I knew they'd checked everything already and would check everything again. Cliff already told me they suspected the killer might have run into the woods, but they hadn't been able to find any evidence that indicated that path of escape.

"Excellent," Amy said. "Now who's going to take me out for breakfast? Cliffy?" She smiled at him.

Evan cleared his throat uncomfortably. I looked up at him.

"Should I be worried?" I said with a smile and my own wink.

"I don't think so, but she sure makes me uncomfortable," Evan said, returning the smile.

I looked at Cliff. He happened to look my direction at the same time. The fact that the scene being investigated was the result of a murder made everything far too serious to joke or even smirk, but Cliff did send me a quick look that confirmed that I had nothing to worry about.

"I'd be happy to take you out for breakfast. In fact, I'd love to take your whole crew," Cliff said.

Amy looked around at the non-talkative group of men. "I suppose they can come, too. We going to that charming place down the street? Bunny's, is it?"

"Will that work? It's what's open this early."

"Yes, that will be fine. We'll meet you there. Come along, troops." Amy signaled, and the others followed her obediently to the van parked in front of Jake's office.

I hadn't noticed that Jake was observing, too, but he stood on the boardwalk across from me and Evan and waved when we made eye contact. I was glad to see him. Amy's idea had made me think of something that I wanted to do, and if he was available, he'd be the perfect partner.

As Amy and the others loaded into their van, Cliff walked toward me and Evan.

"It'd be great to have you both join us for breakfast," he said.

Evan and I shared another conspiratorial smile.

"You want some hometown support, don't you?" I said.

"Wouldn't hurt."

"As much fun as it sounds, I'd like to talk to Jake. You okay if I pass?" I said.

"Of course. Evan?"

"Sure. I'm hungry, and nothing else is calling me away," Evan said.

"That's great news. Thanks."

"I must admit," I said, "she was interesting to watch in action."

"She's very good at her job," Cliff said. "She's just very . . . assertive."

"This'll be fun," Evan said genuinely.

Evan had come to Broken Rope after losing his family to a terrible tragedy. Though a shadow of sorrow was still his constant companion, there were moments when it seemed that shadow might be waning

317

slightly. Because they'd worked together on solving a decades-old mystery surrounding a fire at a famous bakery, he and Cliff had also formed a solid friendship. Cliff, Jake, Evan, and I had had a few dinners at Bunny's together, and it had been good to see Evan begin to come out of his shell. I couldn't imagine the pain he'd experienced and probably would experience for the rest of his life, in one way or another.

"See you later?" Cliff said to me.

"For sure," I said, before I hurried over to Jake. "What are you doing up so early?" I asked him.

"Just awake," he said with a forced, casual tone.

I looked at him.

"Hang on. You haven't been home, have you? You spent the night with Esther, didn't you? If you were upset with her about what I told you, you got over it, didn't you?"

"Betts, I'm not good at this sort of thing. You know I don't like to talk about it, but it's not what you think. Yes, we were together, but not *together*-together. After our talk last night, Esther and I ended up talking, too. We've only just met, Betts. I didn't expect us to have so much to discuss, but it seems we do."

"Just talk?"

"Yes."

"Well, that's too bad."

"Betts!"

"Jake, you are amazing. The fact that you don't kiss and tell makes you even more wonderful. I hope you enjoyed your evening."

"I did."

I wanted to ask more about what Esther had said about her and Teddy and the significance of a letter, but I didn't want to risk ruining Jake's good mood. I'd ask later if I still wanted to.

"Good. Now, want to come with me to the campsite?" I said.

"Sure, but why?"

"I need to talk to Orly again."

"About?"

"His gun collection."

"Okay. You sure we shouldn't bring Cliff?"

"We could wait for him, and we probably should, because we're going to be asking about firearms, but Orly did me a favor by taking me to Teddy before the world knew about the beating. I'd like to keep my suspicions to myself until I know for sure that the police might need to take a closer look. I think there will be plenty of people around. We'll be fine. Cliff's taking the crew from St. Louis to breakfast; he'll be busy for a while."

"Let's go."

The two campfires had already been lit, and from the smell of things were warming cowboy coffee and cooking bacon and eggs and probably some biscuits. A couple trails of smoke reached up to the blue sky as I parked the Nova on the back road, close to Orly's tent and across from the Express station. My mouth watered with all the breakfast scents.

"You think the ghosts are all gone?" Jake said as he glanced at the station. On the way to the campsite, I had told him the details of our ghostly encounters and departures.

"I haven't seen or heard from any of them this morning, but it's early."

"They left without the answers they were looking for? That's a first."

"I know. It bothers me, but there's nothing I can do about it. I hope they'll all come back someday and we can learn more."

"If Joe knew Astin, and Jerome had an idea where Astin's remains were located, we were so close to answering some interesting questions. I must have been wrong about the letter or the reasons for the letter."

I laughed. "Jake, trust me, none of this

320

ghost business is predictable, and much of it is frustrating. I'm trying not to let it bother me too much. I'm sorry if involving you has made you emotionally invested, too. I probably shouldn't have done that to you."

"Are you kidding? I love my involvement. I just wish I was even more involved."

"Come on, maybe we can figure something else out, something from the world of the living," I said as I threw the Nova into park.

The morning was as perfect a spring morning as you could get in southern Missouri. The smells from the campfires, the breakfasts being cooked, and the coffee being boiled made me want to find a comfortable chair somewhere and listen to someone recite some cowboy poetry. Of all the activities, skits, and poetry that had surrounded me over the last little bit, I hadn't taken the time to enjoy the true creativity that the convention had to offer. But neither had Norman Bytheway, and at least I'd still have more chances.

Orly exited his tent just as we closed the Nova's doors. He waved us over. He wore the same type of clothes I'd already seen him in: jeans and an embroidered cowboy shirt. But the typical vest and hat were missing. He looked incomplete without them.

He carried a blue tin mug. I thought that coffee probably tasted a hundred times better out of those mugs than any others. I hadn't had my own cup yet this morning, though, so that might have just been caffeine withdrawal speaking.

"Betts and Jake, goodness, it's early. Come on over, we'll round up some breakfast for you."

Orly unfolded a few chairs that had been leaning against the front pole of his tent.

"You two here for something specific or do you have time to sit a bit and chat?" he said as he placed the chairs in a comfortable triangle.

Jake looked at me. I still hadn't told him why we were there.

"Both," I said.

"Good enough. Sit." Orly signaled someone down a neighboring aisle.

Gary appeared a second later. He tipped his hat at me and said. "Miss."

"Hi, Gary, how are you today?"

"Right as rain rolling through some mane," he said with what I thought was a hiccup, even though there was no indication he was drunk or had been drinking.

"Good to hear."

"Gary," Orly said, "would you grab our guests some breakfast from one of the fires?"

"Yes, sir," he said before he turned and walked away. The hitch I'd noticed the night before was still present.

"You met Gary?" Orly said.

"I did. Nice man," I said.

"He is. So, tell me, friends, what can I do for you?" Orly asked.

"I have a question, Orly, and it's a little uncomfortable to ask it, but I hope you'll forgive me if I offend you."

"Of course."

"You brought some guns to the convention, didn't you?" I said.

"I did, Betts, and I might know what you're getting at, but I showed them to the police after Norman was shot. They said he hadn't been killed with any of them, and they chastised me something fierce for bringing the shotgun out yesterday. I didn't think the police meant 'shotgun' when they confiscated all guns. I was under the impression that they meant handguns. I didn't fire yesterday, though."

"Do you know the kind of gun Norman was killed with?" I said.

"No."

"A .38 Special," I said. I watched him closely. His eyes pinched but only briefly.

"That's quite a weapon," he said.

Gary reappeared quickly and handed Jake

and me each a plate overflowing with bacon, eggs, and sausage, and our own blue tin mugs of coffee. I balanced the plate on my lap and took a sip of the hot and perfect coffee. When the gun had been dropped the night before, I hadn't allowed myself to think too long or hard about how horrible the outcome might have been. We could easily have had another tragedy on our hands. But later last night, long after I'd talked with Cliff on my back porch, an idea had sprung to my mind. Even though everybody was supposed to turn in their firearms to the police, apparently not everyone had. Orly had the shotgun, and the convention attendee's gun, even with his good intentions of showing it to the police, had been loaded. He'd dropped it. Guns had been forgotten, accidentally and maybe even on purpose. And I'd come to learn that Orly probably never wanted to be forthcoming with the police. It was partially the way of the cowboy, partially just plain old stubbornness.

"You ever have one of those? A .38 Special, I mean," I said after I swallowed.

Orly looked younger without the hat and the vest, but my question pained him so much that he suddenly looked older than he had in the short time that I'd known him.

"I was afraid of that," he said.

"You brought one with you?"

"I wasn't sure if I had or not. I thought I had one in the equipment box of my truck, Betts, but I wasn't sure." Orly shook his head. "I'm ashamed to admit that. I should know where every gun is, and whether it's loaded or not. When Norman was killed and I didn't see the gun in the truck, I thought there was a chance I hadn't brought it. There's no one at home I feel like I can ask to check the gun case. The police wouldn't tell me what weapon was used on poor Norman, but . . . Well, now I just hope it wasn't mine. Maybe I should have told them that that gun being here was a possibility, but I thought . . . well, I should have said something."

"I'm sorry," I said. Suddenly, I wasn't hungry, even with the smells wafting up from my plate. It appeared that Jake wasn't either.

"I didn't kill him. If it was my gun that was used, it was stolen," Orly said.

"I'm betting on the fact that you're telling me the truth, Orly. I don't think you killed him either, but I do think you should tell the police." I looked at Jake. He nodded. "Orly, just call Jim or Cliff right now and tell them that you just realized that a gun was missing from your truck. Let them know. They'll question you, but hopefully you can come up with a few specific people who might have had access to the equipment box."

His truck and storage box had been accessible to everyone at the convention, parked outside, but maybe there were others who he'd let borrow the vehicle.

"I can do that," he said with a small, barely noticeable cringe.

"Orly?" I said. "There's more, isn't there? You know more? Maybe exactly who took your gun?"

Orly had probably played a game or two of poker over the years, but he must not have done well. He had the worst poker face. The small cringe transformed into a worried frown.

"Isabelle," a voice said behind me.

I turned quickly and said, "Jerome, you're back!"

Of course, neither Jake nor Orly could see the ghost. There was so much light that I barely could.

"Excuse me?" Orly said. "Do you see someone you know?"

"I found him, Isabelle. Can you come with me? Now? I think we need to hurry," Jerome said.

I turned back to Orly and Jake. Orly was looking over my shoulder, and Jake held his cup of coffee halfway to his mouth, his eyes open wide.

"I'm sorry, Orly. Jake and I have to go. I know I'm acting strangely. Forgive me. But whatever you know, you need to call the police and tell them. Right away." I stood and placed the plate and cup on my chair. I wasn't even going to offer to wash up. Gram would be disappointed. Even though Jerome had come back or perhaps hadn't truly left, he might not be staying long. I truly didn't think Orly had killed Norman or beaten Teddy. I hoped not. I even hoped the murder weapon hadn't been his gun. I prayed that leaving Orly to call the police on his own wasn't a stupid move.

"Of course, Betts," Orly said as he stood, too.

Jake, Jerome, and I made a strange and awkward departure.

"You can count on me, miss." Gary had followed us to the car. "I'll make sure the scoundrel calls."

Scoundrel?

"Thank you, Gary," I said with one last look at Orly, who watched us as he stood with his hands in his front pockets.

"May we go now, Isabelle?" Jerome said.

"Sure."

I smiled quickly at Gary, hoping we weren't hurrying away from something else he wanted or needed to tell us, too. I hoped I wasn't making two mistakes at once by leaving that campsite when we did.

As I turned the car around and drove away from Orly's tent and Gary's friendly wave, I pulled out my cell phone and called Cliff. Surprisingly, the call went straight to his voice mail. I left a message about him needing to talk to Orly about the gun. I hoped he'd pick it up soon.

Jake said, "That was strange. I'm guessing Jerome is with us."

"He's in the backseat."

"Excellent. Good to not see you again, Jerome."

Jerome laughed, the anxiousness I'd heard in his tone now mellowed, most likely because we'd done what he said and were quickly on our way. "I like him, Betts."

"He likes you," I said.

"I like him, too, especially if he shows us Astin Reagal's remains."

Jerome laughed again. "He drives a hard bargain."

CHAPTER 25

"I've at least figured out the general vicinity of where the remains were located," Jerome said. "I don't understand why it became such an obsession for me, Isabelle, but it did. More important than you, than the memories I've had of Elsa, I've felt the undeniable need to find this man's bones. I've been looking since I left the campsite last night. I'm sorry you thought I'd left to go — well, left to wherever I go when I'm not in Broken Rope."

"You were MIA last night when another ghost showed up. Astin Reagal himself. I think he and the other ghosts did leave."

Jerome huffed an ironic laugh. "That figures. I can't stop looking for his remains and he showed up when I wasn't there."

"I doubt he could have helped much. He wasn't there long and his memory was still pretty weak."

"I couldn't have abandoned my search

even if I'd wanted to. I was compelled to be where I was."

I nodded and looked in the rearview mirror. Jerome's attention was focused outside the car, off to the left.

"Where should we look, Jerome?" I said.

"Out there." Jerome pointed toward the east, the left. "Out toward my old farm."

Before now, I'd never considered visiting the site of Jerome's old farm. I'd never even asked about it. I didn't know what might be left of it, but initial appearances told me that nothing was left.

"It's been unused for a while, right?" I asked.

"I think since I farmed it, but I can't be sure."

"No farm, Jake. Just land," I said.

"I thought as much," he said as he leaned forward and looked out toward the wide open space that was somewhat woodsy with trees, but mostly just covered in tall grasses.

"Should we go look?" I said.

"Yes, but first I need to tell you something. A story of sorts," Jerome said.

I conveyed the comment to Jake and told him I'd share the story as soon as Jerome finished.

Jerome began. "You said not long ago that the rules for 'your' ghosts keep changing. I think this is another one of those changes."

"Uh-oh."

"It's not too bad. Really. It's just something new and different, and frankly, not about you at all."

"Okay."

"Strange things always happen, right? I mean, life is full of surprises, and even mysteries."

"That's true. So is death, apparently."

"Apparently. Something happened to me, Isabelle, something when I was alive. I only remembered it right before I came to find you this morning. I think it's what put me in such a hurry. I suppose the incident shouldn't be too much of a surprise considering the state I'm currently in, but I have a distinct memory that I was haunted when I was alive."

"Really?" I sat up a little.

"I think so — and I think by the ghost of Astin Reagal." Jerome chuckled once. "I wasn't as welcoming as you've been to me, though. If I remember correctly, I was scared silly."

"Well, your experience didn't include an immediate, though mysterious, attraction." I smiled.

Even though he wasn't in on both sides of

the conversation, Jake sent me a withering look.

"No," Jerome said. "I suppose if my ghost had been a pretty redhead, I might have been more curious than scared. Anyway, he wasn't pretty at all. It was a brief encounter. I was out in my fields. Corn, I think. I had much better luck with cattle than I did any crops, but I surely tried.

"I was working away in the hot humidity and thought I saw something at the end of the row. I left the horses and the tiller because I thought maybe I'd seen a man, a hurt man. I ran to the end of the row, which bordered a patch of trees. There was a road a ways farther down and I know it used to be a path that was heavily traveled, but at the time I didn't make all the connections.

"The man that I saw was on his side on the ground, and I was certain I saw twisted legs and a bloody face."

"That's sounds terrible."

"It's why I ran. But when I got to the trees, the image disappeared. I thought I was being overtaken by the heat. Perhaps I just needed some water, maybe some food. But then I heard a voice. It said, 'Please find me. I'm right here.' Of course I looked around again for the man, the body, anything attached to the voice. I didn't find anything right off, but I was surely shaken."

"You think it was Astin Reagal?" I asked.

Jerome nodded. "I do now. At the time, I tried to forget it. But later on, I searched, out of curiosity more than any other reason. I didn't find anything in the area where I thought I saw the man, but farther out, more toward where the path had been and the road was, I did find something. This all happened close to the time I died, and there were so many other things that were more important that I didn't have an opportunity to tell anyone but Elsa what I'd found. And she wasn't interested in the least. She was with child and not feeling well. She couldn't have cared less about the remains of a long-dead man, even if they'd been in her own house and haunting her personally."

I looked up into the mirror again. I'd seen pain cross his face before, but his current memory of Elsa might have caused him to feel a whole new level of anguish. Even though he was so transparent, it hurt him deeply to experience those memories, and I could see it.

"I think I came back this time just so I could help find the remains again," Jerome said. "I understand that some other strange things have happened — a Pony Express ghost and a descendant of Astin Reagal in town, and now a visit by Astin too. Perhaps one thing is spurring on another, I don't know."

"That's possible."

"I wonder if all your ghosts were also haunted when they were alive. I'm not sure what that might mean, but it might be something you have to contend with at some point."

"Good question. Maybe I'll start asking."

"Stop here." Jerome seemed to need to gather himself for a moment. "Look for the trees that make a heart. Let's go find Astin," he finally said.

"Look for the trees that make a heart, Jake," I said. "Point us in the right direction, Jerome, and we'll take credit for the discovery. Okay, I'll let Jake take the credit."

We were out in the middle of nowhere; the road I'd stopped on was not used anymore, and was now a wide dirt path. Where there were woods, they were thick woods, and any open space had tall grasses sprouting from uneven ground. Jake and I both walked slowly over the tangled and bumpy earth.

"Almost there?" I asked after only a few ankle-twisting minutes.

"Just up ahead. There's no place for an automobile, but we're not far now."

Jake had the small shovel from my trunk over his shoulder, and I was carrying a couple partly full water bottles that had been rolling around on the backseat. I'd told Jake what Jerome had said about being haunted and he'd responded with his normal thoughtful interest.

It was still spring enough that the Missouri giant prehistoric bugs — my description — hadn't come out of their hiding places yet. The journey wasn't completely bug-free, but nothing I saw made me question evolution.

Without much warning, we were suddenly in a wide clearing that was covered more in short weeds than tall grasses.

"There, past that bunch of trees was my farm." Jerome pointed.

I shaded my eyes with my hand and peered through the trees. There was another clearing on the other side of them. The remains of an old small house still stood, its nubby corners the only things left.

"Jerome's farm was over there," I said to Jake.

"That was a ways out from town."

"Were those things part of your house?" I asked.

"I think so," Jerome said. "I don't know what happened to the place after I died. Miz might be able to answer that better than I can."

I tried to imagine Jerome there, standing in front of a house or a cabin, or perhaps plowing the earth or wrangling cattle. The mental pictures were clear. He'd never fit into my own time, and "seeing" him there, on his land, was easy and almost expected.

"That's kind of cool," Jake said. "We'll explore it sometime."

"I'd like that," I said.

"But for now, are those the heart trees he was talking about?" Jake pointed to the far right of the cabin remains.

"Yes," Jerome said.

"Affirmative," I said.

Jake led the way again and we stepped over rocks and earth until we finally stopped by the trees. The branches of two different trees had bent and come together so symmetrically that they did, indeed, resemble the shape of a Valentine heart.

"Right there." Jerome pointed at the ground at the bottom of the heart. "I think that's something."

"Here," I pointed for Jake.

Jake and I crouched. Mostly we just saw ground, but there was something else. Maybe. Something about three inches wide stuck out of the dirt. It was too uniformly shaped and sized to be something organic, but it was also too heavily caked in dirt to be recognizable.

I grabbed the item and rubbed it with my thumb. Only a few seconds later it became clear that we'd found what was probably a leather flap.

"What should we do?" I asked Jake.

He sat back on his heels and inspected the space.

"Probably nothing. We should probably contact the authorities. I imagine you think we've found the same thing I think we've found."

"A *mochila*? Probably Astin Reagal's?"

"Yep, we're on the same wavelength. And if his *mochila* is around here, maybe so are his bones."

"You're not going to look more closely?" Jerome asked.

I paraphrased. "Jerome thinks we should dig and explore."

"I do," Jerome said.

"We'll be careful," Jake said.

It hadn't taken much to convince him.

Jake moved slowly and carefully as he put the tip of the small shovel into the ground. He dug up only a little bit of dirt at a time, moving it aside with care and reverence. I would have moved much more quickly and with much less care, but his respect for history was even bigger than his curiosity. I bit back my desire to tell him to hurry, but Jerome and I did share a weary look or two.

"I'm not seeing any bones," Jake said when the pocket seemed to be almost fully uncovered.

"But I'm sure that's the pocket to a *mochila*," I said.

"Me, too. Should I keep digging?" Jake said.

"Sure," I said. "It might have nothing to do with Astin Reagal."

Jake looked at me with one lifted eyebrow.

"I know, it's probably his, but even if there were bones, it's been so long, maybe there'd be nothing they could tell us," I said, but I truly had no idea what I was talking about. I wasn't sure what long-lost bones could and couldn't tell anyone. I just wanted Jake to keep digging.

"I think we're curious enough not to care too much. I'll still be careful, but the rest of whatever is attached to the flap is straight down. I'll just dig that way, try to keep from digging too wide."

"Sounds great," I said.

"It'd be good to get on with it," Jerome said. "My goodness, I'm dead, and even I'm getting a little tired."

I smiled but didn't say anything.

True to his word, Jake had the rest of the *mochila* out of the dirt in another half an hour. It was well caked in grime, but it was clear that the case had been much better preserved than the flap. Even with the layer of dirt, the leather of the case was darker than the faded part of the flap that must have been exposed to the elements for a long time.

Jake sat the freed *mochila* on a clear patch of ground and ran his hand over it.

"It's amazing. Betts — and Jerome — this is a real part of history. Not just words, but an actual artifact."

"I think we should open the pockets," I said. I was much less impressed by the old item, but I did appreciate Jake's point of view. But still, I wanted to see what was inside.

"Okay." Jake placed his hand on the flap. He took a deep breath and let it out slowly through his nose.

Jerome smiled at me.

Jake lifted the first flap and a dirty dust cloud puffed around the *mochila*. He held the satchel up and peered inside. He did the same with the other pockets. A moment later he looked at me.

"Nothing."

"Nothing?" I said as I reached for the *mochila*.

"Absolutely nothing."

I peered inside, too. Jake was correct. There was nothing in the case. It was empty except for a few grains of dirt. The inside had, of course, been even better preserved than the outside, but some bits of its surrounding burial place had found their way into the pockets.

"Do you think some letters might have fallen out?" I said as I leaned over and looked into the hole.

"I doubt it. But think about it, Betts. If he was on his way home, he might not have had anything to deliver. After he made his run, there might not have been anything for him to bring back. Not as much junk mail back then. It's conceivable that no one in Broken Rope had a letter coming to them."

"I suppose." I put the *mochila* back on the ground and closed the flaps. I tried to look for markings like those on the *mochila* in Jake's archives, but there were none currently visible. There might be some, but it would take a careful cleaning to find them. This was probably more evidence that Joe wasn't Astin Reagal. Joe's bag had letters. If this was truly Astin's, the real incarnations of the ghostly letters were nowhere to be

340

found. Even considering that inconsistency, though, as well as Astin's appearance the night before, a small part of me couldn't let go of the notion that they might be the same person.

I looked at Jerome. "What else, Jerome? What else should we do? Dig some more, look for bones?"

"Well," Jake said, jumping in before Jerome could answer, "I don't think we should do much more than take this back to town. I can get experts with the proper equipment out here to look for any remains. This find in itself will be enough to get the proper authorities quickly involved."

"All right," Jerome said, but I could hear disappointment in his voice.

"We'll find him if he's here, Jerome, but Jake's right. We don't have the proper equipment, and I don't want to do anything that might harm evidence that could help us better understand what happened to Astin."

"I understand," Jerome said with a little less disappointment.

"I think it'd be great to show this to Esther," Jake said. "She'll be beyond thrilled."

"Let's take it to her right now," I said.

We stood and Jake held the *mochila* out as he inspected it again.

"This is an amazing find, Jerome," he said

341

to no space in particular. "I'm sure this will lead to Astin's remains. We just have to get the right people out here to look."

Jerome nodded.

"He understands," I said. "Come on, let's get back to town."

I carried the shovel so Jake could be extra diligent as he carried the *mochila*. Jerome looked back to the spot we'd been digging as we made our way back to the Nova. I looked, too. Had our discovery also uncovered a ghost? It didn't work that way as far as I knew, but nothing would surprise me.

No new ghosts appeared, though. There was no sense that anything unusual stirred the air. There was no new smell.

My last look behind was at the house's remains. I knew there was nothing to find there, but I also knew I'd come back out and explore the posts and the overgrown weeds. Would I find something of Jerome's? It was unlikely, but I needed to look for myself. Not today, though. There was plenty of other business to attend to today.

CHAPTER 26

"I'm thrilled that you might have found Astin, Betts, and I'm glad Jerome hasn't left, but Orly called and wants me to come out to the campsite. He wants to show me something," Gram said.

"Something about what?" I readjusted the cell phone so I could hear her better.

"I don't know. That's all he told me — something."

"Gram, Jake and I were out there earlier. I had a strange hunch and asked him about owning a .38 Special — that's the kind of gun that killed Norman. He said that one potentially went missing from his truck. I told him to call the police. Don't go out alone. Wait — Jake and I will meet you out there. Give us about ten minutes before you leave," I said in quick-speed staccato. My foot pressed harder on the accelerator as my words became more hurried.

"That's fine. I'll see you there," Gram said

before she hung up.

"Why would Orly want to talk to Gram?" I said as I put down the phone. Jerome was in the backseat and Jake was double-checking that his seat belt was secure.

"Didn't it seem like Orly kind of liked Miz?" Jake asked.

"Well, maybe, but his timing bothers me," I said. "We're going back out there."

"And, apparently, we're going to break all speed records to get there," Jake said.

I handed my phone to Jake. "Here, hit the button for Cliff. Please."

Jake did as I asked and I took the phone back. Cliff's voice mail picked up again after only one ring.

"Hey, meet me at the convention campsite if you get this before nine or so. Thanks." I hung up.

"The campsite is well populated, Betts. Miz will be fine," Jake said.

"I guess I'm overreacting a little bit, but something's not right."

"Maybe," Jake said. "What could go wrong, though? Miz will be careful; extra careful after your call. There are lots of people around all the time."

"If there are always so many people around, how did Teddy get beaten up without any witnesses?" I said.

344

"Good point." Jake pulled out his own phone and pressed a couple buttons. "Hi, Jenny, it's Jake Swanson. Yes, I'm fine. I'm just wondering if there's a quick way to get a hold of Jim, or maybe Cliff Sebastian. Sure. Yes, actually, if you could just ask one of them to call me, that would be perfect. Thank you. Uh-huh. Thanks again. 'Bye."

"Was that Jenny, the dispatcher?"

"Yes."

"You know her?" I said.

"Everyone knows her."

"I mean, you've seen her in person?"

"I've had coffee with her. She's a sweet lady."

"She's a terrible police dispatcher. And I don't even know what she looks like," I said. I'd never met her, but I'd come to know her through her dispatch position. Recently, she'd failed more than once to get a message I'd called in to the police in a timely manner. Gram disagreed with my poor opinion of her. Apparently, so did Jake.

"How is that —"

"Isabelle!" Jerome said from the backseat.

I stepped hard on the brake pedal. The Nova did stop, but first its tires squealed and slid. Fortunately, all wheels stayed on the road, though before we came to a safe halt, the car was at a ninety-degree angle from where it should have been.

"What happened?" Jake said.

"In the road. Joe and his horse are in the road. I'm sorry, Jake. I couldn't have hurt them, but I was so surprised. I forgot they were ghosts."

"We almost joined them," Jake said.

"Sorry. You okay?"

"Fine."

"I'm going to go see what he wants. I'll be right back," I said.

I got out of the car with shaky legs and a too-rapid pulse.

"There might have been a better way to let me know you wanted to talk to me, a better way to reappear. Just showing up in the middle of the road isn't the best idea."

"You found Astin?" Joe said, ignoring my admonition.

"Maybe. We found a *mochila,* and we suspect that Astin's remains are in the general vicinity."

"Take me to him," Joe said.

"I will. Later. I need to get to Gram right now."

"No, Betts. Now."

I blinked. "No, Joe, not now. I've got to get to Gram." I turned and went back to my car.

"Stupid ghosts," I muttered to Jake.

"Sorry, Jerome," I said to the rearview mirror.

"What's wrong, Isabelle?" Jerome asked.

"Joe wants to be taken to Astin, right away."

"I can take him," Jerome said. "No. No, I can't. I think I'd better stay with you, Isabelle."

I looked in the mirror.

"You *can't*-can't, or don't want to?"

"I can't," he said.

"That means my life might be in danger?" I said.

"Betts, tell me what's happening," Jake said.

"I'm not sure," I said. "Jerome?"

"I don't know, Isabelle. I just know I need to stay with you."

"Let's go," I said as I turned the key.

Nothing happened.

I turned the key again. Nothing. Not even the click of a dead battery.

"Betts?" Jake said.

I peered out my side window at Joe, who sat tall on his horse and looked at me with firm distaste. I was beginning to really not like this ghost — well, even more than I hadn't liked him before.

"Can you guys make cars not start?" I asked Jerome.

"Not that I'm aware of."

I got out again and hurried to the ghostly form.

"Have you done something to the Nova? Is that even possible?"

"I've waited a long time to find Astin's remains, Betts. I don't want to wait any longer."

"Who are you? Tell me why you need to find him so badly," I said. I was fuming, literally breathing too heavy for my own good. I was about to prove whether or not smoke could truly come out of ears.

Joe's face softened. "I can't tell you. It's part of . . . I don't know, maybe it's part of my punishment. I don't understand it, but I know I have to find him. Once I do, the last letter will be complete and things will be set right. For him, too. I just know."

"Were you responsible for his death? Did you kill him?" I said.

"No, Betts, I would never have killed him."

"Listen," I said. "You're dead, he's dead. I'm sorry to have only a little sympathy for that situation, but I'm worried about Gram. She might be in danger, Joe. Come on, whatever you've done to my car, undo it. Now. I promise we'll attend to Astin the second I know Gram is safe. She's been there for you for years. You owe her . . . holy cow, Joe, you owe her everything. Without her, you wouldn't have been able to do anything about any of the letters. You can't let me abandon her. *You* can't abandon her!"

Joe's face twitched and then softened more.

"All right, but just as soon as Miz is taken care of, we'll come back."

It wasn't a question, but I still said, "Yes."

"Go. I'll follow."

I hurried back to the car.

"Jerome, can you get to Gram?" I said.

"I need to stay with you, Isabelle. I'm sorry."

I nodded. "Jake, call everyone — Cliff, Jim, Jenny. Don't call Teddy. Don't call Opie. But call everyone else. Get them to the campsite."

The car started with the first turn of the key. I straightened the tires and sped my way toward the campsite. Joe and the horse followed behind, looking like what I imagined most Express riders looked like when they'd delivered letters. I'd seen it a little when we'd gone to visit Opie, but the visual was even stronger now. He was bent over the horse as the front flap on his hat flew back from the effort, and his eyes were focused straight ahead, forward on the path that would take them to their next stop, their one and only destination in mind. I was cooling off from my scorching anger, and I managed to take a moment to wish Jake could get a glimpse. Because, no matter how many pictures one sees, no matter how many reenactments one might participate in, there is nothing like the real thing. And seeing the real thing in my rearview mirror suddenly made me understand and appreciate it on a level I'd never been able to reach before. The riders had given their all, and it seems that in some cases, their all had included their lives. The horses had given their all, too. I'd seen something in the eyes of Joe's horse, something that had made me wonder just how highly intelligent the creatures were. Though it was too light outside and the horse was moving too fast for me to see his eyes, I knew he was just as intent and focused on the ride as Joe was. History books would never be able to do the Pony Express justice.

We were a few minutes later than I thought we would be. Joe's barricade hadn't diverted us for long, but I hoped that Gram had waited for us before looking for Orly.

I parked in the same spot I had earlier and bolted out of the car toward Orly's tent. I yanked the flap open.

"Betts?" he said as he sat on a stool and held a pair of underwear over an open bag. "Everything all right?" He noticed the underwear and placed them in the bag before he stood up.

"Gram? Has my gram been here?" I said.

"Not yet. I called her, though. I think she's on her way. She said she'd be here." Orly stepped forward.

I backed out of the tent and into Jake. Behind him were Jerome and Joe and the horse.

"I called the police, too. I remembered the people I thought had access to my truck. I had to leave a message with someone named Jenny, though. I'm sure I'll be able to talk to Officer Morrison or Sebastian, your boyfriend, soon though."

"Okay, so why did you call Gram?" I said.

Orly blushed. "I hoped to spend a little more time with her. I thought Miz and I could chat over coffee and maybe she'd want breakfast or something. It's a quiet morning, but I'm not sure the afternoon will be the same. She'd mentioned that she was an early riser. I took a chance that that was so and called her."

"She said that you said you wanted to show her something," I said.

"Oh, yes. Hang on, I'll grab it." Orly disappeared back into the tent.

I looked at Jake and then at the ghosts behind me. At the moment, we were a rather pitiful group of heroes.

"I wanted to give this to her." Orly said as he emerged with the item he wanted to show Gram.

"It's a Dutch oven," I said.

"Yes," Orly said, "it is. It's one of the best ones I've ever had. I wanted her to have it for all her trouble over these last few days."

"That's very kind of you," I said.

Between Joe's trick in the middle of the road and my concern over Gram, my heart was still beating too fast, and I suddenly noticed that I could hear its pounding rhythm. I took a deep breath.

"Can we go back to Astin now?" Joe asked.

I shook my head, but not so much that Orly would wonder what I was doing. I wanted to see Gram arrive safely for myself before I left again.

"I'll be right back. I'm going to find Esther," Jake said as he patted my arm. He stepped through the horse as he set out.

"I'm sorry I barged into your tent," I said to Orly.

"It's fine," Orly said. "Can I round up some more grub for you?"

"No thanks," I said.

The engine of Gram's Volvo purred down the side road. We all turned to watch her park behind the Nova. She didn't have her stereo turned up, so neither of her two favorite country singers, Toby Keith nor Tim McGraw, accompanied her arrival. Today, she wore a University of Utah long-sleeved T-shirt. The bright red of the shirt looked great with her gray hair.

"Excuse me," I said to Orly. "Give us a second."

"Of course," he said.

I greeted her halfway.

"Hi, Gram."

"Betts. Everything okay?"

"I think I'm a little on edge this morning. I'm sorry if I sounded crazy."

"No problem." Gram smiled and waved at Orly and the ghosts. They all waved back. "After I spend some time with Orly, I would like to go out and see where Astin's remains are. Sounds kind of interesting, actually."

I glanced back at the crowd watching us.

"It is interesting. In fact, we think we found his *mochila*. It's in the Nova's trunk. I'll show it to you when you're done."

"Oh! Wonderful. Let's have a quick look now." Gram sent the one-minute signal to Orly, who nodded and then busied himself with straightening up the camping equipment outside his tent.

"Sure."

We ventured back to the Nova and I opened the trunk.

"Oh, Betts, that's extraordinary," Gram said.

"I think it's cool, but you think it's that big a deal?"

"Absolutely." She reached in to touch it, but she moved carefully. "In the first place, these are rare finds, but that's more the reason Jake will appreciate it. To me, well, it represents so much of my time with Joe, the other rider. I'm thrilled to touch a real one and know what it feels like."

I didn't mention to her that Jake had one in his archives, because I didn't want to lessen her excitement.

"We're guessing it was the one Astin was carrying when he died. We didn't see any remains, but we think we found the spot where they'll be found."

"What did Joe say?"

"He wasn't there at the time. We saw him afterward, and he's anxious for us to show him the spot."

"That's a shame he wasn't there. Where was he?"

"I didn't ask. Go ahead, hold it. Jake's not around, so he can't cringe or chastise."

I lifted the *mochila* out of the trunk and handed it to Gram. She was gentle and more curious than I would have predicted she'd be. She opened two flaps on one side and looked inside. When she turned it to look into the other two, something fell out and to the ground.

"Oh, no. Sorry," Gram said.

"A letter? Jake and I looked through it thoroughly, Gram; there was no letter."

"You must have missed it. Let's see what it is. Be careful. It will probably be very delicate."

"Should we call Joe over? I mean, it's a letter from a *mochila;* maybe he should see it too?" I said as I crouched to pick up the weathered envelope. Time had made it look like someone had spilled coffee on it and wadded it up before straightening it again.

"Makes sense to me," Gram said.

I held the letter as I stood up with the intention to signal Joe to join us. But as I glanced over at the group, I was stopped by the look on Jake's face as he talked to Orly. Something was wrong.

With letter in hand, and with Gram and the *mochila* behind me, I made my way back to Orly's tent.

"What's going on?" I asked Jake.

"I couldn't find Esther. I told Orly, and

he said that he saw her with Vivienne earlier, walking along the back of the campsite."

"I told them to stay out of the woods," Orly said as if to somehow appease Jake.

"And then he mentioned that Esther and Vivienne were two people who had access to his truck," Jake continued, worry now pinching his voice.

"Well, yes, but they're on a list of about six people, Jake. I'm sure those two are fine. I didn't mean anything by it. Sorry."

I wasn't sure they were fine. And I wasn't totally aware of what I was doing as I stuffed the letter into my pocket. I wanted to find Esther and Vivienne before I did anything else.

"We'll find them," I said to Jake. "Come on."

Those who were paying attention would have seen me, Gram, Jake, and Orly tromping toward the thick woods. But Gram and I both saw that Jerome and Joe and a horse were part of the pack of explorers, too, though they were mostly silent. I sensed that Jerome was somehow out of sorts, but he stayed close by.

"Orly, how far away are we from the spot where Teddy was found?" I said.

Orly shrugged. "I didn't find him."

He had mentioned that, and he'd men-

356

tioned that one of the cowgirls had found him, but I'd never asked for a name. I remembered that I had been so worried about Teddy's state that I'd missed that important question. I couldn't believe I hadn't, but I didn't hesitate to ask it now. "Who found him? Which cowgirl?"

"Vivienne," he said. "She helped him back to the tents."

I looked into the copse of trees and felt small and unsure. I'd been in the woods plenty of times, and I could easily find my way out, but there were so many options as to which path Vivienne and Esther might have taken if they had, in fact, gone into them.

"Should we split up?" I said. "Orly, you go with me or Jake. We know our way around in there. We won't get lost."

"Wait a minute, Betts," Joe said at the same time Orly said, "I'll go with Miz."

"Let me look first. I can ride much more quickly than the rest of you can walk. I can do this, I can find them," Joe said with such emotion that Gram, Jerome, and I looked up at him. Was he going to cry?

I nodded and then turned my attention back to the others. Orly and Jake, of course, hadn't heard Joe, so I responded to Orly's comment about going with Gram. "Okay,

357

but Jake, you go with them, too. Hang on a second, though. Gram, how about you take the short path around to the south end and then back up again?"

"Will do," she said, knowing that trail was easy and wouldn't take them long.

Once she and Orly set off, I held on to Jake's arm to keep him back a moment. I quickly turned my attention to Joe. "Go, I guess. Find them and yell for us. Hopefully Jerome or I or Gram will hear you."

Joe's mouth formed a straight intense line before he said, "I will find them. I was supposed to find Astin, Betts. I was supposed to find him. I won't fail again."

He nudged the horse with his heels before I could ask any questions.

"He said it had been his job to find Astin," I said to Jake. "Maybe Joe was a law enforcement officer from that time and it was his job to find the downed rider. He said he wouldn't fail again."

"I haven't researched that aspect. I can, but right at the moment I'd like to find Esther," Jake said.

"I understand. Go on. Catch up to Gram and Orly." I nodded.

But a scream cut through the trees and stopped us in our tracks.

The scream came from the direction I'd

sent Gram and Orly. It had only been less than a minute; they couldn't have gone far, but I didn't see them.

"Gram!" I said before I set off into the trees. Jerome and Jake probably followed behind, but I didn't take the time to look.

Chapter 27

Even though I knew the woods, the worn paths weren't all that well-marked and I had to jump and dodge through and around nature's obstacle course.

"Gram!" I yelled as I ran.

It was as if they appeared out of nowhere, but in fact, Gram and Orly simply stepped out from a turn in the path. Orly grabbed me just as I was about to run over Gram.

"Betts, I'm okay. It wasn't me," Gram said. "But we need to find who it was. Come on. This way."

She turned and stepped away before I could even catch my breath. She wasn't running, but she was moving at a good clip.

"You all right?" Orly still had his hand around my arm.

"I'm fine. I thought . . ."

"I know, and I understand, but I need to go catch up to Miz. You sure you're okay?"

I nodded.

Jake stepped around me. "She's fine, Orly. Let's go."

Jerome and I followed behind them.

"Do you have any idea what's going on?" I said to him.

"No, I don't, and I don't mind saying that I'm more than a bit uncomfortable about it. I tried to go find who was screaming, but I can't seem to leave your side, Isabelle."

"Which means I'm in danger," I said.

"That's my only guess."

The sound of rhythmic horse hooves from up ahead caught Gram's and my attention.

Joe brought the horse to a halt in front of Gram and said, "They're in the Express station. The two women."

Gram turned and said, "I think they're in the Express station. We need to hurry."

If Orly wondered why Gram thought what she thought, he didn't ask the question.

If we hadn't stepped into the woods in the first place, we could have gotten to the station quickly and easily. But now we had to decide if we wanted to continue through the woods and take a roundabout way to the station, or backtrack and go the other way. Time-wise it was probably sixes. Gram chose to keep moving forward, so we followed behind.

Though we moved quickly, it felt like our

feet were having to be pulled from thick mud. It was only a minute or two later when we reached an edge to the dense woods. We stepped out into the clearing and hurried to the Express station. When we reached it, Orly stepped in front of Gram and put his hand on the door.

"Why don't you all just cross back over to the campsite. I'll go in and see if they're in there and what's happening. You all try to get ahold of the police again."

"Excuse me, Orly, but I'm not waiting for anyone," Jake said as he gently pushed Orly aside and opened the door. He was in a second later. Orly followed him. Gram and I looked at each other and the ghosts. We weren't waiting either. Another second later, Gram and I and the ghosts, the horse included, joined the others.

Unfortunately, we walked into a situation that was much more dire than any of us had predicted. If we would have taken at least a moment to hoist ourselves up to a window so we could see that a gun was being held to one of our visitors' heads, we might have all chosen to stay outside instead and make that extra call to the police. And even more unfortunately, it became quickly clear that we weren't going to be allowed to escape.

"Stay back, Isabelle," Jerome said as he

put himself in front of me. I quickly put my hand through his arm.

"How many more are out there?" Vivienne said. One of her arms was tight around Esther's neck. The other hand held the gun, and currently it was aimed at me.

"The police are on their way," I said.

Esther's fair skin was even paler than normal, and she was bleeding profusely from her arm. I assumed she'd been shot. I didn't think I'd heard gunfire, so I wondered if she had been shot before we'd returned to the campsite.

"Then we have only a few minutes. Here's what's going to happen: You are going to let me and Esther get out of this building, and then I'm going to leave. I'll leave her where you all can find her and get her to a doctor."

"Fine, Vivienne," I said. I hoped it would actually play out that way and no one else would get hurt. The space was too small for us all, and gunfire could be extra deadly.

"What's going on, Vivienne?" Orly asked. "What's the paper on the floor?"

I truly hadn't noticed the piece of paper, and I wished Orly hadn't either. If only we could just get out of there.

Vivienne laughed. "Ask her." She squeezed her arm a little tighter around Esther's neck.

Vivienne nodded to the piece of paper close to her left foot.

"Esther?" Orly said.

Esther shook her head. She either didn't want to tell what the letter was, or she couldn't because she was in shock or in pain — or both.

"It's what brought her here," Vivienne said as she kicked the letter away.

It floated in the air a second and then it landed at Jake's feet.

"Go ahead, pick it up," Vivienne said.

Jake did as she instructed. He read over the letter silently and then said, "It's a letter that tells her she's a descendant of Astin Reagal, a Pony Express rider who was lost on the trail," Jake said. I thought he was angry that Esther was hurt, that she was being held, that he couldn't figure out what to do to help her. Tension straightened his back and tightened his voice.

"So?" I said.

"Really?" Orly said. "I'm a descendant of Astin Reagal, too. It's part of the reason I came to town last summer. Do you remember me asking you about him?" Orly looked at Jake.

"I don't, Orly, but I get a lot of visitors and a lot of questions."

Vivienne forced a chuckle this time. "Of

364

course you are, Orly. And let me introduce you to your daughter. Esther, say hi to dear old dad."

"What?" Orly said.

Esther blinked, and a tear fell from the corner of one of her eyes.

"That's right. That's why I got her and Norman here. They're yours, Orly. Twins, of all things, parted at birth and given away for adoption. My mother was their biological mother."

"Vivienne, I don't understand what is going on," Orly said. "But I don't think it matters. Let's get Esther to a doctor and we'll sort it all out."

"Right. The police are going to let me go, even after I killed Norman and shot Esther? I doubt it."

"Why did you kill Norman? Why would you hurt Esther?" Orly said.

Vivienne laughed again, even more maniacally this time. "I didn't even mean to kill Norman. I meant to kill Cody."

"Why?" Orly said.

"Because he knew what I was up to. He found out I was trying to get Norman and Esther to buy into my idea and blackmail you."

"I don't understand."

"I would ruin your reputation if you didn't

pay up, but they had to be in on it with me. It wouldn't have worked otherwise. Both Cody and that other guy, Teddy, overheard what I was doing. I talked Cody into helping me with Teddy, and then I knew I had to get rid of Cody, too. I thought Teddy was dead. I tried to kill Cody, but hit Norman instead."

I thought about Amy's measurements and her words. She thought that an accident or a mistaken aim might have been a possibility.

"Why in the world didn't Cody come forward?" Orly asked, but it was more to himself than to Vivienne.

Jake had said that Cody was one of the better actors he'd seen in Broken Rope. Apparently his appraisal had been spot on. Cody had acted the goofy innocent so well that almost everyone, including myself, had believed his act.

"Ended up I had to promise him some money, too. I brought Esther out here today to try to convince her again that you owed her something, anything. But she wouldn't listen."

"So you shot her?" I said.

"I was only threatening her with the gun. It went off by accident."

I wanted to say something about Vivienne's horrible gun-handling skills and suggest that she should never, ever again carry one, but it didn't seem like the right time.

"Now, here's —" Vivienne said as she wielded the weapon at Orly. Evidently she was going to tell us again what we were all going to do. I hoped Orly would just listen this time and we could all get out of the small space without further injury. I thought about pushing my way out the door and running for help, but I was afraid that Vivienne just might shoot at someone because she was angry I'd tried to escape.

But before she could finish, the world shifted. It was as if the light dimmed a little and we were all suddenly inside a walled-in cave.

"What's going on?" Vivienne said.

"I don't know," Orly said.

"Uh-oh." I looked at Gram and then at Jake. "You seeing this?"

"Yes," Jake said. "Totally."

Not only did the sights transform, but so did the smells. Suddenly, we were in something like a real station, one from olden times, but without distinct walls, and so were a couple horses — seemingly real horses. The scents that went along with horses, their feed, and their riders were all around us.

"Miz, what's going on?" Orly asked.

"Everyone will be fine," Gram said. "Just hang on. We're about to see a show, I think."

Gram and I had both experienced something similar with the old bakery, but the other living souls in the room had probably never seen a real ghost or been part of a real ghostly experience. Jake was clearly interested, but his concern for Esther took priority. Esther was having a hard time remaining conscious, and though she was a small woman, was becoming heavier and heavier for Vivienne. Vivienne was just as perplexed as Orly and wasn't sure where to aim the gun or what to do with the body she was trying to keep hold of. I sidled my way that direction with the hope that I might be able to get either Esther or the gun away from her — or both. Jerome stayed close by my side.

A loud rumble preceded the arrival of who I hoped was our last ghost of the day.

"I'll be jiggered," Astin Reagal said as he pulled his horse to a strong-reined halt on the open side of the station. The space had become bigger than it would have been in reality and the walls had all but disappeared into a muddy murkiness. He looked behind himself at some of the murkiness and laughed, and then looked at us.

"Hello," he said with a blink. "Where's my man? Where's the next rider?"

"Astin," Joe said as he got off his horse and walked to Astin's side. "I'm here. I'm here, Astin." Joe turned to me. "You have a letter, I presume." At first, I had no idea what Joe was talking about, but then I realized that he meant the one I'd put in my pocket. I nodded. "Read it. Now."

I pulled it out. It was in terrible condition, but I carefully opened the flap and reached inside for the small piece of paper.

I looked around at the confused and concerned faces in the station. I wanted to get this over with, but I saw no shortcuts. I was going to have to read the letter.

"My dearest Josey. If you find this, I'm sure I will have passed to the great beyond. I fell off the horse, sweetheart. I took a shortcut and somehow the horse's legs got caught in some bramble and I went down, and broke both my legs. The horse ran off. I'm sure to die if no one finds me soon, and I don't see that many people will travel this way. I love you and our dear son. I'm sorry to leave you. Astin."

Sure to die. They were the few legible words from Joe's last letter. This must somehow be the same letter.

I looked up to see Joe removing his hat. His — no, *her* long black hair cascaded down her back. Her grimy face became distinctly ungrimy and very pretty — that's what I'd been seeing, a watery version of the beginnings of that transformation.

"I searched for you, my love," she said as she looked up at Astin. "I searched for so very long."

"Oh, Josey, I'm so, so sorry."

"No need to be. I found you now." Josey looked at Gram. "I couldn't tell you. It was . . . well, I don't know why, but I think it was some sort of punishment for abandoning my remaining family, but I just couldn't say the words. I couldn't admit to who I was until I did what I'd set out to do. My name is Amelia Josephine. Astin always called me Josey or Joe. I hope you understand."

"I do," Gram said.

Josey looked at me. "I'm so terribly sorry for the trouble I caused you, but I'm beginning to think that if it weren't for you, we still might not have a solution. An end to my torture. Thank you."

"You're welcome," I said.

"I think things are good now," Josey said.

"We had our fun over the years. Thank you, Joe. Josey," Gram said.

"We did. And Astin and I will be back someday, I'm sure. And we'll be together,"

Josey said.

"We'll see you down the road, then," Gram said. "And, Josey, I'm ever so glad you aren't alone anymore."

Josey's horse stomped and looked directly at me. Our eyes made contact, and I was certain he was trying to tell me something. It was too bad that even in the midst of all this weirdness, it seemed that animals still couldn't speak. I wish I could have known what he was trying to tell me right before he faded away completely, but I'm going to go with gratitude. The horse was either happy to have the truth come out or was so fed up with the rest of us for not being able to figure out that Joe was a she and not a he that he needed one last look of "sheesh." No, I'm going to go with gratitude.

Astin pulled Josey up onto his horse. She sat behind him and wrapped her arms around his waist. They smiled at each other as he heeled the horse and pulled on the reins to turn it back toward wherever he came from. In a moment, they were all gone, except for Jerome.

The stress of the haunted moments, as well as holding the now-completely-passed-out Esther, had worn on Vivienne. As Astin and Amelia Josephine and the horses completed their disappearing act, Esther slid

371

from Vivienne's arms. The unconscious woman fell backward onto Vivienne's knees, causing her to fall over, too. On their way down, the trigger of the gun got pulled.

The next thing I knew I was flat on the ground with my face in the dirt, and Jerome was on top of me.

"What happened?" I said.

"The bullet was headed your direction," Jerome said. "It missed you."

"But it got you, young man," Orly said as he crouched down next to us.

Jerome rolled off me and then sat up. I pulled myself up to my knees and looked at the hole in his shoulder. It wasn't bloody. It was just a hole.

"Oh, Jerome, I'm so sorry," I said.

"I'm fine," he said with a smirk. "Can't die twice, remember?"

"Excuse me," Orly said.

"Look, you two need to kiss and get this over with. We need to help Esther," Jake said. Gram had the gun, and Jake held Vivienne's arms behind her so she wouldn't get away.

I looked at Jerome. "You think you're done here?"

"For now."

I tipped his hat back and leaned toward him. I held his face, now so real and stubbly with the paranormal juju all around. I kissed his forehead. I felt him and he felt me. The light around wasn't bright daylight again, but it was bright enough that we shouldn't have been able to feel each other. But we did. Some things just might never be understood or explained.

"I have a boyfriend. I'd better stop kissing other boys on the lips," I said.

"That you'd better. Good-bye for now, Isabelle and Miz. See you next time," he said before he disappeared.

"I can't wait," I whispered.

"Holy moly, what's going on?" Orly said.

The scene shifted again. We were no longer in a cave-like tunnel. There were no horse smells. We'd made it back to the place we belonged.

"I'll explain later," I said to Orly. "It's a darn fun story."

"I bet."

The police weren't there quickly. We had to call them again. Fortunately, Cliff answered his phone this time, because Jenny had left her post and no one answered the dispatch phone.

Once Esther was taken care of, we knew we'd have to live up to what I'd promised Orly — a darn fun story. And I thought we did okay.

CHAPTER 28

"If I'd noticed that his wife's middle name was Josephine, we might have figured it out sooner," Jake said. "Or if I'd had time to do a complete genealogy for Esther, maybe."

"Maybe," Gram said. "I'm not so sure I would have ever thought Joe was a Josephine. It was a real surprise for me. I never once sensed that he was a she."

"Seems like we're full of surprises lately," I said.

"I have another one," Jake said. "They found some human bones out by where we found the *mochila*. It's too soon to know much about them, but there will be a thorough investigation."

"Must be Astin's," I said.

Jake shrugged. "Probably, but having seen the real man, well, almost the real man, I suppose, I'm not sure I find the bones as interesting. We'll see what conclusions the forensic team comes to."

Gram, Jake, and I were in Bunny's. Orly and Esther would be joining us soon, but the rest of the cowboy poetry convention attendees had gone home and the big plot of land behind the high school was now vacant and, I thought, lonely and far too empty.

Orly *was* Esther's biological father. Norman's, too. He'd had a fling with their mother at a convention twenty-five years earlier. Their mother, also Vivienne's mother, already had one child at the time — Vivienne — and no husband.

As Vivienne got older, she remembered back to the time when she was very young and her mother started gaining weight. Then she went to the hospital and came home thinner. Vivienne never put the pieces together when her mother was alive, but after she died Vivienne found half-written and never-sent letters to Orly in an old shoe box. Choosing to give the babies up for adoption had been difficult for Vivienne's mother. From the letters, Vivienne determined that her mother didn't want to burden Orly over a one-night stand, but there was no way she could have afforded to raise the babies on her own. She and Vivienne were struggling as it was. Ultimately, the letters weren't sent and the babies were given up for adoption. Orly never knew about them. He was never put into a position where he could have offered to help financially or in any other way. When Vivienne found out Orly was a well-off Kansas cattleman, she thought she might be able to use her knowledge of his fatherhood to her advantage, and she thought his offspring would only help her with her plan.

It didn't take her long to find what had happened to the babies and where they were currently living. And Vivienne researched Orly from top to bottom, once reading an article that mentioned that he was a descendant of a Pony Express rider from Broken Rope, which was coincidentally where the cowboy poetry convention was going to be held this year.

Vivienne got both Norman and Esther to the convention by writing them letters that mentioned their Astin Reagal ancestry, and by promising them that they'd find out even more information about their birth families if they attended the convention. Norman thought it would be fun to also get an acting job, and Esther just thought it would be a fun and interesting vacation. Neither Esther nor Norman knew about each other, and until Vivienne told them at the convention, they had no idea that Orly, the man running the convention, was their biological father.

The best we can put together is that Teddy overheard Vivienne telling Norman about Orly. He also overheard Norman tell Vivienne that he didn't want to have any part of blackmailing Orly. Norman and Vivienne hadn't been interested in each other romantically, but they'd had a passionate and heated conversation or two. Vivienne couldn't believe that Norman wouldn't help her with the blackmail scheme. Teddy is only now remembering that Vivienne was upset that he overheard her blackmail ideas. The reason she made such a scene of yelling at him that night at the convention was with the hopes she would diffuse any accusations he might have toward her. She had no idea that his memories had been jumbled enough that she had nothing to worry about.

Cody hasn't given the police all the details yet, but we learned that Vivienne told him that Teddy accosted her the night before their brutality toward him. Cody was taken by Vivienne's beauty enough that he believed her lie and went along with her request to help get Teddy out to the woods and beat him up. They'd hoped to death. Cody's criminal record might not have been violent, but he had easily crossed over to that side of things.

Teddy didn't remember the specifics of what happened to him. I hoped he never would.

Apparently, Norman had been a longtime fan of Orly's and his poetry. He'd known about Orly the poet for years, but Orly being his father was news that didn't necessarily bother him, though was still not something he could easily accept. He hadn't had a falling-out with his adoptive parents, and we learned that they had spoken frequently over the last year. Jim wasn't happy to hear that he had misinformation from the Kansas City police. Apparently, the morning Norman was killed, the morning that Jake found him on the boardwalk talking about a "make-or-break" day was the result of a phone conversation with his adoptive parents. They'd told him they loved him and were glad he'd found his biological father and welcomed him into his life if that's what made him happy.

Vivienne hadn't been the cowgirl to bring Teddy back to the campsite. It had been the old guy, Gary. Gary wasn't quite "right in the head" according to Orly. He left Teddy on the edge of the campsite, close to Orly's tent, afraid that he'd be accused of the beating. Orly found Teddy with Vivienne standing over him. When she saw Orly, she took the credit for finding Teddy in the woods and bringing him back to the campsite. Orly had no reason to question her, and at that point Teddy didn't have any idea what was going on. Cliff and I had tried to make Gary's odd story/poem fit with what he'd done, but it still didn't make sense.

We think Cody panicked when he learned that Teddy was alive. Vivienne probably thought there was a chance he would go to the police about the beating, and place the blame on her. Vivienne's plans to kill him failed, but her act of getting rid of Norman scared Cody into silence. It was no wonder he wanted to get out of town so badly.

The gun used to kill Norman was Orly's .38 Special. Vivienne had stolen it out of Orly's toolbox. I doubted he'd ever forgive himself for that, but we'd tried to make him understand that it wasn't his fault.

After she pulled the trigger and realized what happened, she ran into the woods and threw the gun under a rock beside the same river that Jerome and I had been fishing in, but a good ways down from where we fought the catfish. Vivienne hurried back to town and found Esther, and the two of them went into Stuart's shop. Vivienne hadn't been faking the "damsel in distress" act. It had been real, just more real than anyone knew — she was overwhelmed and distressed by what she'd done.

Esther also wasn't interested in blackmailing Orly, but she was much more distressed by the news that he was her biological father than Norman had been. Shocked, in fact, but then deeply curious about her biological heritage. Before she received the letter from Vivienne, she had no idea she was a descendant of Astin Reagal's. In fact, her last name wasn't even Reagal — she'd been adopted by the Andersons of Kansas City. And it wasn't until after the bullet wound on her arm was attended to that she learned that Norman was her twin brother. Vivienne had told them separately about Orly, but never about each other, apparently with the hope that they wouldn't conspire together and leave her out of whatever plans they made.

Esther had lied about who she was to Jake because it simply seemed like the best way to get more information about Astin Reagal and still maintain her privacy — something she thought was important after Vivienne told her the shocking news about Orly. Later, and when she realized she really liked Jake, she felt badly about the lie and wasn't

quite sure how to get out of it without looking deceitful at best, and somehow guilty
about something at worst, considering all
the violence that had been occurring at the
convention.

Esther had also made up the story about
Astin helping deliver a baby. She just
thought she needed to sound like she knew
more about him than she truly did.

Esther's discussion with me at the fish fry
was mostly fabrication, too. She wanted to
do something to shine a light of suspicion
on Vivienne without mentioning the true
specifics of blackmail and potential murder.
Esther suspected that Vivienne had had
something to do with Norman's murder,
but she couldn't prove it.

The morning Vivienne shot Esther in the
arm had started off with a friendly invita-
tion. Vivienne asked Esther if she wanted to
take a walk, maybe look at the Express station. Esther said that Vivienne actually
apologized to her for bringing up the blackmail idea, that it had been wrong to even
consider something so awful. Esther hadn't
even noticed the gun Vivienne had placed
in the waist of her jeans that was hidden by
a long T-shirt until they were inside the station, and for whatever reason Vivienne
brought out the gun to show to Esther. Es-

ther thinks the shooting was what Vivienne had said it was, an accident, but no one is completely sure, of course.

Additionally, and much less important, Esther had never been romantically interested in anyone but Jake. Not even Teddy, even if she did think he was cute.

Jezzie hadn't been interested in anyone but her boyfriend back home. She was probably the happiest of anyone to get out of town, even if she had missed her family dinner with Cliff.

Orly told me that he hadn't had romantic thoughts for anyone since his wife had died, certainly not for anyone at a convention. He mentioned, however, that he sure hoped for the chance to know Gram a little better.

No one has figured out how the snake got into the cooler full of fish. I think Vivienne was involved, but I can't figure out why she'd do such a thing except that some people are just prone to mean and violent behavior, and she's one of those people.

It seemed that what I'd heard was going on at the convention had been misconstrued and misinterpreted. There'd been arguments and heated discussions, but Teddy hadn't misbehaved and had actually attempted to help when he thought help was needed. It was easy to understand how the stories got jumbled, what with those lies mixed in with all that beautiful poetry and those moonlit nights.

After Esther was shot, the convention came to a quick close and most everyone went home, except for Cody and Vivienne, who were both arrested.

The biggest mistake Vivienne had made was that no matter how much research she did, she didn't truly know Orly. She had no idea that he would have stepped up to the plate and made good in whatever way — financially included — that his biological children, or their biological mother, needed him to. He had already set plans in motion for Esther to meet his other two daughters.

Orly and Esther came through the front doors. Esther's arm was in a sling, but she walked with a pep in her step and a smile on her face. She would recover fully.

They joined us in the large round booth and we all ordered burgers and fries for lunch. Esther and Jake shared a smile, as Gram and Orly shared their own smile. I was a fifth wheel, and I was just fine with it.

We replayed the whole story again, and Orly smiled at Esther. "Thing is, I'm tickled to my hairy toes to know this young gal's my daughter, and I'm sorry as can be about

Norman. I would have welcomed them both into my family. Shoot, I would have welcomed Vivienne, too, if she'd just come to talk to me and was straight about everything. The biological part wouldn't have even mattered. I've got enough to share. I would have felt responsible for some of her and her mother's hard times. My kids would have been okay, too. They're a good group of people."

We spent some time small-talking our way to the one question we knew Orly had. Apparently, Esther had missed the entire ghostly scene in the stable, so she had no questions about it, but Orly did. Vivienne was in jail, so no one was listening to much of the strange stuff she was spouting. And Jake had been so worried about Esther that he hadn't appreciated the fact that he got to see three ghosts at once — even more if you counted all the horses. He said he would think on it and appreciate it someday.

But Orly. We were sure Orly wanted the truth, and he finally came around to asking the question.

"Betts, Miz, what happened? Y'all said you would tell me," he said after the plates with the burgers and fries had been placed on the table.

"Orly, we've been chatting, and we're hoping you'll be all right with the story that we want to tell you," Gram said.

"Yes, ma'am," Orly said.

"Broken Rope has a glitch somewhere. We hold on to our past a little too much. It can bite us in the behind sometimes, surprise us, you know," Gram said.

"Not really, but go on," Orly said.

Esther just listened, her eyes wide and curious.

Gram sighed. "Sometimes, the past just demands that things be worked out, and that glitch in Broken Rope allows weird things to happen. In fact, they happen more than we'd sometimes like. That's what went on in the stable. Some things from the past needed to be worked out."

"I see," Orly said doubtfully. He turned to me. "You kissed that man who saved your life. Who was he?"

"An old friend," I said carefully.

Orly nodded. He looked at Gram, at Jake, at Esther, and then at me. He smiled. He was a lot like an older version of Jerome, I thought. I liked him. Gram really liked him. He liked Gram.

"Well, I'll tell you this much, the only reason I'm not going to ask any more questions is because what you are saying is making sense. It looks like I had to come to

385

Broken Rope to work out some things from my past. I'm awful heartbroken about Norman, but there's something about what you're telling me that makes me think I just might get another chance to know the boy. Maybe that's all I need to know." He looked at Gram.

"Can't be sure, Orly, but anything is possible," Gram said gently.

"That's good enough for me. Let's eat." Orly winked at me.

I patted my pocket with my lucky coin, the one from Jerome's long-ago treasure, the one I found the first time I met him and now kept with me always. I pulled out my phone and texted Cliff, telling him I was excited to see him later. He still hadn't asked to know more about the distraction between us, but if he ever did, I was ready to tell him everything.

Orly wasn't the only one heartbroken about Norman; everyone was. But Gram, Jake, and I were going to do our best to enjoy the new people in our lives, even if they weren't ghosts.

AFTERWORD

The entire but brief history of the Pony Express is wholly fascinating. From the brutal ride across the western United States to the romantic ideals embodied by the riders and their horses, the country and the way its citizens communicated were transformed during the months the Pony Express was in business. Among other challenges, financial troubles, business logistics, and the invention of the telegraph brought the days of the Pony Express to an end in 1861, only eighteen months after it began.

The pieces of actual history I included in *If Catfish Had Nine Lives* were manipulated a little to fit with the story. In fact, the Southern Missouri location of the fictional town of Broken Rope would not have had a Pony Express station. However, the actual route did begin in St. Joseph, Missouri. The historical stable is still there, and has been turned into a terrific and interesting museum for curious visitors. Also, sending mail via the Pony Express was an expensive venture which made it difficult for the average person to use. Many of the items that rode inside the *mochilas* were government documents. I like to think that the letters I put in the story were important enough that the characters would have seen fit to pay any amount necessary to get their messages to the proper recipients in a timely manner. Just like real life, though, obstacles can be thrown up and put in the way of good intentions. Important correspondence doesn't always make it to its destination. And when that happens, everything can change.

DUTCH OVEN COOKING

Cooking with a Dutch oven is a fun and tasty adventure. The adventure begins, of course, with the oven itself. Some outdoor Dutch ovens are made of aluminum, some of cast iron. There are pros and cons with each type of oven, but I prefer the heavier, cast-iron variety. Some Dutch ovens have legs; others don't. I prefer legs, and that's what you should use outside. There are also Dutch ovens that are meant for indoor use (no legs on these), using your kitchen oven and stovetop. But I'm only going to talk about outdoor cooking.

Learning how to cook using a Dutch oven isn't difficult, but it takes time, experience, and experimentation. There's always something special about cooking food outdoors, and using Dutch ovens is a great way to make your outdoor cooking full of flavor and comfort — you just need to have patience and care while learning the ins and outs of the process.

There are lots of books and websites devoted to Dutch oven cooking, but the following is a beginning crash course with some fun recipes. If you're a beginning Dutch oven cook, you might want to research materials and methods a little more before you dig in. If you've cooked with Dutch ovens before, these recipes will be great additions to your repertoire.

MATERIALS NEEDED

Dutch oven — I like cast iron, with legs, shallow, with a 12-inch diameter. The oven should be cleaned and seasoned. There are a number of ways to do this, but I use the heat and vegetable oil method.

A lid lifter

Heavy duty leather gloves

A pair of long-handled tongs for the coals

A bag or two of charcoal

Lighter fluid (some people are against using lighter fluid for the briquettes, but I like having the charcoal light and heat up quickly)

A couple surfaces to cook on. You need two spots that are in the open air and are placed fairly close together. You don't want to use charcoal in an indoor or closed in space. I work on my back patio. Two surfaces — one to cook on and one to prepare the charcoal briquettes on.

These surfaces can be made by using paving bricks or a couple sheets of solid gauge sheet metal. When you're camping, you can use some hard, clear ground. Soft dirt won't work. Fire pits are frequently used.

The way you cook the food is by placing the Dutch oven over or on prepared briquettes, and by also placing prepared briquettes on the top of the lid. The underneath briquettes should be placed in a circular pattern, but with no briquettes underneath the very center of the oven. The lid briquettes should form a circular pattern moving inward from the outside of the lid. I also put a briquette on each side of the handle. So, on one of your surfaces, you light the briquettes. When they're ready, you use your tongs to move them to your cooking surface. You always want to be preparing at least a few new briquettes, in case you need more heat or some of your first briquettes don't last long enough.

Following is a temperature/number of briquettes chart using a 12-inch Dutch oven. It should be fairly accurate, but when you're outside other factors can come into play — wind, humidity, elevation, etc. Of course, always check your food to make sure it's prepared thoroughly. Again, experimentation is a big part of Dutch oven cooking.

TEMPERATURE (FAHRENHEIT)	TOP BRIQUETTES	BOTTOM BRIQUETTES
300°	15	7
325°	16	7
350°	17	8
375°	18	9
400°	19	10
425°	21	10
450°	22	11
500°	23	12

I've never cooked with any temperature higher than about 375 degrees.

Have fun!

RECIPES

PEACH COBBLER

2 cans peach pie filling, or equivalent fresh
  peaches
1 package vanilla cake mix
1 stick margarine or butter
2 cups water

Empty the pie filling into greased Dutch
oven. Sprinkle the dry cake mix over. Cut
up the margarine and dot over cake mix.
Pour the water over all. Don't stir. Bake at
350°F for an hour. Serve with whipped top-
ping or ice cream if desired.

  You can use any kind of pie filling with
any complementary cake mix flavor, such as
cherry filling with German chocolate cake.

Serves 4–6

APPLE CRISP

6 apples
2 teaspoons cinnamon
2 teaspoons nutmeg
3 cups quick-cooking oats
1 cup flour
2 cups brown sugar
1 teaspoon baking powder
1 teaspoon salt
1 cup butter

Slice apples. Mix the apple slices, cinnamon, and nutmeg in a bowl. In another bowl, mix the oats, flour, sugar, baking powder, salt, and butter to make the crust. Press half the crust into the bottom and sides of the Dutch oven. Pour the apple mixture over the crust, and cover mixture with the remaining crust mix. Bake covered about 45 minutes at 350°F, until top crust is light brown and apples are tender.

Serves 6–8

BEEF POT ROAST

3-pound rump roast or pot roast
3 tablespoons vegetable oil
3 big potatoes, peeled and halved
3 carrots, cut into 2-inch pieces
2 onions, halved
1 teaspoon salt
1/4 teaspoon pepper
1/2 cup water

Place the vegetable oil in the Dutch oven. Add the roast and brown on all sides — you do this without a lid and by placing the oven on prepared briquettes. Remove the roast from heat. Place half of the vegetables in the bottom of the Dutch oven. Place the roast on top of the vegetables. Season with salt and pepper. Add remaining vegetables and water. Cover and cook at 300°F for 3–5 hours, depending on how well-done you like it.

Serves 6–8

COWBOY STEW

1 pound ground beef
1 onion, diced
3 potatoes, cut into 1-inch cubes
1 15-ounce can green beans
1 15-ounce can baked beans
1 15-ounce can black beans
1 15-ounce can tomato soup
1 15-ounce can corn
1 15-ounce can diced tomatoes
1 teaspoon chili powder
1 teaspoon cayenne pepper
1 bay leaf
Salt and pepper

Preheat Dutch oven to 350°F, using just the underneath briquettes. Brown the ground beef and onion in preheated oven. Add all potatoes and canned items (don't drain). Add spices to your taste. Cook for about 45 minutes, until potatoes are soft, stirring contents every 5 minutes or so.

Serves 6–8

MONKEY BREAD

2 cans Pillsbury biscuits
1/2 cup sugar
1/2 cup brown sugar
3 tablespoons cinnamon
1 stick butter, cut into pieces

Preheat kitchen oven to 350°F.

Tear the biscuits into quarters. Mix the sugars and cinnamon in a plastic bag. Drop biscuit quarters, one at a time, into the bag. Shake and coat well. Place all coated pieces into the Dutch oven. Place butter pieces over the tops of the biscuits. Bake for 35 minutes.

Serves 6–8

HONEY MUSTARD PORK CHOPS

8–10 pork chops
touch of oil, if needed
1/4 cup Dijon mustard
1/2 cup honey
1 tablespoon liquid smoke
1/2 cup melted butter
1/2 teaspoon garlic powder
1/2 cup chicken broth
1/2 teaspoon salt

Brown the pork chops in the oven at 400 degrees (16–20 briquettes, bottom only). A little oil might be needed. Mix together the rest of the ingredients until well blended. When the chops are browned, pour sauce over the top and cover and cook. Move two thirds of the briquettes to the top of the lid. Cook 25–30 minutes or until the chops are tender. Add more broth if needed while cooking.

Serves 4–6

ABOUT THE AUTHOR

Paige Shelton is also the author of the national bestselling Farmers' Market Mysteries. She lives in Salt Lake City, Utah, with her husband and son. When she's up early enough, one of her favorite things is to watch the sun rise over the Wasatch Mountains. Visit her at paigeshelton.com.

CPSIA information can be obtained
at www.ICGtesting.com
Printed in the USA.
FFOW04n0331050315
11596FF